STRIKE: DAX

ROCKSTAR SERIES BOOK 2

HEATHER C. LEIGH

SHELBYVILLE PUBLISHING, INC.

Strike
Rockstar Series
Book 2, Dax

By Heather C. Leigh
Copyright © 2015 Shelbyville, Inc.
All rights reserved.

PRINT ISBN: 978-0-9985209-2-6

Cover by Mayhem Cover Creations

✿ Created with Vellum

QUOTES

There is no such thing as a lost cause or a dead end, through persistence, attitude and creativity, there is always an escape route.

 —**Urijah Faber** (MMA World Champion)

Forget about past mistakes and focus your energy on the victories of tomorrow.

 —**Carlos Gracie** (creator of modern Jiu Jitsu)

Know the rules well so you can break them effectively.

 —**Dalai Lama**

The more anger towards the past you carry in your heart, the less capable you are of loving in the present.

 —**Unknown**

To everyone who loves Syd and Drew as much as I do, it means the world to me that you brought them into your hearts and homes.
disclaimer

I would just like to clarify what you will be reading in STRIKE Dax is British. I am not. I have done my best to keep the language true to his heritage, however, keep in mind that I will not be using British spellings or always use the British vernacular for certain words. I don't want to confuse the non-British readers or explain what a clanger is or what Gordon Bennett means.
I will be using friends from the U.K., for reference now and then, but I can't ask people to repeatedly edit my book and fix every single Briticism. I made some creative changes to the school system in the UK among other things. Let's not nitpick the small stuff.
Happy reading! Cheers!

HC Leigh

DESCRIPTION

Dax Davies has one job to fulfill in the Davies household. Earn money at the family business. The problem is that the family business is illegal underground fighting. His future is in the cage, not on stage where he dreams of being.

KATE CAMPBELL LOVES one thing in life. Well, two. Soccer and Dax Davies. Growing up in the poorest part of London, soccer is her personal escape from reality and the fact that Dax doesn't seem to know she exists.

KATE DOESN'T plan on ever getting a chance to know Dax as more than an unattainable dream. After a mutual acquaintance finally brings them together, it only takes one ill-fated night at the fight club tear them apart.

THIS IS a standalone novel in the Rockstar Series.

THIS BOOK CONTAINS hot British curse words, sweaty, muscled cage fighters, and a feisty female footy player.

1

D^{ax}

I WAS eight years old when I broke my first bone. My older brother is the one who did it, while my father watched, criticizing my fight stance as it snapped.

If you're male and born in the Davies household, you have one and only one job—to fight. My parents have *four* boys, which means most of our childhood was spent beating the absolute shite out of each other. As the youngest, and for a long time, the smallest brother, I've had so many fractured bones I'm not sure if there are any left that haven't been cracked at least once.

"C'mon lad, you're up."

Out of the corner of my eye I see my dad poke his head into the tiny locker room of his underground fight club, his bushy eyebrows raised as he waits for my response. The strong scent of antiseptic stings my nostrils when I take a few deep, calming breaths.

"I'll be out in a second."

He glares at me. "Don't make me come back in here, Dax. There's a big crowd and a lot of money riding on you tonight. Plus," his angry face breaks into a grin. "I got a nice reward for ya afterwards, aye?"

Fuck calm.

A blaze of heat rushes up my chest and neck. "I said I'd be out in a second!" I'm not sure exactly who it is I'm yelling at as my dad is long gone, the doorway he was standing in is empty.

I can't help my short temper. My dad wants me this way, molded me to be this way, the same he did my three older brothers. Pent up frustration leads to domination in the ring, and my dad is an expert at making you frustrated. He dictates everything —what I eat, who I fight, he even has a system for when I can get laid.

The rules.

I'm so fucking tired of being told what to do. I ache for the day that I can be in charge—dictate, and be as bossy of a prick as I want.

A loud roar surrounds me as I make my way to the ring. The energy seeps into me, my body itching for some kind of release— physical release—whether sexual or not, I need relief.

Heavy hands slap my shoulders and back, sharp voices wish me luck or yell at me to fuck up and lose so they can collect their fifty quid. I stretch my neck from side to side, hopping on my toes once I hit the small set of stairs that leads into the cage. I'm ready and all too willing to set the beast inside me free.

My opponent tonight is hideous. Not just any kind of ugly, mind you. He's a right minger. Ewan Blair—eighteen, black hair, black beady eyes, acne scars all over—and the meanest bastard I've ever met.

"Ya ready for me to pound yer arse into the floor, Davies?"

The dull roar of the crowd fades into the background as I calmly stare at Ewan and his big, bloated face, following dad's rules to the letter. Even if you're bleeding from every orifice and your kidney is falling out, if you're angrier than a bull with a red flag in it's face, you keep yourself under control, never let your emotions show. It's part of *the rules*.

Rule 1—Family first.

Without saying a word, I stare at Ewan's hideous face. My brother, Liam, puts in my mouth guard and leans close, his massive arm coming round my neck. "Nasty prick is weak on his left. He never remembers to keep his chin down when he throws a right uppercut." I already know this, but reviewing your enemy's flaws is part of the ritual dad beat into our skulls. Literally.

I nod and shrug Liam off, more than ready to get this fight going. I feel like I might explode I'm wound so tight. The ref for tonight is one of dad's regulars, Tommy MacGregor. He's an okay bloke, fair enough, lets the fighters have a go without interfering too much. Plus, he's a Scot, which holds more weight than anything else in dad's eyes.

Tommy raises his hands in the air, motioning us forward. "Fighters to the center!"

Ewan and I walk towards each other, converging in the middle. My training takes over, as natural to me as breathing. I'm thinking about that reward. Like one of Pavlov's dogs, my cock is already anticipating it, twitching in my shorts.

I never break eye contact with my opponent, studying, intimidating, showing him I'll never back down. Tommy's voice booms over the sound system and I simply stare when Ewan frowns. The noisy crowd falls silent as he announces the match.

"Tonight you're in for a great show. We have two former youth champions meeting up as adult fighters for the first time."

Loud hoots and hollers bounce throughout the open space of the warehouse that holds the fight club. Tommy thrusts a finger at Ewan.

"In the black corner, we have our challenger, last year's

welterweight under eighteen London Underground champion, at six foot even, weighing eighty-eight and a half kilos or one-hundred ninety-five pounds, Ewan Blaaaaair!"

Ewan does a three-sixty spin for the crowd, holding up his hands and air-punching as he goes round. What a tosser. The idiots in the audience eat it up, going wild for Blair. Dad told me the betting was especially heavy tonight, with me only getting a slight edge in the odds. Ewan and I have never fought before because until recently, I hadn't been in his weight class—that plus I used to fight without the thin, fingerless gloves I'm currently wearing.

Tommy turns from Ewan to point at me, once again doing a bang up job of whipping the crowd into a frenzy.

"Aaaaand in the red corner, standing six foot three inches, weighing in at ninety kilos or two-hundred pounds, we have last year's London Underground seventeen and under bare-knuckle boxing champ, Dax Daaaaaavies!"

Wild shouts come from all sides of the warehouse. The men (and quite a few women) who bet on me call out their cheers of approval. Mingled in are a few boos and hisses, but I could care less. I'm going to shred this prick and I'm going to do it quickly. Yep, I'm a fucking cocky bastard, but I've earned every bit of it.

We step to the center, tap gloves, and it's on.

Kate

I'VE BEEN in love with Dax Davies since the moment I laid eyes on him in year three of primary school at the tender age of seven. Sadly, I'm not sure if he even knows that I exist.

Now, we're in our final year of school, newly turned eighteen, and he still hasn't said more than a few words to me here and there and when he has, it's only because we shared a class so he didn't have a choice. He's on an entirely different level of exis- tence than I am, beautiful, perfect, girls throwing themselves at him. It's not surprising that he never noticed plain, boring Kate, the least girly female in school.

It's the first day back after the winter holiday break, so I'm desperate for a fix of Dax's gorgeous face. I mentally cheer for myself because lucky me, this term Dax ended up in front of me in class. I can't help but stare at his wide, muscled back, defined perfectly under his tight T-shirt, as we wait for Mr. Patel to take roll call.

They always seat us alphabetically first thing in the morning. Since my name is Campbell and his is Davies, Dax either sits several seats behind me, or, like this year, the beginning of the next row. Obviously, I prefer him to be in front so I can ogle as much as I want without anyone knowing how pathetic I am.

"Kate Campbell?"

"What?" I jerk my eyes away from the back of Dax's head and drop my hair, which I had been twirling in my fingers nervously.

"Are you with us today, Miss Campbell? I've called out your name three times."

Mr. Patel stares at me from behind his wire-framed glasses with a bemused look on his face. Most of the class turns to gawk at me and I hear a few giggles from them, but it's when Dax's dark eyes meet mine that I feel the burning shame spread up my face and cheeks. He doesn't look amused, he looks... well, hot, but he's always hot, even with the dark bruise that spans the length of his jaw. No, scratch that, he looks... totally uninterested. Bored to death. By me.

I shift in my seat, utterly humiliated. "I-I'm here. Sorry Mr. Patel."

Well, Dax certainly knows I exist now—as the class imbecile.

Mr. Patel clears his throat and everyone quiets down, my stupidity seemingly forgotten. Dax has already turned back towards the front of the classroom, likely thinking I'm a total nutter.

The bell rings sharply, dismissing us for first period. I wait for the room to clear before gathering my things and heading for maths.

"Kate! Wait up!"

My teammate, Tasha, comes dashing up the hall like a maniac, nearly crashing into me. We've done girl's football together for ages so I've known her a long time. My mum says I've always had too much energy, been impossible to keep still. They signed me up for footy as an outlet for my insatiable need to be on the go.

"Tasha, I've told you to stop drinking so much caffeine." I almost never drink caffeine. I can hardly keep still as it is. If I drank my favorite tea with milk, I'd be off the wall.

She throws her head back and laughs, tossing her long dark hair over her shoulder. I smile wistfully. I've always wished I were more exotic looking like Tasha, with her almond-shaped eyes and creamy white skin. But no, I'm not flashy or girly. I'm just boring old me. Boring brown hair, too big for my face murky greenish-brown eyes, average height, average weight, average... everything.

"I haven't been drinking caffeine, silly. I'm just excited. All last term was footy this and footy that, around nothing but girls all the time. Now, since it's off-season, we can flirt and find blokes to chat up and have fun."

We had been walking towards class, but after that comment I stop to face Tasha. "Firstly, we still have football, just not as much. Practice starts next week. Secondly, *you* can flirt and find a bloke. I'm not interested. I need to get out of this town." It's a partial lie. I *do* want a bloke, a specific one. Only he doesn't want me. Letting out a huff, I continue down the hall to the maths classrooms.

"Hey." Tasha grabs my elbow, pulling me over to the side of the hall so we don't block traffic. She lowers her voice and leans in close. "He's an idiot to not notice you, Kate. You're bloody gorgeous, smart, and fucking brilliant on the pitch. Either forget about Dax or make a move. I've heard he's a cold, soulless bastard anyway. This is our last term together and we're going to have some fun if it kills us."

While I'm glad to have a friend like her who knows what I'm thinking even when I don't say it, hearing her insult Dax ruffles my feathers a little. Yeah, he seems unapproachable and icy, but there's something there. I just know it.

Regardless of how she feels about him, Tasha always lets me prattle on and on about Dax Davies and his magnificence and never once makes me feel stupid or obsessed—even though I'm ashamed to admit I'm both. "We're going to have fun, huh?"

"Yeah." She grins.

I pull my hair out of its elastic, run my fingers through it, and immediately whip it right back up in a ponytail. Nervous habit. "Right. You're right. We are." I'm not sure if I'm convincing Tasha or myself.

"Good. I'll see you at lunch. Lucky us, they're welcoming us back with that dodgy shepherd's pie you love so much."

I wrinkle my nose at the thought of eating the horrid school lunches for another term. Oh well, could be worse. I could be eating nothing for lunch—something I've had to do many, many times.

"See you then."

When I reach my class I notice that my streak of misfortune continues—making a fool of myself during attendance, dodgy lunch, and to top it off, Dax is already seated in the back row of my maths class, running one of his huge hands over his short, dark blonde hair. His round, well-defined bicep flexes as his arm moves, making my mouth practically water. Brilliant, I'll be spending the entire term thinking about Dax and his perfect muscles, sitting behind me. I'll probably fail maths whilst I daydream.

Make a move or forget about Dax. Yeah right, not a bloody chance.

DAX

"No, no, no! Lad, are you payin' any attention to what yer doing? He's gonna leather you if you lower yer right hand!"

Aggravated, I take a step back into the corner of the cage, praying that my temper will lessen. I know my dad's angry—really angry, because his Scottish brogue is so bad it's almost unintelligible. That says a lot since I grew up with the sorry prick. I should know what he's saying after eighteen years.

"Look at me, ya numpty!"

Gritting my teeth, I control my face before I turn towards my old man.

"Freddie, take a break," he snaps at the bloke I'm sparring with, never once breaking our eye contact. Fred silently exits the cage, disappearing somewhere in the massive old warehouse my dad uses for his underground fight club. You wouldn't believe how widespread and organized the illegal fight scene is in London. There are tournaments and everything.

My dad steps over until we're nearly chest-to-chest. I'm a huge bastard, six foot three and over fourteen stone. Dad? He's tall enough to look me right in the eye. If he were younger, I could possibly be scared of him.

Who am I kidding? I *am* scared of him, or at the very least greatly intimidated.

My dad only knows one way—very controlling, very painful, and absolutely terrifying. He's a decent man, mostly. It's just that he puts fighting over everything else, including us. Plus, if there's one thing I absolutely loathe, it's being told what to do.

Unconsciously, I shift my gaze away from his dark, piercing

stare. Faster than you'd think the old man could move, his hand whips out and catches my chin, yanking it until I look at him.

"Face me like a man, lad. Never let yer opponent see weakness."

Opponent... what a joke. He's my fucking father. He's supposed to be on *my* side. He's the only man on earth that can intimidate me. With everyone else, I'm fearless.

Rule 2—Never let your emotions show.

He stares for what feels like forever, searching my face for something. Looking in my eyes as if they hold the answers to all of his questions. I wait, not daring to move an inch. You never, ever flinch.

He narrows his gaze. "Did you have a shag?"

"What?"

"You heard me. Did you get fucked?"

I shake my head, hardly able to move with his thick fingers still squeezing my chin.

"Did you have a wank?"

"Dad! No!"

Horrified, I try to pull my head out of his tight grip, but it only makes him clamp down harder. His normally light eyes are nearly black as he scowls.

"You know the rules, aye?"

"Yes."

Of course I know his bloody rules. They've been beaten into me since I was a kid.

Rule 3—No fucking, shagging, wanking, sucking, or getting off for seven days leading up to a fight.

You want your reward? You better win.

Dad shoves me away by my chin, making me stumble back, disgust clearly written all over his face. "I want ya ready for Friday night, Dax." My dad's thick finger points at me, "No slappers, no fucking, keep yer hands off yer dick."

I nod, swallowing down the rage that boils in my gut. He's a fucking genius. He *wants* me furious, determined...an outright demon in the ring. He knows the best way to get results is to keep me angry and horny.

"Go'n do the bag. An hour. Not a minute less."

"But—"

"Don't bloody argue with me, lad!"

The venom in his voice keeps me from talking back. Silently, I leave the cage, stalking over to the heavy bag in the corner, and start punching it, pretending it's my father's face I'm hitting instead of cracked old vinyl.

As I do the various punches and kick combinations, each one in a specific order long ago committed to memory, I allow myself to imagine getting out of this place to have a life of my own. Where I get to choose what I do, who I fuck, and where no one else will have a goddamn say.

For now, I go along with dad's way simply because it's easier. The money is good and I get pussy brought right to my feet. Regardless, I cannot wait until my gig Saturday night. It's the beginning of my plan to leave Hackney, and the club, behind.

Sweat is pouring off my face and body, making it difficult to see, but I keep pounding that sodding bag, too stubborn to back off and let my dad think he's broken me.

"Oi!"

I give the bag one last good whack before snatching up a towel to wipe myself off. I need my brother giving me a pep talk like I need a second cock—It seems like a good idea until you realize it's fucking useless.

"What do you want, Ethan?"

"Hey! Who put a goalpost up your arse?" He holds his hands up in mock offense.

I glare at my oldest brother. He can be so fucking stupid sometimes. Of all of us, Ethan is the only one who looks like dad —dark hair, light eyes, intimidating as fuck all. The rest of us are big like them, but blonde with dark eyes like our mum.

"Let me guess. *Dad*, of course. Who else would have you this aggro?" Ethan chuckles under his breath, but there's no humor in his tone. "You have to ignore ninety percent of what the old codger says, Dax."

"Easy for you to say. He's not riding your ass like he is mine."

I strip off my fingerless bag gloves, tossing them aside to grab my drink. Too late, I see Ethan's hand whipping through the air.

"Ow!" My instinct is to rear back and punch my brother after he slaps the back of my head, but I suppress it, knowing Ethan will give as good as he gets. "What the hell was that for?"

"Because, you stupid knob, we share a room. Or have you forgotten?" My only answer is a rude grunt. "I work here with him every damn day, Dax. At least you have school and your music as an escape. You don't hear him getting on me because you're not here all the time."

"School," I scoff. "Yeah, that's a real relaxing break from the club, Ethan. Stuck with a perpetual stiffy while surrounded by girls that I can't fuck for fourteen days out of every month." Scowling, I grab my water bottle and drink most of it in a few large gulps.

My oldest brother's gray eyes soften, reflecting an age much wiser than his twenty-two years. "Trust me bro, take advantage of the freedom school gives you while you're there. This..." he spins around with his arms spread wide, "is no paradise."

Well crap. If this is the best it's going to get, I need to get moving on that plan.

Kate

"THIS IS SO EXCITING! I'm so glad I wore this dress, it shows off my body perfectly."

I stifle a giggle when Tasha hides her face and rolls her eyes so I can see it but Willa can't. Willa is... well, let's just say she only thinks about one thing—herself.

"Ellie, you alright?" I elbow my newest, and somehow suddenly my closest, friend, bouncing my knees with anticipation. Ellie and I live in the same building so we've bonded by walking to school together or doing class work. Ellie turns in her seat to face me, her big blue eyes wide with anxiety.

"Yeah, I'm fine," she responds with a worried frown.

I must be scowling because she adds on to her statement, sounding somewhat more convincing. "Really, Kate. I'm brilliant." I watch her wipe her hands on the super tight jeans I made her wear.

Fine. Hmph. She couldn't be less fine if she were walking naked across the stage at the Royal Albert Hall.

Not wanting to start an argument on our girls' night out, I keep my observations to myself. Frankly, I'm just chuffed that she came out with us. Ellie is... reticent to say the least.

The tube slows to a stop and Tasha jumps to her feet when they announce the station. "This is ours!"

We file out, laughing and chatting about everything and anything. The excitement of seeing a live band at a popular London pub has us all wound up like little children on a sugar high. Most of us are just over eighteen, so this is our first chance to go.

At the front entrance of the bar, we meet up with some of our other teammates and head inside. The Drunken Kitten is a noisy, jam-packed little place in a bohemian area of London, filled to the brim with people of all sorts.

Tasha leans close so I can hear her. "Let's get a good spot!"

I nod at Tasha and grab Ellie's hand, making sure to hold my pint up in my other so the crowd doesn't jostle it.

"Perfect," I declare when we carve out a little section right near the tiny stage. "I've heard these blokes are talented."

"No, you've heard that they're smoking hot," Tasha says, laughing as she sips her lager.

"Shut it, Tash." If it were bright enough in here, I'm certain everyone would see how red my face is. "So what? Yeah, they're supposed to be good-looking. Is it a crime to want to watch hot guys sing?"

Willa comes gliding through the throngs of people, sidling up to us. "I'm *so* going to shag one of the hot musicians," she announces.

Ellie frowns at Willa, but the rest of us have learned to ignore her. Willa's only here because she overheard one of the girls discussing our plans during football practice. Otherwise, not one of us would have dared to invite her.

The lights dim causing the packed crowd to whistle and yell. After initially stumbling over his own feet, the first musician hops onto the small, lighted stage. Right as it hits me that I recognize him, I spot another man with a guitar following close behind.

Dax Davies.

I'm struck dumb. Rooted to the spot like a total idiot. I'm so shocked I don't even remember to fidget. In the background, I register that my friends are screaming for Dax and his friend Adam, and they're screaming loudly. Everything after that becomes a blur. I'm sure there's singing, clapping, hollering, dancing... I hear and see none of it.

Instead, burned onto my impressionable brain forever, is the glorious sight of Dax in a tight white T-shirt, his ripped, sinewy bulk flexing as he strums his guitar. His jeans are frayed, the waist barely holding up on his narrow hips. I can't tell if he's any good at playing because the only sound I hear is blood rushing behind my ears as my poor heart works overtime to keep me on my feet.

"Kate. Kate!"

My unfocused eyes find Ellie, standing in front of me, blocking my view of Dax and his perfection.

"What?"

"I don't feel well. Do you mind if we take off? My stomach…"

I glance back up at Dax and my mouth goes dry at his magnificence. Then my eyes find a group of scantily dressed females congregating around the stage exit, Willa included. My stomach does a back flip, accompanied by a horrid feeling of despair.

What's the point of sticking around? So I can watch Dax snog someone else? Put those huge, talented hands on another girl's body? I can't compete with them. They're all posh and gorgeous. Why would he want me when he could have one of them?

My gaze drops back to Ellie. *Christ*, she really doesn't look well at all. "Yeah. Let's go, El."

What was supposed to be a fun night out has made me depressed as hell. Instead of having a laugh, I tortured myself for nearly two hours watching my walking dream get eye-fucked by every girl in the audience. I need to get it through my thick skull —Dax Davies doesn't love me and never will.

It's better that way, I'm sure. But coming to grips with it? Well, that just plain sucks.

2

D^{ax}

"DAD! I'll be ready for the fight. I'm always ready. Stop bleedin' jumping on me!"

I stuff my head under my pillow, not wanting to hear my brother argue with my dad.

"Yer not ready. Ya look like ya were whoring about last night. Forget the rules, Liam?"

Fuck me. I let out a groan. The thin pillow can't block out the shouting. Liam has a match tonight and I swear the old bastard is more obsessed with his rules than ever. Right now, he's pushing his favorite rule on Liam, the one we hate the most.

Rule 3—No fucking, shagging, wanking, sucking, or getting off for seven days leading up to a fight.

Naturally, with four randy sons sporting constant hard-ons in need of relief, dad has had a difficult time drilling that particular rule into our heads. Hell, Ethan told me that dad had expected him to be completely celibate once he was old enough to fight at the club. When that plan failed miserably, with Ethan running around behind the old man's back shagging anything that moved, dad conceded to no sex for one full week before a fight. He insists it keeps the primal drive to win heightened. There's something to it, especially his rewards. I just happen to think it's cocked up when your dad is plotting your next suck and shag.

Sighing, I glance over and notice Ethan's small single bed is empty in our cramped room. My eyes find the digital clock on our shared nightstand. Crap. It's already noon. After last night's gig, I let some tart suck me off in the loo. That meant I didn't get home until late. Adam, well, Adam went straight home, too obsessed over this Ellie girl from school to chat up anyone at the DK. After he noticed her in the audience, he went looking for her. When he couldn't find Ellie anywhere, he was done for the night.

"Dax! Get yer arse out here ya skiver! Your lie-in is over, son!"

I punch my pillow miserably. My day has officially begun.

"YOU NEED HELP?"

My brother Liam ignores me, choosing to stretch his own muscles instead of answer as he readies for his fight.

"Fine," I snap, using Liam as an outlet for my irritation. "I don't give a rat's arse if you're tight and pull every muscle in your body!"

Liam doesn't fight often. He's not weak by any means. He honestly just doesn't care enough to win, which makes our dad mental. The intense, burning fountain of rage and testosterone that the rest of us feel before a match doesn't seem to extend to this particular Davies. Somehow, Liam maintains an even, Zen-like attitude no matter how much our dad berates him or how hard he works him. He doesn't have to hide his emotions like the rest of us do.

"Will you shut yer hole, Dax?" Shaun's huge form barges into the tiny locker room, all puffed up and set to defend his less aggressive twin brother.

"Fuck off," I say lightly. Shaun glares at me, but his lips twitch just enough that I know he's amused not angry. Thank god, because fighting Shaun is a nightmare. He's ruthless.

Shaun turns his attention to Liam. People say they can't tell them apart, being identical twins and all, but for me it's easy. Maybe it's the way Liam's eyes shine with compassion and warmth while Shaun's are hard and cold. Hell, I'm Shaun's little brother and the teeny tiny smirk he just gave me is about as much of a laugh as I've ever seen on his face. Polar fucking opposites, those two.

They put their heads together, nodding and whispering and doing that strange twin thing they have with each other. Now I feel like an intruder. I have to get out of here. "I'll be out by the cage," I growl as I leave the suddenly stifling room.

Liam and Shaun have each other. Ethan is never around anymore and with him being the oldest, I was always just the annoying kid brother. Dad only cares about the club and mum is too busy taking care of and feeding five huge, hungry men to worry about me.

I live in a crowded fucking flat with five other people and I feel completely alone. Really, the only attention I get is when I'm fighting or when I get my reward. Right now, I live for those fucking rewards. It's the only human contact I get that doesn't involve punching, and the only time in my life when I have some sort of semblance of control.

After Liam's fight, I trudge down the dark streets towards my flat. By the time I'm nearly home, I feel guilty. I probably should have gone out to celebrate Liam's win with the rest of my family. This particular match was such a big deal even my mum went with them to the local pub.

Rule 1—Family first.

Whatever. So I broke a rule. I'm the youngest, the defiant one, the one they always expect will go left when they say go right. I'm sure no one thought I'd turn up anyway. I told them I'd meet them out at the pub and came home instead. Any punishment dad comes up with won't break me. I'm used to his methods by now. Yet those sodding rules still gnaw at me like Catholic guilt, popping into my thoughts every time I do something that doesn't follow their restrictive instructions.

As I approach my crumbling old building, I see the dark shadow of a person sitting near the graffiti-covered entrance. No matter how good I am with my fists—and I'm good—I'm still wary of getting into a street fight with a bloke on the piss or a nutter who went off his meds. When I get close I have my hands clenched and ready for whatever comes next.

A low moan breaks the silence and the figure turns his head towards the dim streetlight.

"Adam?"

Fuck! I sprint the remaining distance, dropping to the cold ground next to my best friend. My heart seems to clog up my throat, making it difficult to breathe. Something is *very* wrong.

"What happened? Are you hurt?"

Adam wheezes, wincing from the effort, but doesn't answer. Gravel digs into my knees as I check him for injuries, but I ignore the sharp pain. All I can see are a few scrapes on his face, some worse than others. It's not nearly enough to have him looking this pale or to render him practically unconscious.

"Adam!" I lightly shake his shoulders.

Still no answer. Adam's hazel eyes are glassy, unfocused. Panicking, I yank up his thin jumper, exposing his undershirt to the cold air. My mouth dries up and I let out a gasp, bending over in pain as if I were punched in the gut.

Holy fuck!

It's dark out, so the shiny, dripping wetness on his white shirt looks black. But it's not. It's blood. Loads of it. So much so that I can smell the metallic tang in the crisp January air.

"Adam! I need to get you to hospital."

I reach down to help him up, shoving one arm under his arms from the back and the other in front. I'm easily able to hoist him to his feet. Miraculously, he doesn't collapse even though I'm supporting most of his weight.

Adam whispers in my ear, so soft it's just a faint rasp.

"Come again?"

I can hardly hear him, but his words are clear. "No. Hospital. Danny."

His own brother? Bastard!

I tense up, squeezing with my arms, which causes Adam to hiss in pain. "Danny did this?"

Adam can't respond. He passes out, his head dropping forward and his body becoming slack in my arms. Lucky for me Adam is fairly thin and I'm fit, or else I wouldn't be able to manage. It takes almost half an hour, but I get him back to his flat and into his bed. I can't keep him at my place, my parents would insist on going to A&E. They've known Adam forever and care about him as if he were another Davies.

By the time I get him home, get to the all-night chemist to retrieve some supplies to clean his wound, and get back to Adam's flat, we're both drenched with sweat—me from exertion, Adam from shock.

Shaking, I sit on the edge of Adam's bed—just a dingy mattress on the floor—and hold my head in my hands. My best mate was almost killed tonight. Something has got to change.

Kate

I WATCH RUEFULLY as Dax and Ellie walk away from school

together, threading my fingers through the end of my braid. Never in my life did I think I would hate football, but today I do. I'm stuck at practice, in the freezing cold, while Ellie gets escorted round town by the boy I want more than anything in the world.

"Oi. What's that about?"

I turn to see Tasha staring at Dax and Ellie, her brow wrinkled in confusion.

Shrugging, I play it off. "Don't know. He's been walking her to Adam's flat every day. She said it has something to do with Adam being out of school. He takes her to visit."

"Adam? Adam Reynolds?"

"Yeah."

Tasha gives me an incredulous look as if she doesn't believe their story. That it's a cover for some sordid affair between Dax and my best mate.

"Ellie's not with Dax, Tash."

"Hmph. What does a god like Dax Davies see in a boring little mouse like Ellie?"

I startle, not realizing Willa had joined us on the edge of the pitch. Both Tasha's mouth and mine fall open at Willa's rudeness.

She takes note of our shocked expressions and sneers, curling her lip up in disgust. "Well, it's true. Didn't you see all the girls at the DK waiting to get a piece of him? They were all way better looking than her," Willa sniffs, tossing her hair over one shoulder.

Annoyed, I defend my friend. "How can you say that? Ellie's flat out gorgeous, Willa." God, I could slap that condescending look off of her face.

Jealous cow.

"Is she? Then how come it was *me* sucking him off after the concert and not her?" She arches one of those perfectly groomed eyebrows of hers, shoving her superiority in my face.

My heart crumples in on itself and nosedives right into my hollow stomach. "You... you..." I can't manage to finish my sentence. All at once I'm feeling humiliated, jealous, and seething with anger. Despite the cold, my face is burning up. My gaze flicks over to Tasha, catching the look of sympathy she's giving me. It's clear she already knew about Willa and Dax.

Willa smirks as I take off across the pitch towards the street. Screw practice. I can't look at that bitch without wanting to kick her teeth in, and I certainly don't want anyone to see me break down and cry, which is exactly what happens the minute I get out of sight.

My throat is tight and my tongue feels thick as I run in my footy boots. Past broken down cars, past abandoned buildings, past the shoddy cornershop where filthy dossers try to scam you out of your money—not that anyone round here has any.

I hate bloody Hackney! Living in London's worst, most crime-ridden neighborhood can suck the life out of you if you let it. Mine's not been sucked out. It's been hoovered out by Dax Davies and his man-whore ways.

By the time I reach my dingy flat, my lungs are burning and tears cover my freezing cheeks. I might be hurt, but I'm also determined. I head straight for a pile of scholarship applications with a singular purpose.

To get the hell out of Hackney so I can forget all about Dax Davies.

∼

"WHAT?"

I literally can't believe what I'm hearing. When I look into Ellie's large blue eyes, I know she's not lying

"Adam was stabbed, Kate." She sniffs and tries to hold back tears. How did I not notice that my best friend was falling apart? Her eyes are swollen and red-rimmed. There are dark circles beneath them telling me she hasn't been sleeping well. Her nails are chewed down to stubs, and frankly, she just looks exhausted.

"How? I mean why? Hell—I have no idea what to say, El."

I feel like a total failure as a friend. After Willa enlightened me to Dax's extracurricular activities, I *had* to know if Ellie was another notch on his headboard. Apparently, I love to torture myself. What she confesses instead literally renders me speechless.

"I still don't understand. What does Adam being stabbed have to do with Dax walking you home every day?"

Ellie sighs, flopping back on my bed. Our families live in the same crappy council flats, so we tend to see each other a lot, usually to walk to school, but sometimes for a chat. When I invited her over to gently finagle some information out of her about her after school walks with Dax, I had no idea she was going to drop a bomb of this magnitude in my lap. Make that *two* bombs—Adam was stabbed and Ellie was attacked.

"It's a long story, Kate." Ellie's eyes glisten with moisture and her lip begins to quiver. My best friend is falling to pieces and all I can think about is my selfish desire to get with Dax.

Some friend I am.

I lay back on the bed next to El, taking her trembling hand in mine. "I'm here to listen, El. Tell me everything."

I am floored, literally gob smacked by Ellie's story. Right when the school term started, Callum Murray attacked her in a vacant lot and the only reason she wasn't defiled was because Adam and Dax intervened at the last second. They beat the crap out of Callum and his mate Ryan, which explains why Callum is holding a grudge against Ellie. And why Callum and Ryan looked so banged up a few weeks ago.

To keep Ellie safe from Callum, Adam made an arrangement with his drug-dealing brother Danny. Everyone at school knows about Danny and his criminal activities. Heck, half the kids buy from him. In exchange, Adam had to run Danny's drugs for him. That's when Adam was jumped, Danny's drugs and money nicked, and Adam left for dead.

Dax has taken Adam's place in walking Ellie home every day so Callum won't try to get her again when no one is looking. I always knew that Callum Murray was a complete prick. I'm glad Adam and Dax hurt him. Now I feel about two feet tall for thinking Ellie was hooking up with Dax. Clearly, she loves Adam. The expression on her face can only be described as heartbroken.

"I know you fancy Dax, Kate."

I blink rapidly, opening and closing my mouth like a fish at the abrupt change in topic to focus on my embarrassing lack of a love life. Ellie's eyes bore into mine, open and honest. There's no use denying it. Not to my best mate. Especially not after she opened up to me like she did.

I shrink back, the weight of everything pressing down on my body. "Yeah. Since we were kids."

Ellie scoots to lie on her side, propping her head up on one hand. "Why haven't you ever talked to him?"

I snort. "Right. Chat up Dax Davies. Okay, El." The familiar cracks in the ceiling distract me enough to keep the tears at bay.

Her brows pull together as she stares at me. "I know he acts like he has no soul," she giggles, "but honestly, he's a nice bloke. Give me a good reason why you won't talk to him?"

"Would you walk up to Adam and chat him up?"

Her cheeks redden and her gaze drops to my faded quilt. "I did. On the first day of school. He yelled at me for looking at his sketchbook. It was humiliating."

I can't help it. The laughter bubbles out uncontrollably. Soon, Ellie joins in and it feels great to be able to have some tiny bit of joy in our lives when it seems everything around us seems to be crumbling to dust.

DAX

"So we're going to have a practice this Saturday morning at the DK. That way we can see how we sound in the pub for the gig that night."

I nod at Adam as he goes on and on about the band. This is only his second week back at school after missing a week recuperating from being stabbed. He looks better, not great, but functional. He can't fool me with his happy act. I've known him too long, plus, *I'm* an expert at hiding pain, having been busted up in the cage many, many times. I know all the signs. Adam is in agony, but he's a passionate bastard, unwilling to let anything keep him from his music—or from Ellie. And since she's at school, that's where he wants to be.

"Right. Gavin and Hawke seem to fit in okay."

Adam frowns when I mention the two Americans that have joined up to complete our band, Gavin Walker a blonde bloke who looks more like a posh model than a bass player, and Hawke Evans, a tattooed, pierced drummer with a geek chic fetish.

I'm about to tell Adam for the millionth time that he doesn't have to worry about Gavin or Hawke making a move on Ellie because I already threatened them both within an inch of their lives, when a warm, curvy body presses up against my back, long fingers reaching out to wrap tightly around my arm.

"Dax, when are you going to let me have another go at you, you sexy thing?"

I don't bother to turn around in the crowded school hallway. It doesn't matter who's whispering in my ear because the answer I give would be exactly the same.

"Never, so bugger off." I shake whoever's hand it is off of my arm and stay silent until the girl takes the hint and leaves.

A glance at Adam shows him covering his mouth, trying not to laugh. Fuck him. Maybe he likes to stay friends with his shags, but not me. They serve a purpose—one purpose—to get me off during my dad-sanctioned weeks. After that, I don't need them for anything else.

Rule 4—Women who act like slags can be treated like slags.

That's what Adam doesn't understand. Any girl willing to disrespect herself by getting to her knees the second you meet isn't worth the effort it takes to be nice. In trying so hard to *not* be a bastard like his father, Adam's kindness has the potential to be easily taken advantage of. If nothing else, my dad was right to teach me that lesson.

"You're such a cold bastard, Dax."

"I know. You could learn a thing or two."

"No thanks," he says dryly.

"Adam!"

I follow Adam's gaze to see Ellie hurrying towards us, towing a friend by the hand. Ellie immediately latches on to Adam, prattling on about something or other. Tuning out the happy couple, I take a moment to check out Ellie's friend, Kate. I've seen her around, mostly with Ellie, but she's in my maths class as well. In fact, now that I think about it, we've been in school together a long time.

The fact that I didn't remember her until now makes me frown, which in turn, makes Kate's eyes go wide with fear. The girl is fiddling with her hair, pulling it up into a ponytail. She's clearly uncomfortable around me, so, being the heartless prick that I am, I decide to make it worse.

"You're Kate."

When impossibly green eyes shoot up to meet mine, big and innocent looking, all of the smartass comments I have at the ready fall away. Smooth, lightly freckled skin flushes pink and full lips part, making my cock sit up and take notice. It's then I realize I've never really *looked* at Kate before.

How did I not see how gorgeous this girl is? She's not obvious or flashy—no, she's very... girl next door. Sporty and fit with tawny brown hair always pulled up on her head, showing off two very high cheekbones. I'm surprised how affected I am by her. My heart has begun thumping hard and my palms are sweaty. How angry would Adam be if I shagged Ellie's best friend?

Probably very. Not that I care much what he thinks.

While I'm thinking of how she looks naked, she gathers herself together and answers my question. "Yes. I'm Kate." Shit, even her voice affects me—soft and slightly scratchy in a sexy kind of way. Now my dick is throbbing, pressing uncomfortably against my zipper. I need to hear that voice again.

"I'm Dax. You're in my maths class."

Those emerald eyes get even wider and her jaw hangs open. "How do you know who I am?"

Huh?

"Why *wouldn't* I know who you are? Haven't we been in the same year for ages?" I furrow my brow, trying to decide if I'm thinking of a different girl. But no, it's her, I'm sure of it.

"Y-y-yes. Since third year."

I hold back a smile, keeping my cool exterior. At least I got that right. "Well then, apparently I'm not as stupid as some might say."

Kate's fingers untwist from her hair, settling on her hips. Lush, ruby lips turn down in the corners and her eyes narrow. She looks downright offended. "Who says you're stupid? You're in my advanced maths class, so I know that can't be true."

For once in my life I'm speechless. No one ever gives me the benefit of the doubt or defends my intelligence. Do I bother explaining to her that most people associate a big, muscled guy with an empty skull? Add in the underground fighting and they assume I've taken enough hits to the head to be rendered daft and dumb.

No one talks about it, but the teachers here know what I do— what my dad's business is. I am the fourth Davies son at this school after all and they treat me accordingly. They don't even bat an eye at the bruises anymore.

I tilt my chin to look down at her. Kate's not at my eye level, but for a girl, she's fairly tall—maybe five foot seven or eight? In those eyes, eyes as green as the stripes on the Davies family tartan, I see something I haven't seen on a girl's face in... well, *ever*. Admiration? Respect, maybe? Is it possible Kate *respects* me? That she sees past my intimidating exterior to the man beneath the brawn? That she sees more than just a conquest to brag to her friends about?

One of dad's rules pops into my head.

Rule 2—Never let your emotions show.

I lock down the surprise on my face, keeping it to its usual icy façade.

What if she doesn't like what she finds? I don't know why I care, but suddenly, I don't want Kate to know about the fighting, the girls, my family... those goddamn rules. For the first time in my life I'm not proud of my wins, of all the girls I've shagged or had suck me off at the club or behind the school. For once, I'm truly ashamed of what I am.

Kate

"They never stop, yeah?" Dax's elbow gently pokes my ribs.

I tear my eyes away from Adam and Ellie, who are cuddling up close on the bench across the table from my seat. Heat rushes into my cheeks at the fact that Dax caught me ogling my friend making out with her boyfriend.

"No," I admit.

Dax frowns at my one word response. He's probably sick to death of being forced to hang out with me. I'm so intimidated by him that I can't ever manage to say more than a few words when he's around. My hands never feel comfortable, so I'm extra fidgety. Especially when those dark eyes are fixed on me. Like they are right now.

"Did you want another cuppa?" He motions to his empty mug.

"Sure. Decaf—"

"With milk. I know."

I have no response. Dax Davies knows how I take my tea! I'm such a social idiot. Dax will never want to be near me again if I keep acting like such a prat.

"Where'd Dax go?" Adam asks.

"Oh, so you've stopped snogging long enough to notice your best mate is missing?" I snap. Catching the hurt on Ellie's face, I quickly apologize. "Sorry, Adam. I'm out of sorts today."

Ellie's eyes flick over to where Dax is waiting in line at our favorite café, then back to mine. I caution her with a look, praying she doesn't say anything about Dax to let on that I like him.

When he slides back into the booth next to me, my left thigh and arm ignite where we touch. My body reacts instantly. My heart fluttering as if it's going to fly out of my chest and my breathing becomes fast and erratic.

It's so embarrassing to have such little control over my body whenever Dax is around, especially if he's touching me, which doesn't happen often. My face is certain to be five shades of red right now, pointing out my ridiculous infatuation with him like a blinking neon sign.

Dax leans in, unknowingly unleashing the overwhelming power of his beautiful yet utterly masculine face. His perfect, curved mouth is only inches away from mine. Those lips, soft looking yet surrounded by a rough late day stubble, are so tempting, I'm about to close the gap and see if they taste as good as they look.

"At least they've stopped swapping saliva long enough to have a bit of air, yeah?" he stage whispers conspiratorially.

My breath stutters, then I burst out laughing at his unexpected humor. Dax joins me while Adam and Ellie pretend to be offended.

And just like that I'm irreversibly hooked on my drug of choice, Dax Davies.

DAX

"DAX! Do you need me to tape your hands?"

Shaking my head, I remain seated on the rickety bench in the tiny club locker room, not answering my brother, Shaun, as I methodically wind the hand wrap through my fingers. The sharp scent of sweat and menthol sports rub stings my nostrils.

"If you want to win, then you need to—"

"Shaun," I snap. "Sod off! If I want you to do them or hear your advice, I'll bloody ask!"

Anger clouds his face. I know I'm pushing it with Shaun. A quick glance at his fisted hands lets me know that he's itching for a fight. He's the hot head of the family. Loves everything about this place—the fighting, the women, the money, and the thrill of doing something illegal.

"You're bloody lucky you're fighting tonight, or else I'd fuck you up for speaking to me like that." His dark eyes are cold, lacking any kindness. His twin, Liam, is completely opposite him in personality even though they look identical. I'm truly shocked they get along so well.

"Whatever Shaun. Just tell me when it's time."

My brother grinds his jaw, the muscles twitching under the light stubble on his face. Without another word, he turns and leaves.

"Fuck." I exhale loudly and drag a wrapped hand down my face. Picking a fight with Shaun is not smart. The man is ruthless, explosive, and doesn't care if you're family when he starts swinging.

I know I'm being a whingy prick, but I don't want to be here.

After spending the past week hanging out with Kate via Adam and Ellie, chatting about out mutual love of Arsenal football, I've begun to resent my dad and this whole fucking scene. More so than usual. I really want to shag her, more than any girl before, but if I'm honest with myself, I could see myself dating someone like Kate. *Exclusive dating*, something I've never even considered before.

There's something about Kate that's different than the tarts that normally chat me up—something that makes her better than them. She's much too good for a bloke like me. I'll end up fucking it all to hell somehow, I'm sure. Yet, she makes me want to take all the rules and toss them out the window.

Fighting was never my choice, yet I always thought it was something to be proud of—being fit, winning matches, getting the attention of loads of girls—*my rewards*. Now, the fighting is like a noose around my neck, pulling tight and holding me back when I want to be free to be with Kate. I want to be the one who decides.

All my life I've been playing by my father's rules. Now it's time to do what I want, when I want, who I want.

And I want her.

3

K ate

"C'MON. It'll be fun! Just this once take a break from studying, El. It's Saturday night." My best mate stares at me as if I've grown a second head. "Please?" I beg. "I've come all this way to see you, don't make me sad."

"All this way? Rubbish. You walked a single flight of stairs from your flat to mine," she huffs with a smile. I grin, knowing I've won. Ellie rolls her eyes. "Fine. But if I fail chemistry, it's your fault." Ellie shuts her book, stuffing it into her bag.

"Thanks! I'll love you forever." I wrap her up in a big hug.

"You'll love me forever anyway," she laughs. "You don't have to pay me favors."

"True." I let go, pushing her towards her wardrobe. "Now, get changed. We don't want to miss any of the show."

"Alright, alright! Give me a minute."

I walk into the tiny washroom and check my reflection—boring and plain, as usual. Oh well.

"Ready?" Ellie asks.

"Let's go!"

The tube to the DK seems to take forever tonight, probably because I'm nearly crawling out of my skin to see Dax perform again. Yeah, last time sucked. Watching the groupies stalk Dax and Adam from the edge of the stage was a nice solid punch to my ego. But the fact that I've spoken to Dax a few times since has given me a microscopic sized amount of courage that I plan on exploiting once I have a pint or two.

"Bugger. They've already started," I complain, hopping from one foot to the other. I twist my hair nervously around my hand.

"What's the big deal? We've seen them before," Ellie asks.

I shrug, not wanting to discuss my enormous, pathetic, decade-old crush on Dax. "You get to see them practice nearly every day. I've only seen them the one time." Ellie hands me a pint of lager, which I down much faster than I should. I need to relax or I'll combust.

"Jeez, Kate. Thirsty?" Ellie is raising a questioning eyebrow at my empty glass.

"Oh. Yeah. I was. Sorry. Let me grab another and we can move closer to the stage."

Five minutes later, we're situated a few meters from where Adam and Dax are singing and strumming their hearts out. The two new blokes are good as well, making them sound like a proper band.

"They're really good with the Americans joining up!" Ellie shouts in my ear so I can hear her over the music. "They even wrote some more songs now that they have drums and a bass!"

"They are good!" I yell back. Personally, I liked the acoustic set they did a bit better. But she's right. They do sound like a proper band. Professional. The fact that all four of them are strikingly gorgeous in their own way doesn't hurt their popularity one bit.

I know the exact second Adam notices Ellie in the crowd. When he sees her, he smiles like he's found his reason to live. He sings to her and her alone, exposing his heart and soul with each beautiful note.

It's almost uncomfortable to watch, as if I'm intruding on an intimate moment. A seed of unease blooms in my chest. No one has ever looked at me like that. I can't even imagine what that level of devotion would feel like.

My eyes leave Adam to focus on Dax. He's singing and playing as much as Adam, but Dax keeps his emotions sealed up tight—if he even has emotions. His face is as expressionless and distant as it's been every single day I've known him. In fact, the only time I've seen that cold, unreadable face change is when he talks to Adam or his band mates. Never for anything or anyone else.

That's not entirely true, he had a laugh with me the other day at the café. Of course, Adam was there, but still. I saw it, and it was breathtaking.

Iceman. I giggle at the thought.

As Dax's eyes roam the crowd, they land on me and freeze. Too late to hide it, I see his eyes widen in surprise. To my complete and utter shock, Dax winks at me before returning his attention to the music.

My chest is suddenly full, and it's not from that seed of doubt. No, it's from hope. The hope that maybe, just maybe, I'm no longer invisible and Dax Davies might actually see me.

～

"YOU SURE you're okay going home? It's a long way and I don't want to feel like I'm ditching you."

I smile at Ellie. "You're not ditching me, El. I'll be fine."

"I'll make sure she gets home, Ellie. No worries, yeah?" Dax has silently edged up next to us, apparently overhearing our conversation. He doesn't seem to think twice about his offer. I stifle a smile. Surely Dax must realize I've been walking around Hackney by myself my entire life?

Ellie's gaze shifts from me to Dax and back. I see an impish sparkle in her blue eyes right before she smirks. "Thanks Dax. I was worried, but Adam wants to—"

"Adam wants to what?" Ellie's boyfriend, Adam Reynolds, wraps his arms around her waist, leaning his lightly stubbled chin on the top of her blonde head. He's exactly what you want for a lead singer, tall and lean, with tousled black hair and a permanent grin. Charming as well. "Spend time with his girl?" Ellie tips her head back so Adam can reach her mouth, giving her a quick kiss.

It takes everything in me not to squirm or fidget as they give us another peek inside their relationship. A prickly heat creeps up my neck and into my cheeks. If Dax weren't standing so close, close enough to catch his alluring masculine scent, maybe it wouldn't be so uncomfortable, but Adam and Ellie are *always* snogging when Dax and I are around. Their intense heat combined with Dax's close proximity makes every cell in my body ache to spin around and press against his huge, muscular form.

"Ummmm, yeah," I stammer. "Go. Spend time together. Be happy and loving and snog all night. I'll find a way home. No need to bother Dax." I have to allow him an out. He isn't my keeper and isn't responsible for me.

I can't bring myself to look at Dax directly. If I do he'll see right through my lie. He'll know I want him to insist on taking me home. That it will make me feel that a teeny tiny piece of me somehow belongs to him.

Dax immediately rebuffs my option. "Nonsense. I'm taking you home." Even though I can't see his face, I can tell from his voice that our discussion is over. Somehow, I knew he wouldn't allow me to walk home alone, and that controlling, possessive streak of his brings a smile to my face that I can't hide.

"Fine. See El? Dax is taking me home. Go." I bodily push her and Adam out the door of the DK. Hawke and Gavin, their American band mates, have already left. Only Dax and I remain in the cramped back room.

"Ready?"

Dax has gathered his guitar and is holding open the door for me. "Yes, I suppose," I say, flashing him what I hope is a sexy smile and not an awkward grimace. A second later, I feel utterly ridiculous in my pathetic attempt to seem flirty. I'm not flirty, not even close.

My attempt must not be as pathetic as I thought, because Dax's usually glacial expression lights up and he grins back. "After you."

Wow. Being able to pull that single smile from him gives me a heady sense of power. Dax doesn't smile for just anyone. In fact, I've only ever seen him smile for Adam and... me.

Forgetting about my inadequacies for a change, we chat comfortably all the way to the tube station, have a laugh at the confused tourists on the train, and jostle each other playfully as we make our way to my flat. In fact, we're having so much fun we don't realize how handsy we're being with each other our joking has me pulled against Dax's wide chest, my head tilted back to stare into his molten brown eyes.

Our laughter cuts off abruptly. Something flickers behind those dark irises of his. Something that sends tiny sparks zinging down my spine, flooding my body with warmth. He looks as if... as if he's going to kiss me. But he wouldn't do that, right? I'm the sporty girl. The boring one. Not the gorgeous type a bloke like Dax would go for. Yet there's no mistaking the heat in normally ice-cold his eyes.

Dax lowers his head, his nose brushing against my cheek. An uncontrollable shudder wracks my body and goose bumps cover my skin. His breath is hot on my ear. The contrast between hot and cold overwhelming my body is as thrilling to feel as it is confusing to see in Dax's ever-changing moods. "Kate..." He inhales a ragged breath, as if merely speaking is painful.

Before I can blink, Dax's huge, calloused hands are framing my face and his mouth brushes across mine. At first it's just a whisper, a tease, the contact barely there. Then, I hear him inhale sharply and his lips press down forcefully, melding with mine, urging me to open up with quick flicks of his tongue. I melt against his solid body as he dominates the kiss, completely under his spell to do with as he wishes. It seems to go on and on—a small slice of paradise in this blighted spot of East London.

When he finally pulls back, greedily stealing a few more nips at my mouth, he closes his eyes and moans. "I knew you'd taste like heaven. You're an angel, I just knew it." His voice is so quiet I wonder if he meant to say it out loud.

Naturally, I stand there like an idiot, saying nothing... doing nothing. I've been kissed into complete stupidity.

Dax swipes the pad of his thumb over my damp lips. "See you at school tomorrow." Without giving me a single hint of what he's thinking, he turns and leaves. I touch my mouth, running a finger over the same spot Dax touched. My heart leaps into my throat, fluttering so fast I fear it may explode.

Great. I'm ruined. My first kiss and it was nothing less than brilliant. Dax Davies just ruined me for every other man from now until the day I die.

DAX

FINALLY. I have nine days before my next fight, so if I play my cards right, I can get Kate to drop her knickers for me before the seven day no shagging period. I swear I've become obsessed with her. For some reason Kate's tall, athletic body and natural beauty are all I think about day and night. Even that husky voice of hers makes me hard. At this point, no other girl will do.

Fuck. I need to get laid. I've spent the last four days imaging Kate beneath me, naked and sweaty and screaming my name. Now, there's only half an hour left of school and it feels like it'll never end. My dick can't take much more of a wait. It's about to burst through my trousers from my lewd and frankly, quite creative thoughts.

"Oi! Dax!"

Adam claps his hand on my shoulder as I stuff books into my locker. "Yeah?"

"I can't make practice today. Ellie asked if I'd hang with her. Her mum's expecting some test results today and she doesn't want to be alone."

Ellie's mum has cancer, which just plain sucks. They're good people, her parents.

"No worries. Are you going to her place?"

"Nah, we're going to have a bite or something."

Now I have a reason to speak to Kate. I'll offer to walk her home.

"See you later, then."

"Right. Cheers." Adam nods and ducks off into the crowd to find Ellie.

As if the gods are determined to help out my poor, neglected cock, Kate walks down the hall towards the doors. I sprint into action, catching up to her with a few long strides.

"Hey."

Great opening line, you numpty.

"Uh, hello." Kate is looking at me oddly, her petite, freckled nose scrunched up in confusion.

"What?" Lovely. I must have offended her by forcing myself on her the other night. That means my chance with her today is hovering at right about zero.

Kate giggles. "No. I'm wondering... forget it. Did you need something Dax?" Those green eyes, so hopeful, so trusting, are looking up at me, waiting for me to speak.

Every slick word I had ready to get into Kate's drawers sticks in the back of my throat. My gaze roams over her face, innocent, yet somehow so provocative at the same time. She pushes all my buttons, turning me into a horny bastard, yet I want to cherish her at the same time.

Damn. I pick now to grow a conscious?

Yes, apparently I do, because I can't bring myself to feed her a bunch of lines. Even though I know I could have Kate in my bed within the hour, something inside me doesn't want to taint someone so pure.

"Uh... I was just going to see you home. Since Ellie and Adam left already."

Kate smiles shyly, and my breath catches. Fuck, she's bloody gorgeous. My cock twitches, protesting the change of plans. It was really counting on getting some action today.

Crap. I'm a fucking bastard, a heartless one at that—but I can't be the one to manipulate and take advantage of such a sweet, innocent girl. Kate's not a slag, not even close. I won't treat her like one.

Rule 4—Women who act like slags can be treated like slags.

Right. "Ready to go?" I ask, willing my rock hard cock to go down.

Kate stares at me one last time, as if deciding whether or not trusting me is a good idea. She seems to come to the conclusion that I'm safe. With a practiced move, she hikes her bag up on her shoulder.

"Yes. I'm ready."

Oh love, you really shouldn't trust me. I'm most definitely not safe.

I hold open the door to the school. "Let's go then."

∾

"Oi! Dax."

I let go of the pull-up bar and drop lightly to my feet.

"Shaun."

Buggar. Of course he'd pop by while I'm in a shitty mood. Everything goes tits up right quick whenever my brother Shaun is around.

"I was about to have a go at the bag, but if *you're* here..." He gave me one of his evil smiles, the kind that makes you think he's deciding where to stash your body once he's offed you.

Fuck. Shaun and I haven't been in the cage together in months. We don't mesh well, me and him. Last time we went at it, both of us ended up in A&E—me for a busted nose and Shaun for a hairline fracture of his thumb. Still hasn't forgiven me for that one, even though it was his own fault for hitting me without making a proper fist.

I look over at the empty cage. It's calling to me, begging me to step inside and forget about everything else. To forget about my sexual frustration, self-inflicted by way of a newfound conscious. To forget about how I felt when Kate looked up at me with such trust in her emerald eyes. To forget about the fact that I'm just a poor Cockney bastard with no fucking future outside of this club.

Without another thought, I grab my thin gloves and yank them on. "Fine. Do we need a ref?" Shaun prefers to fight 'street style', meaning without rules or referees. He hates being told what he can and can't do.

Predictably, my brother's eyes narrow and he steps up into the cage. "No."

Certain I'll regret this come morning, I follow him up the stairs, slamming the cage door behind me.

Shaun grins from his corner, smacking a fist into an open palm. "Sure you're up for this? Your fight is in what... a week?"

"Nine days," I snap. Not that I'm counting.

"Hold up!" Shaun laughs. "Don't get your knickers in a twist.

Dad'll murder me if I injure you so you can't fight. I'm just wondering how hard I can hit your tender face, that's all."

"Fuck off, Shaun. Are we going to have a chat over tea or are we going to fight?" I move towards the center of the ring with my fists up.

Shaun shakes his head, smiling. "Always a glutton for punishment, aren't you? Fine, on three...two...one."

We both come out swinging.

It's the shortest fight either one of us has ever had.

Kate

"WHERE IS THIS PLACE?"

This is so cocked up. I have no idea what I'm even doing here. I'm so frightened, I can't even answer Tasha's question. A quick glance around at the neighborhood that surrounds us has me shivering in fear. Each street is getting scarier than the last.

I feel exposed and vulnerable in this part of Hackney. It's not known for its friendly atmosphere, that's for sure, and after dark isn't the time for a couple of girls to be wandering the streets. We're actually disturbingly close to the street known as Murder Mile.

Briefly, the image of Dax holding me close and keeping me safe while he fights off criminals flashes though my head. Another shiver wracks my body, but I'm certain this time it isn't from fear. No, it's definitely desire that has me shaking. That and my superhero fantasies.

Even though he's walked me home every day for the last week, Dax hasn't tried for another kiss or anything else. Honestly, I wish he would. All that talk of him being such a big ladies' man must be just that—talk. Otherwise, he would certainly have made a move on me by now. Unless... maybe he isn't interested in me in that way.

Maybe he was in an experimental mood that night. The thought is damn depressing. Or maybe the massive split lip and bruised chin he was sporting earlier this week kept him in check. Who knows?

Reaching into my pocket, I fish out the scrap of paper with the directions scribbled out. Directions. *Ha!* It's a bloody illegal fight club. You're not supposed to know where it is. There's not exactly going to be a big sign out front now, is there?

"Second building after Parson's Laundrette," I mutter, feeling significantly less confident about this plan than I was a few minutes ago. One kiss and I'm bloody stalking a bloke in the worst part of town. Hell, he probably kissed me out of pity—threw me a proverbial bone.

"This is so crazy, Kate. I can't believe we're doing this!" Tasha glances around nervously as we walk, but I can hear the excitement in her voice, feel it in her step. She always wanted to be the rebel, the bad girl. Now she's getting her chance. I've given her the perfect excuse to let loose and embrace her inner wild side by mentioning the club. Hell, *she's* the one who suggested we find it.

We come to a stop in front of a large, abandoned brick structure. It's completely dark, not a single light is on inside.

My head swivels around, looking for any signs of humanity. Nothing. Just the eerily silent night, mocking my desperation with its darkness. "This can't be it."

"Maybe—" Tasha's thought is cut short by a man's voice. We quickly huddle behind an overturned rubbish bin.

"Oi! Joe! Get yer arse in 'ere!"

I whip around just in time to see a bright light shine out of a crack on the bottom level of the building. A man ducks inside what appears to be the outline of a door then it closes behind him, plunging us back into blackness. Fear grips me—hard—slithering down my spine in icy, probing tentacles.

We should not be here.

"Why did I let you talk me into this, Tash?"

As much as try, I can't blame Tasha for our situation. After spending the last few weeks getting to know Dax, as Ellie's best friend of course, I want the chance to see him one on one, without Adam and Ellie around making me feel like I'm on a supervised non-date. Naturally, when I confessed my thoughts to Tasha, she came up with this brilliant plan.

Tasha and I had heard the rumors of Dax's involvement in illegal fighting over the years—and on more than one occasion seen the bruises on his face and hands. So she persuaded one of our less upstanding classmates to tell us how to get to the fight club and what nights we could find Dax there.

"Do we just—knock?"

Tasha shrugs. She doesn't know any more than I do. She just knows how to act the part. Bolder than I could ever be, her arm thrusts out past my shoulder to bang on the metal door, the loud clanging piercing the silence.

"Bloody hell, Tash. What the—"

My words die in my throat when I find myself face-to-chest with a wall of solid muscle. Tasha takes my elbow and pulls me back a step.

"What do ya want?" The large man looks mean, terrifying actually, and a small, condescending smile lifts one corner of his mouth. Strangely, when I look at him, I'm reminded of Dax. Except this man's brown eyes are cold and unwelcoming whereas Dax's are slightly warmer and friendlier. The reality of where I am and what I'm doing takes hold, causing my stomach to cramp with anxiety.

"I-I-"

Tasha gracefully steps in front of me, slithering right up close to the huge man. I let her take over. My nerves are shot to shit. It's quite clear—I'm not cut out for illegal activities.

"We're here to see Dax." She says it so casually that even *I* believe she has every right to be here demanding to be let inside.

An odd look passes over the man's handsome face, then it lights up with some sort of understanding. He looks us up and down lustfully, making the hairs on the back of my neck stand up. His scrutiny makes me feel as if I were naked and splayed out in front of him. I feel cheap and more than a little pissed off.

"Of course you're 'ere fer Dax. 'Nuff said, yeah?" He smiles, opening the door wider, letting us enter. "Two, eh? Dad's gone all out tonight. Dax will be quite pleased, I'm sure. *If* he wins that is." Big and Creepy lets out a deep chuckle, sending another round of goose bumps across my neck.

Tasha plays the part perfectly, going along with whatever he says. "Yes, he will."

The man grins and I have to hold in a gasp. He really does look just like Dax. One of his brothers, maybe? I know Dax has several. I just don't know their names, not that I'm about to introduce myself to Mr. Scary.

He nods his chin toward another door at the end of a short hall. "Thanks," Tasha tosses over her shoulder, walking confidently towards the door, swaying her hips as we pass.

"It's me pleasure, or should I say, Dax's?" He gives us one more lecherous look and winks before returning his attention to the entrance.

"Creepy, but hot," Tasha whispers. I nod, still too frightened to speak. Behind the next door we can hear the dull roar of a large group of people. Tasha reaches out and grips the doorknob, pulling it open slowly.

As we step through, the crowd howls with delight. It's so loud I have the urge to cover my ears with my hands. The place is packed with people, every one of whom has their full attention on the elevated ring in the center of the room. The ring is brightly lit with spotlights, standing out in the sea of darkness surrounding it.

My senses are so overwhelmed I'm not sure what to do first. Thank god for Tasha. She grips my arm and pushes me forward.

"Right. C'mon, then. Let's watch your man fight."

Her words break me out of my trance, as does the constant jostling of the other patrons as we make our way up front. "He's not *my man*, Tash." Not for lack of wishing.

"Well, not *yet* anyway," she says, smiling as we weave in and out of the lively crowd. "Maybe by the end of tonight."

Great. Now I feel all awkward and pressured to make an impression on Dax. It's bad enough that not only did I sneak off to an illegal fight club, but I also let Tasha do me up like some tart in order to make Dax think I'm desirable. I run a nervous hand down the tight-fitting shirt and jeans she made me wear, hoping to hide my overwhelming anxiety. What if I vomit? God, that would be just like me, ruining everything with a bout of sick.

"Look! Dax is fighting next. We almost missed it!"

We're finally close enough to see what's going on in the ring—honestly, it's more like a cage than a ring. Elevated a few meters off the cement floor is a boxing ring, but there's some sort of tall, black chain link around the perimeter, extending up a good ways above us.

"This is so awesome!" Tasha bounces up and down on her toes, clapping like a kid in a candy store.

"Awesome?" I stare at her incredulously. "This is going to be barbaric!"

"Pfft, lighten up Kate. It's hot to watch two built guys fight." She glares at me reproachfully. "It's sport, no different than our footy matches."

Not wanting to argue the blatant differences between football and illegal fighting, I stand in place gaping, my eyes glued to the cage. Tasha has gone mental. There's nothing hot about this. Scanning the area, my eyes find Dax, standing in one corner, rocking his head back and forth on his shoulders. He bounces around on his bare feet while punching the air in front of him. And he's doing it *shirtless.*

Watching his sinewy muscles stretch and flex with each movement does something to me. Fiery heat licks up my body, starting from the bottom of my feet and traveling all the way to the top of my head. Suddenly, it's very, very warm in here.

Tasha laughs. "See, admit it. It is hot. You're blushing so hard right now!"

"Shut it, Tash," I grumble, attempting to look unaffected. Who am I kidding? Of *course* I'm affected. It's Dax! A nearly naked Dax—every muscle of his perfect body on display for my viewing pleasure. I lick my lips at the thought of tasting that tan skin, from his ripped shoulders down to the glorious six-pack that tapers on his waist.

"Ladiiieees and gentlemeeennn! Tonight is your lucky night. Right now, we have a great fight for you! Most of you know that tonight is our welterweight championship fiiiight!"

Everyone around us explodes with excitement, cheering and yelling and whistling in response.

"In the blue corner, weighing in at one hundred ninety-nine pounds we have—" he pauses dramatically, "Noaaaaah Bakerrrrr!"

Half of the large crowd boos and the other half cheers excitedly. We're jostled about as the punters scramble to get a drink or put in their final wagers. We get more than our share of lewd stares from pervy blokes who are much too old to be looking. Even I have to admit, Tash and I stick out in this club like a nun in a brothel. Especially with our tight clothing and Tasha's liberal use of makeup.

"Now, in the red corner, weighing in at two hundred and one pounds—our own Dax Daaaaavies!"

"Oh my god! It's starting!" Tasha is so excited she's practically pulling me to the ground.

"Shhhhh, Tasha, I can't hear." I wave her off, annoyed at her for distracting me.

"Kate, it's loud as hell in here. Me talking isn't going to change whether or not you can hear. You just don't want me interrupting your ogling."

"Whatever," I snap, knowing she's exactly right.

The referee finishes up describing the rules and sounds the bell, starting the fight.

Dax and his opponent circle each other slowly. I can't take my eyes off of Dax, his body arching and gliding like a lethal jungle cat. Even from several rows back, I can see the primal instincts glinting in his dark eyes as he watches his enemy. Without warning, Noah strikes out, two quick punches that Dax deflects easily.

They continue this dance for a while, Noah advancing, Dax rebuffing. I'm beginning to wonder when the actual fighting will start when it happens. In the blink of an eye, Dax lets loose a series of jabs, knocking his opponent back.

Once the man is pressed into the chain links of the cage, Dax pounces—striking Noah over and over with his fists, raining them down all over the man's head and torso. Somehow, Noah regroups and is able to push Dax off right as the bell sounds.

Oh. My. God.

Now I see what Tasha meant about watching two men fight being a turn on. My skin is tingling with heated desire and a knot of pleasure begins swirling low in my body, begging to be let loose. A big blonde bloke that looks exactly like the one who let us in the front door wipes down Dax's face and squirts some water in his mouth. Dax nods as the man speaks in his ear. Before I know it, the bell sounds again and the men are back on their feet.

The crowd is clamoring for more, their shouts and whistles so loud I can't hear anything else. But I'm so entranced by Dax's smooth, sweaty skin, my eyes taking in every single bare inch, that I don't notice the noise. I don't notice anything, actually, until

Dax's opponent is on the floor and the announcer holds up Dax's hand in victory.

"Winner, by knockout, the new light heavyweight champion of the London Underground fighting circuit, Dax Daaaaavies!"

Tasha grabs my arm. "Did you see that, Kate? That was incredible!"

I blink rapidly, not understanding what just happened. "No. What?"

Her eyebrows pinch together. "Dax just pummeled that guy to the mat. You didn't see it? How could you not?"

Certainly, I'm blushing again. Or I would be if my skin weren't already flushed from staring at a half-naked Dax and his gorgeous muscles.

"Oh, I see," Tasha smirks. "Too busy getting an eyeful of Mr. Davies' arse to watch the action."

I huff in protest. "No. I was watching the action. I just didn't comprehend what was going on."

"Mmmmm-hmmm. Riiiight, Kate."

"Whatever, Tash. Don't be cheeky." I huff, feigning annoyance. She's right... I *was* watching Dax. He was stunning up there, like a sculpture come to life. His body was fluid and graceful, even as he used it to execute an extreme level of controlled violence.

"Oi! You aren't supposed to be here!"

Startled, Tasha and I whirl around to see Mr. Big and Creepy, the bloke from the front door, storming over to us with a daunting scowl on his face. The punters in the crowd dispersed immediately after the fight, either to collect their winnings or go home as losers, so our safety in numbers has been blown.

"What do we do?" I whisper to Tasha.

"Leave it to me." Tasha grins at the angry man, projecting complete confidence. "Where do you want us?" She flutters her eyelashes ridiculously.

Jeez, she really does want to walk on the wild side.

"After the fight, you're supposed to be in the back room with my brother." He hooks a thumb over his shoulder, indicating a lone door on one side of the large open space.

So he *is* Dax's brother. That explains the matching glacial expressions.

"Sorry, love. We were just chatting," Tasha says with a flirty tone in her voice.

The man's frigid exterior melts a tiny fraction at Tasha's playfulness. "Yeah, well, don't lounge about. Get moving. You can't keep a bloke waiting forever."

"Sure thing, gorgeous." Tasha takes my hand, walking me towards the door. On our way past the large, menacing man, she drags a painted fingernail across his chest and purses her lips. "See you later."

He grunts, and I swear I wouldn't have believed it had I not seen it with my own eyes, the man smiles. The big scary iceman has feelings, who knew?

Once we're out of earshot, I whisper to Tasha, "What in bloody hell are we doing?"

"I don't know," she whispers, panic in her voice. "I just played it by ear. It seemed safest to do what he said." Tasha looks me in the eye as her hand rests on the doorknob.

"We don't know who or what is in there, Tash." I'm shaking all over. The adrenaline rush from watching Dax fight is gone, leaving me to deal with its uncomfortable aftereffects.

"It seems a better choice than dealing with that bloke. Although, he is rather sexy, don't you think?"

"No, Tasha. I don't think that!" I hiss.

I look over my shoulder and see Mr. Big and Creepy staring directly at us, waiting for us to open the door. He has a knowing expression in his dark eyes. Something about it is telling me to be worried what we'll find on the other side.

"Here goes nothing." Tasha turns the knob and pushes the door open.

We both freeze at the sight in front of us. This room is clearly some sort of locker room or changing room—how I manage to notice my surroundings I don't know, but I do. The walls are covered with shelving stuffed with equipment. Gloves hang on various pegs and there's a pile of towels in one corner. But it's what is seated on the small wooden bench in the center of the room that catches our attention and crushes my heart.

Or should I say *who*?

Dax is sitting, completely naked, with his head thrown back and eyes closed. Droplets of water cling to his body and his hair is damp, indicating he just took a shower. His lips are parted in ecstasy, the angled planes of his jawline clearly visible. This is not the cold, hard façade I'm used to seeing.

Soft grunts can be heard as they escape from his throat, his Adam's apple bobbing when he swallows. Dax's large, bruised hands are buried in the blonde hair of the girl kneeling between his legs, controlling her movements as she loudly and enthusiastically sucks his cock.

"Holy—" Tasha whispers, not meaning to speak but too shocked to keep quiet.

Dax's head snaps up, those deep chocolate eyes locking onto mine even as the girl's head continues dipping up and down in front of him. As the tears begin to well up, the horrible scene in front of me goes fuzzy. Not enough that I don't register the horror on Dax's face before the tears are too thick to see. Unable to do anything else, I turn and run.

I realize I've put Dax up on a pedestal all these years without ever really knowing a thing about him. Now that I've seen who he is—*what* he is—I'm done. I am getting the hell out of this sodding town, leaving Dax Davies and my shattered heart behind.

4

S *ix months later*
Dax

"GORGEOUS, AREN'T THEY?" I have my arms around two girls, one on each side. They want me so badly they're practically humping my legs. Getting women in L.A. is easy. I don't have to work for it at all. Hawke says it's the British accent. I have to agree. It makes American women strip their clothes off faster than you can say *'shag me'*.

"Lovely," Adam growls, in a piss poor mood again.

I stifle a growl. "Ladies, excuse me for a moment." They giggle ridiculously as I grab my mate's arm and shove him into a corner of the loud club.

"Fuck off, Davies." He drains the rest of his drink, slamming the glass down on a nearby table.

"When are you going to start having fun? You going to spend the rest of your life moping around because Ellie broke up with you? It's been two months, Reynolds. Haven't any of those American pussies made you forget about her yet?" I lean into Adam's space, practically snarling at him.

"What do you care? Go fuck your tarts and leave me be." Adam sounds angry and determined, but his eyes tell a different story. They're the eyes of a broken man. I would know. I see the exact same thing in the mirror every day since I fucked up with Kate.

It's why I'm so cheesed off at his behavior. When I see him self-destruct, when I watch him try to fuck Ellie out of his head, I'm reminded of my own actions, my own hurt, my own screw-ups with Kate.

I shrug off the memories. I don't need her or any other girl. I've got a successful band, my father doesn't have any say over my life anymore, and I have more women available than I ever could have imagined.

So why do I still obsess over one woman in particular?

"I care because you're my best mate and you're miserable! I care because the band needs you and you're bloody rat-arsed all the fucking time! I care because you're a mess and I'm tired of having to mind you all the damn time!"

I don't shout out that I need him to move on and stop reminding me of the girl I left back home. A girl who is now in the same city as me. Thinking about Kate makes me feel like the biggest fucking bastard in the world.

Adam's brows come together at my chastising. The dark look he gives me is shocking. Adam is always happy. It's not always genuine, but he puts up a good front. Tonight is the first time I've ever seen such a furious expression on his face.

"You're not my keeper, Davies! I'm not your bloody responsibility. If you don't like what I'm doing, then don't fucking watch!" He shoves past me, knocking me back with his shoulder as he heads for the bar.

Stunned, I return to the two attractive girls I left on the edge of the dance floor, my mood now dark and dangerous. "Ladies, I'll have to take a rain check. Sorry," I growl.

They pout, but I'm halfway to the exit so I don't hear their protests. The familiar agitation roars through me, flooding my veins with rage. The same feeling I used to get back in Hackney when I had no choice but to follow my dad's orders. If there's one thing that can unsettle me and drive me over the edge, it's not being in control of my own life.

I don't care about people. Ever.

These fucking feelings of helplessness, of giving a shit that I let Kate down, of not being able to just let it go and be the cold prick I know I am—it has my skin crawling and my fists eager for a fight.

Outside, I hail a cab and give the address of a run down gym near my flat. It's for serious martial artists, boxers and the like, open until after midnight most nights. While the driver weaves in and out of heavy L.A. traffic, I think about that night in Hackney. The night that took everything I knew to be true about myself and turned it all into a lie.

My cock was buried deep in the throat of the slag my dad hired for my reward when the locker room door opened. She was giving me one of the best blowjobs of my life, yet all I can remember from that night is the wounded, desolate look on Kate's gorgeous face.

Shit. Pining after a girl. Maybe I'm more like Adam than I thought. Only, instead of using a bottle to bury my pain, I use my fists.

Kate

"You really won the roommate lottery, Kate." My friend Abby glances over at Lila's side of the room with disgust. Designer clothes are tossed everywhere, littering the bed and the floor—even her desk. The sarcasm in Abby's voice is evident.

"You don't know half of it." I throw my Intro to Psychology textbook into my duffel with my footy gear and zip it closed. "She's got a different bloke in here just about every night."

Abby's eyebrows shoot up, "Every night?"

I nod. "Just about. It's so bloody inconvenient. She made a rule that if one of us is in here having it off, you put a sock on the doorknob so the other won't come in and interrupt." I stifle a smile when Abby bursts out laughing. We're in a class together and became fast friends.

"She's unbelievable," Abby chokes out.

I roll my eyes. "Yeah. She's something."

"Why is she even here? At UCLA? Or in the dorms for that matter?" Abby asks as we head for the lifts to take us downstairs. "Clearly she has money. And she isn't here to study."

The doors to the lift slide open. A few students exit before we get on. "I guess she's here for the shagging," I joke, only, that's not far from the truth when it comes to my perpetually randy flatmate.

"Huh. What a waste." Abby is shaking her head. "I'd love to get inside that brain of hers."

We walk outside into the bright L.A. sun. September has just begun and it's hot and sunny, as it's been every day of the last four weeks since I arrived. "You and your psychoanalyzing."

"Hey!" Abby bumps hips with mine. "That interest in psychoanalyzing is going to help you pass Psych 101. Where would you be without me?"

Indeed. Where would I be? I'd be in L.A. alone, no friends, no Dax, no Ellie, no anything. The thought has me resolving to try harder to find out where Ellie is staying. Classes started two weeks ago and I haven't heard a thing from her. I'm listed in the campus directory but still, no call.

Tomorrow, I'll call the Department of Student Services and

see if they can give me any information. I may not have Dax, but I can always count on my best mate. And right now, I could really use another friend. Someone I can lean on.

I never spoke to Dax again after the night Tasha and I literally caught him with his pants down. I couldn't bear to face him knowing that I had absolutely no place in his life. That whatever we had between us was about as important to him as clipping his fingernails and choosing what socks to wear.

"I think I'm going to go on that date with that guy from the men's footy team," I blurt out randomly. Maybe a new bloke will help me forget about Dax. "The one who asked me to dinner last week."

"Really?" Abby sounds confused. "I thought you told him no."

I *did* tell him no. I had still been holding out hope that things may work out between Dax and me. "I told him I had to think about it. Not a flat out no."

"Good for you. So far, all I've seen you do is study and practice. That's not much of a life. This is college. Time to figure out who you are and what you want."

"Yeah," I respond quietly.

Too bad what I want isn't ever going to be mine.

DAX

"DUDE! YOU'RE A MACHINE!"

I ignore the kid who walks up next to where I'm working with the heavy bag. I hit it over and over in the exact same routine my dad had me do back home. Going through the familiar motions gives me peace. It lets my mind focus solely on the power in my body as it comes into contact with the thick, padded surface. Each strike serves as a reminder of who I really am.

My father's son. A violent, unfeeling bastard.

I continue pummeling the bag, kicking and punching over and over again. Sweat is pouring off of me, dripping off my body and onto the mat. Concentrating on making each strike perfect is supposed to keep my mind from wandering. Keep out the unwelcome emotions that surge forward when I think of Kate.

Yet she creeps in constantly. Between each flying kick I remember her bright green eyes. Between each punch I remember the way her face lights up when she smiles. Between each jab, I remember how she tasted when I kissed her. Between each front kick, I remember how I fucked it all up.

I stop, my hands hanging at my sides as my chest heaves up and down. Frustration and anger eat away at me, boiling up like acid inside. Yanking off my gloves, I throw them on the floor, disgusted.

I have total control over my body. It pisses me off that I can't exert that same control over my mind. I don't let anything bother me. *Ever.* I don't allow emotions to control me. This powerlessness over my own thoughts has turned me into raging lunatic.

A male voice snaps me out of the dark place I'm in, bringing my attention back to the gym.

"Hey man, that was awesome! Do you fight professionally?"

After wiping off with a towel, I glance over at the enthusiastic kid standing in front of me. "Who are you?" I've been here dozens of times, but don't recognize this overly excited bloke.

Eager as shit, the kid bounces on the balls of his toes. "Zane. Zane Denninger."

"Dax Davies." I eye him up and down as we shake hands. "You're a fighter?" Kid's way too small to be much good in the cage. Maybe flyweight, but even then I'd have a hard time believing it.

His cheeks turn pink. "Nah. I work the desk here. I do some kickboxing, but only for exercise."

"I see. And the answer to your question is no, I don't fight professionally." I don't see the point in discussing my past with a stranger so I make no mention of my days in Hackney.

"You should," he says. "You're really good."

I stare at Zane curiously. Why is he talking so much? "Nah, I can't. Musician." I hold up my hands. "If I injure them, I'm out of work."

He nods rapidly, up and down, up and down. Christ, the kid has more energy than anyone I've ever seen. He makes me feel old, and he can't be but a year or two younger than me.

"Gotcha. Music, cool. I always wanted to work in the entertainment industry. It's why I moved out here." Zane shrugs. "No talent though." He grins. "Well, I better get back to work. See you around."

With that, he turns on his heel and walks back to the front desk.

People in L.A. are so fucking weird. At least his blathering made me forget about Kate for a whole minute and a half. Now I understand why Adam drinks—to numb the mind, shut it off, have a bit of peace—if only for a little while. Unlike Adam, I'm not willing to sit back and let my life go on without me.

Since I can't stop thinking about Kate, I need to accept that I fucked up and take charge of the situation. If I have to see her and beg for her forgiveness to move on and get this shit out of my head, then that's what I'll do. I'll be damned if I let something as pointless as emotions torture me for weeks, months, or fuck, even years.

Dax Davies doesn't sit back and let shit happen. I grab it, control it, and make that shit mine.

5

K ate

"I'm glad you agreed to go out with me tonight. I had fun." Mateo flashes me one of his brilliant white grins, the dimple in his left cheek visible. It looks good on him. He really is a good-looking bloke.

"Me too," I reply automatically, giving him what I hope is a convincing smile.

Mateo walks me up to the door of my building where we stand a few feet apart, staring at each other awkwardly.

"So, can I see you again?" His dark eyes are fixed on me, unwavering. I shiver with deja vu. I want to run away from those familiar eyes. That wouldn't be fair. It's not Mateo's fault that they remind me of someone else's deep brown gaze.

A sophomore, Mateo is here from Barcelona on a football scholarship—same as me. The girl's footy team does a few events with the men, which is how we met. He asked me out twice before I reluctantly agreed.

It doesn't hurt that Mateo is easy to look at—tan skin, eyes so dark they almost look black, full lips, and perfect teeth. His slightly too-long hair always falls into his eyes, which makes him that much sexier. Plus, since he's a footy player he's super fit. He reminds me of a Spanish version of Oliver Giroud. Only, I can't bring myself to see him as more than a friend.

I'm the only one who gets the friend vibe from Mateo. Nearly all of my teammates are jealous that he asked me out. Yet I can't seem to find the proper amount of enthusiasm. My heart just won't let go of the past. Ten years of believing you were meant for someone else isn't an easy thing to move past. God knows I'm trying.

When Mateo leans in for a kiss, I reluctantly allow it, praying it will wipe away my memories of Dax. My heart is racing when his warm lips meet mine, gently pressing against them. He doesn't deepen it or push for more, yet it feels wrong. Too intimate. Too...different.

Mateo is the only man I've ever kissed besides Dax. Even though it was ages ago it feels as if I'm cheating.

Mateo pulls back, his eyelids heavy with desire. His pupils are wide and his cheeks are flushed. I can tell he wants more, but thankfully, he's too kind to push. Instead, he steps back, releasing me. "Good night, Kate. I'll call you tomorrow."

I nod before turning to fumble with the lock. Once inside I bolt for the lifts and say a silent thank you when a set of doors immediately opens. Inside, I slump against the wall, fighting to keep back the tears.

I'm afraid. Afraid that Mateo will have expectations of things I can't give him. Afraid I'll never be able to love anyone but Dax. Afraid I'll be alone forever because I can't move on from a man who was never mine. Most of all, I'm afraid that my opportunity to be happy has come and gone and no matter how hard I try to forget Dax, I'll be miserable for the rest of my life.

Dax

Sᴡᴇᴀᴛ ᴅʀɪᴘs off of my neck, trickling down between my shoulder blades. Los Angeles is a bloody nightmare of a city. It's hot and sunny all the damn time, which wouldn't be so bad if there were decent public transportation. But after spending an hour and a half making two bus changes to get to the UCLA campus, I'm pretty much done with the heat and the traffic.

It takes me another thirty minutes to cross campus to the section with student housing. A piercing ring startles me right as I stop in front of Hedrick Summit, a tall dormitory on the far side of the university property. Groaning, I fish my mobile out of my pocket.

"Yeah?"

"Dax? Where are you man?"

Jesus, Adam sounds like bloody fucking hell. *Again.* "Adam, I told you yesterday that I was going to see if I could find Kate at UCLA."

His rough voice crackles through the phone. "Oh. I don't remember."

Of course he doesn't remember. He's always on a piss up these days. After Ellie broke up with him this summer for absolutely no reason, he's been self-destructive times a thousand, finding peace in an endless supply of blondes and booze. Not that I'm one to talk. I was so angry and frustrated when Kate caught me getting head at the club that I flipped out the next day and attacked Adam's wanker of a dad—forcing Adam and me to leave the U.K. six weeks ahead of schedule.

"What do you need, Adam?"

"Ummmm, I can't remember, really. I woke up and everyone was gone. Where are Hawke and Gavin?"

My patience is wearing thin. Adam's my best mate and I'd do anything for him, but being his nanny isn't exactly my idea of a good time.

"I don't know. They didn't ask me for permission to leave the flat. Get cleaned up and eat something for Christ's sake. We have a gig tonight. I'll be back in a few hours." Sighing, I rein in my anger, easily trapping my emotions inside where they can fester with everything else in my life that I've repressed under my dad's tutelage.

I snap the mobile closed and stuff it in my pocket. Hawke's uncle, Ross Evans, is now our manager. He gave each of us a mobile to keep in touch in case he needs us for anything. For me, it's become a tether to my fragile best mate.

"Room 1425," I say to myself, trying to work up the nerve to walk inside the looming building. Students bound up the stairs past me, laughing and chatting like the world isn't about to implode. For some reason, I have to make things right with Kate. I have to see her again.

Ever since Kate refused to speak to me after that night at the fight club, I've been a miserable bastard. She literally caught me with my pants down and my *reward* sucking me off in the locker room

Dad's theory that withholding sexual release from us before a fight made us quick-tempered enough to step into the ring. But the promise of a whore to suck us off and rid us of the frustration after? That's what made us determined to *win*. It pissed me off that he taught us that way, but it pissed me off even more to know that he was right.

I nearly took Shaun's head off when he admitted to letting Kate and her friend into the club. In fact, he was the one who directed them to the locker room. To this day, when I think about it, every bit of rage I felt that night comes flooding back.

"S*HAUN, you useless fucking twat! Why'd you let them back here?"* I storm out of the locker room, exchanging embarrassment and shame for red-tinged fury.

My brother's dark eyes narrow as he folds his muscular arms over his chest. *"I thought they were your reward. You know, a twofer."*

I come to an abrupt halt, my mouth gaping open in shock. *"You what?"* He thought Kate was a whore?

"They were all tarted up like a couple of slags. How was I supposed to know?" He shrugs as if it were no big deal to accuse Kate of being one of dad's hookers.

Those words cause my vision to go completely red and I fucking snap, lunging for my brother. I know the only reason I get one solid punch in is because Shaun isn't expecting my attack. My right fist connects with his face with a satisfying crunch. His head snaps back and he tumbles to the concrete floor. Quick as a snake, Shaun is back on his feet, his eyes flashing with fury as he wipes a trickle of blood from his lip with the back of his hand.

Shaun spits blood onto the ground and raises his fists. *"C'mon little brother. I'll give you that one hit, but you want another you're going to have to earn it."*

Shaun is the most dangerous of my brothers, lethal and indifferent. Right now, I could give a shit. I leap at him, determined to take out my devastation on his ass. The pain inside of me is so acute, that I don't feel anything as we exchange hard blows. When his fists or feet connect with my body, it's as if I'm numb. My mind goes somewhere else, watching from afar. An unseen force must be controlling my actions, because something fragile inside me has snapped. The next thing I know, Ethan has his arm around me in a chokehold and Liam has Shaun.

"Fuck you! Let me go!" I gasp, struggling to get out of the tight hold Ethan has me in.

Shaun is somewhat calmer than me, but not much. Then again,

he's not having his air cut off. Liam lets go of his arms, whispering something to get Shaun to back off.

"Dax, stop." Ethan is still trying to reason with me as I buck against his tight grip.

"Fuck off, Ethan! He ruined it for me! He fucking ruined everything!" I wheeze.

"What are you talking about?" Ethan asks, still holding me back as I tussle to get at Shaun and to breathe.

"Kate! That's what! He cocked up my only chance with her!" Shaun smirks from behind Liam. I scream in fury at him taking pleasure in crushing what little light I had in my dark soul. "I'll fucking kill you!"

"Come off it, Dax," Shaun says, that motherfucking smirk still on his face. I'd love to punch it right off for him. "You can't have a girlfriend and you know it. Dad won't allow it. He knows if we get regular pussy we won't want to fight. That's the whole point of the fucking reward, you stupid tosser."

I know he's right but he can sod off. Shaun doesn't know I'm planning to get out of here, that Adam and I are going to leave for America with Hawke and Gavin to further the band. That Kate and Ellie are going with us and I had every intention of pursuing something with her once we were gone. None of them know. Dad would lose it if I told him I wasn't staying to work for him.

Living here, in this shithole? This isn't my dream. Fighting for the next twenty years? I'd rather be dead. It feels as if an important part of my future has slipped through my fingers tonight.

The anger bleeds out of me at the reality of my situation. I'm defeated. Lost. Without a purpose. I'd always claimed my rewards proudly. I'd earned it, it felt good, and no one was hurt so what did it matter? Today, after seeing the look on Kate's face, I realized too late that someone was hurt, and there's nothing I can do to fix it.

It's better this way. I'm no good for a girl like Kate. All I'd do is corrupt something good and pure. I'll suffer now to spare her from the pain I would eventually cause.

IT TAKES a minute to relax my fists at the unwelcome memory. By the time I reach the 14th floor, I'm more agitated than angry— scared to see that hurt in Kate's eyes again. The hurt I put there. It replays over and over again in my mind, haunting me since that day.

I need to do this to take back control, to push out these obsessive thoughts so I can focus on my music. Room 1425 stares me in the face. Holding my breath, I file away my emotions, put up my hand and knock.

"Why hello gorgeous."

A small, bleached blonde girl in an impossibly tiny shirt and shorts is standing in the doorway, giving me a look I can only describe as lewd. Lewd to the point of uncomfortable. So uncomfortable, I actually drag a hand across my chest to make sure I'm wearing clothes.

Clearing my throat, I manage to speak. "Is Kate in?"

The girl's eyes go wide. "You're British! Oh. My. God. Tall, gorgeous, and a sexy accent? My, oh my..." She licks her lips and gives me another once over. Christ, this girl is eye-fucking me and doesn't care if I know it!

"Ummmm, right. So... is Kate here? This is her flat, yeah?"

The blonde giggles, placing her small hand on my chest. I tense up under her touch. If I've learned one thing about girls in L.A. it's that they have no sense of decency. There is no such thing as self-respect or personal space here. Cold, emotionless Dax rears his ugly head, ready to put this girl in her place.

"Kate's not in. I'm her roommate, Lila. She didn't mention anyone stopping by." Her tongue wets her lips in what is likely supposed to be a seductive move. Yeah, she's fit and all, but my mind isn't on her or what she could give me. I want to see Kate.

I let out a huge sigh. I can't be a bastard to Kate's flatmate. Instead, I gently remove Lila's hand from where it still rests on my chest. "Do you have a marker pen? I want to leave my mobile number for her."

"Hmmmm," she taps her tooth with a pink polished finger-nail. "Do *I* get your number too, big guy?"

The shock I feel at her blatant come on is tough to keep from showing on my face. My irritation must be obvious because Lila backs off, but only a little. Desire is still evident in her eyes. "Fine, fine," she gives me an odd smile and waves her hand as if I'm already forgotten and she's moved on to her next potential conquest. "Here." Lila hands me a pen and paper. I scratch down my number and hand it back.

"Thanks. Please, it's important. We're mates from back home and I haven't seen her in a while." I try pleading to Lila's sympathies, praying she'll make sure Kate gets the number.

Lila's hungry expression returns, "Sure you don't want to come in for a few minutes?"

I go rigid, beginning to get more than merely annoyed by Kate's pushy tart of a flatmate. "No, I'm quite sure. I have to meet my mates in a bit."

Lila narrows her eyes into a sly glare. "Oh, well then, no prob-lem..." she glances down at the paper in her hand, "*Dax*. I'll make sure she gets it."

I nod woodenly, wondering if she'll actually give my number to Kate or if she'll 'lose' it in a jealous bid to keep Kate away from the bloke who turned her down.

Fuck if I know. I'm more worried that if Lila *does* give Kate my number, Kate won't use it. If Ellie, who was so obviously in love with Adam, could be so cold and heartless as to break up with him over the phone for no reason, I have no doubt in my mind that Kate might have shut me out for good as well.

After seeing Adam's downward spiral after Ellie and the hurt in Kate's eyes that night, I don't know if I can live with that.

Kate

I FIDDLE with the edge of my textbook, worrying it until it tears off in my hand. This past summer, while traveling Europe with an international girl's footy team, I was able to tuck Dax into a tight compartment in the back of my mind, forgetting everything about him. Well, not *forgetting*, exactly. The memory of Dax sits heavy on me every minute of every day. I remember every second I spent with him, his scent, the taste of his mouth taking mine, the feel of his rough hands on my skin.

Knowing we're in the same city has made it all that more difficult to keep those memories locked away. Even the few dates I went on with Mateo haven't lessened my fixation. I told him I needed to focus on school and the team and didn't have time to date. He seemed to accept my need to stay as friends, but it's still awkward to be around him.

It's not healthy, the way I let thoughts of Dax dictate my actions even though I haven't spoken to him in months. Dax is completely wrong for me—dangerous, heartless—he'd leave me broken with no one to help pick up the pieces.

Mateo is perfect. We have the same interests, the same goals, and he isn't a cold, heartless bastard without any regard for anyone but himself. Yet when I'm with Mateo in a romantic setting I feel restless, like my skin is too tight, squeezing around my chest and making it hard to breathe.

Now, I have to face my fears.

After speaking with my mum last night, I found out Ellie's dad died a few months back and her mum moved away from Hackney. Now I have no choice but to surprise the guys at one of their shows so I can talk to her. I can't find Ellie on campus, the school won't tell me where she's living, and I have no way of contacting Adam. I'm well aware that the best way to find her is to find him. And wherever Adam is, Dax will be as well.

Chickening out on having to deal with Dax back in the U.K. after that horrible scene at the fight club was a mistake that now looms over me. It's somehow grown into a much larger problem than it would have been had we discussed it immediately. Instead, I chose to shut him out completely, refusing to even speak to him or acknowledge his presence.

It wasn't fair really. He wasn't my boyfriend and didn't owe me a thing. My heart however, just couldn't take any more pain watching him shag girl after girl. I needed to distance myself so I could move on.

Unfortunately, time and distance haven't helped at all.

Resigned, I log onto the shabby second-hand laptop my parents scraped together to purchase as a going away present, and go about finding where their next gig will be.

Tomorrow night at the Viper Room.

I figure I can borrow a friend's I.D. and be at that club after the show.

Stupid U.S. and their drinking age of twenty-one.

Hopefully, I can deal with Adam and not have to see Dax. That's nothing but wishful thinking and denial, I know. I try not to remember my time with Dax, good or bad, but I can't help it. In a few short months, we went from hardly knowing one another to good friends, to nothing. I'm not about to lose Ellie because I'm afraid of dealing with Dax.

My best mate has been through so much and I wasn't able to be there for her. I'll be damned if I'm not going to be there for Ellie now, even if it means diving straight into shark infested waters and having my heart ripped right from my chest.

I NERVOUSLY RUN a hand through my hair for the millionth time since leaving my flat to take the bus to the bar down off of Santa Monica Boulevard. Why I care what I look like, I don't know. I shouldn't care. It's not *healthy* to still care. This whole sodding ten-year fixation on Dax fucking Davies isn't healthy yet here I am, obsessing again.

My fake I.D. doesn't even make the bouncer at the Viper Room blink. He simply glances at it and hands it back. When I walk into the crowded club, the first thing that hits me is the overwhelming excitement buzzing through the crowd. *Sphere of Irony* is the headlining act tonight and it's late, so the band is already on stage. I hadn't realized they were so popular, having been avoiding looking them up for fear of feeding my Dax addiction.

The band got to L.A. in April and it's only September. Despite the small time frame, it seems they've got quite the following already. Girls in skimpy dresses and how-can-you-possibly-walk heels are everywhere, crowding around the stage area, their lustful eyes fixed on the guys as they play. The memory of Willa setting her sights set on Dax hits me smack in the face.

I shudder in revulsion.

See Kate? It's better you didn't get involved with him.

There's no way I would have been able to handle this—the girls, the clubs, the crowd—all of them wanting a piece of Dax. It's too far out of my comfort zone. Hell, I'm just a footy-playing tomboy, not a fuck-me heel wearing groupie.

Unfortunately, old habits die hard. I can't keep my eyes off of the man I used to know. I'm drawn to the stage like a moth to a flame. He looks good, really *really* good. Dax's large hands effortlessly move across the strings of his guitar, playing a song I recognize from back home. His dark blonde hair is thick and tousled, no longer in the near-military short cut he used to wear.

Unchanged are his huge muscles, his intimidating presence, that flicker of danger in his eyes... he looks just as threatening as always. Only, I know that this isn't the real Dax. The real Dax is kind, thoughtful, and fiercely protective of anyone he cares about —if he lets you in, which, chances are he won't. For a moment, I wish I could see through that false front he puts up to keep people away.

How can I miss someone so much, yet he was never really mine?

Blessedly, the show ends and the band leaves the stage. Watching them brings back too many memories. Unfortunately, my own personal torture has just begun. I *have* to find Ellie. Without a doubt, I'll willingly put my heart on the line for my best mate. I haven't heard a word from her in four months and since my parents said her mum moved and changed her number, Adam is my only link. If that means coming face to face with Dax Davies, then so be it.

Elbowing my way through the crowd of tarted up groupies is easy with my football skills. I effortlessly slide up to the backstage area, which is protected by a large man, attempting to look intimidating. He doesn't scare me. Not after dealing with Dax and his brother, Mr. Big and Creepy, at the fight club in Hackney.

"Pardon me, I'm a friend of the band from the U.K. Could you tell them I'm here?"

The man looks me up and down disinterestedly and scowls. He says nothing.

How rude. I'm not the most confident or beautiful girl, but you're not keeping me from finding Ellie.

"Hello? I'm speaking to you. Can you get a message to one of the band? We went to school together and I've come to surprise them."

He narrows his gaze, shooting me one of the most contemptuous looks I've ever seen. "Riiiiight. Friends. You think I was born yesterday, sweetcheeks? Hit the road." The idiot shoves a thumb towards the exit.

Alrighty, now I'm good and aggro. I let out my inner bitch, the one that hardly gets a chance to see the light of day.

"Listen you uptight wanker, I've known Dax and Adam since primary school and I *am* going to speak with them!" I dig my finger into his stupid chest. "Let me in, it's important!" I realize

I'm making a scene, but I don't care. I'm going to find my friend and this idiot isn't going to stop me.

The bouncer puffs up his body and his face turns purple. Before he can kick me out or say something rude, someone shoves him aside.

"Kate?"

Dax's dark eyes bore into mine from next to the increasingly hostile looking bouncer. They crinkle adorably in the corners when he breaks into an enormous grin.

Holy shit an actual reaction from the Iceman!

"Kate!"

Dax pulls me around the bouncer, Dax's huge, muscular, six-foot plus frame towering over almost everyone around us, garnering admiring looks from both men and women alike. Dax snags my arm, yanking me into a massive hug and I swear, I hear him let out a sigh of relief once I'm in his arms. I can't take the time to be shocked. I'm too happy to be surrounded by Dax. I inhale deeply, reveling in the fact that he smells exactly the same —spicy, delicious, and utterly masculine.

When he finally releases me from his tight embrace, Dax holds me at arm's length, his fingers gripping my shoulders to keep me in place. He flicks his eyes up and down my figure, making me squirm from the intensity of his stare. Even though we're surrounded by squealing groupies and a scowling bouncer, the moment is as intimate as if we were alone behind closed doors.

It seems as if he wants to say something, but before he does, his expression shuts down, back to stone-faced Dax. He stares, waiting for me to speak. No way do I want to have this reunion out here, so I try to get him to take us somewhere private. Pointing at the backstage door, my question comes out in a rush. "Can we go somewhere else?"

Dax glances around, finally taking note of the small crowd that has gathered. A blush pinks his cheeks as he lets me go, directing me to go backstage first. A blush! Cold, unemotional *Dax Davies,* the Iceman, blushed because of me! Boring, plain Kate Campbell. It's both endearing and an enormous turn on to think I have that kind of power over him. That and the fact he completely ignored the squealing crowd of sluts have my feelings for Dax all jumbled up again.

"How have you been?" he asks, his eyes meeting mine for a fleeting moment before dropping to the floor again as he leads me backstage. There's that blush again. He's going to make it impossible for me to let him go, isn't he? How can I possibly be expected to stay angry with someone that I've loved for as long as I can recall? Especially when his loud confidence and stony indifference has been replaced by this adorable, blushing man.

He leads me to a tiny room crammed full of electrical equipment. Dax shoves a few things off the battered old sofa and onto the floor, clearing a place for us to sit. I tremble, lowering myself to the cushion slowly. The air seems to have gotten scarce, my lungs having difficulty expanding in his proximity. There's just enough left to force out a quick reply.

"I've been good. How about you, Dax?"

His downturned eyes flick up to mine, trapping me, *owning* me. Then again...he's always owned me, heart and soul, hasn't he? Even after that night at the fight club, I never really let go of Dax... of the dream of us being together someday.

Is someday now?

6

D^{ax}

HELL, Kate's even more stunning than I remember. The sunny L.A. weather has done her well. Playing football has her tanned and toned from her head down to her feet, those killer legs of hers perfectly showcased by a criminally short skirt.

My heart has always been an empty shell, until Kate brought out the best in me. Being around her innocence, her radiance, then losing her had me thinking there was more to life than getting off and keeping everything inside.

Without her, I'm back to being a cold and heartless bastard. Any warmth I may have gained in the short time I knew her seeped out long ago. Today, having her right here in front me, the black hole in my chest feels as if it's beginning to recede.

Kate never rang me after I stopped by her dormitory, not that I know if her crazy flatmate gave her my number. I had begun to think I'd never see her again. Unbelievably, I've got Kate sitting next to me, picking at a tiny hole in the hideous sofa backstage at the Viper Room, and I'm not sure what to say.

"You look gorgeous," I blurt out, immediately wanting to punch myself for sounding so bloody desperate. One of the rules flicks through my head. One I have a hard time remembering when I'm around Kate.

Rule 2—Never let your emotions show.

Her wide green eyes find mine for the briefest of moments before they drop back down to the sofa.

Forcing myself to go against everything I was raised to believe, I stupidly put it out there. "I'm sorry, Kate. About—" I swallow thickly, having a hard time putting my feelings in words. "About what you saw. It..." Jesus, I sound like such a wanker. The urge to take what I want, to kiss her until she comes undone is nearly overpowering. Especially after a performance, when my libido is flying high. Having her here is pure torture.

Kate waves her hand dismissively. "It's no big deal, Dax. Honestly."

My heart, which just mere seconds ago was beginning to come to life after years of blackness, has crumbled and fallen in pieces down into my hollow insides at her effortless brush off.

"No big deal?" I snarl, my tone angrier than it should be. So she couldn't care less that she saw my dad's whore on her knees sucking me off? "Bullshit," I challenge her. I know she cared. I saw it on her face. I fucking felt it in my shattered soul. You want to make me prove you cared?

Challenge accepted.

Kate's face and neck are a brilliant shade of crimson—her emerald eyes narrow, flashing with fury. "Excuse me?"

Confident I've gotten it right and refusing to back down even if I'm wrong, I cross my arms over my chest. "I don't believe you. It was a big deal to you. It was and most definitely still is a big deal to me."

Her anger melts away at my very rare show of feelings. "Why

do you care what I think? So you had your cock sucked by some slag. What difference does it make?" Kate's voice is shaky, in fact, when I look down at her hands, now gripping her own knees, they're shaking as well.

Feeling bold, or embarrassed, or maybe just tired of not being allowed to touch her or talk to her, I reach over and pull her into my arms, crushing my mouth against hers. Kate is stunned at first, unresponsive as my tongue demands entrance. Then, as if a switch is flipped, she comes alive, groaning and opening up to me, allowing me access to her hot, wet mouth, letting me relive that perfect kiss we had so many months ago.

Intense fire burns through me, blazing, stoking the instinctive craving for my post-fight/post-gig reward. Our lips move in tandem, sloppy and desperate. She tastes exactly how I recall, the sweet memory burned on my brain forever. I'm about to shift her into my lap so I can feel that perfect body rubbing against my rock hard length when she breaks the kiss.

"Stop."

"What? Why?" I continue to nip at her mouth.

"No Dax. Stop."

Reluctantly, I back off, slumping on the sofa. She looks gorgeous, her lips swollen and wet, her cheeks red, and her eyes filled with unmistakable lust.

"What's wrong?"

"I don't know if I can do this, Dax. I'm sorry. You're not good for me." She moves away, reaching her hands up to right her disheveled hair.

Fuck. She's right, I'm not good for her, but I'm also a selfish bastard. Always have been. I need to fix this so I can have her near me. Inhaling deep, for the first time in my life I dive in headfirst.

"I want to make a go of this. With you." I slide off the sofa, kneeling down between her legs, not willing to give up so easily. I'm stubborn. I get what I want and I want her.

Kate's eyes are wide and unblinking as she thinks it over. "You, you want to make a go of it... with me?"

"Yes."

She lets out a choked laugh. I reach into her lap, holding her hands in mine. "I can't believe this," she says. "I've always wanted you, but you never saw me. Never expressed any interest in me."

I pull our intertwined hands to my lips, kissing them lightly. "I was an idiot. I'm interested now. What do you say?"

Kate hesitates and her mouth twists up into a pained grimace. "I'm sorry Dax. I think it's best we just stay friends." She chokes up, struggling to keep the tears at bay.

This. This is why I don't let my emotions show. It's a weakness that can be used to exploit you, let you down, make you feel shit you shouldn't have to feel.

"Fine," I reply stonily, the mask back in place.

"So," Kate asks, her voice cracking. "Can you take me to see Adam? I really need to chat with him."

"Adam?" So she didn't actually come here to see me tonight. And if her flatmate did give her my number, she never rang either. Kate had no intention of ever seeing me again. This information takes her rejection to another level. She not only crushed my ego, she chucked it to the ground, spit on it, and then ground it to pieces under her boot.

"Follow me," I growl, ducking around her and down the hall.

It takes several frustrating tries to find the room Adam is in. As I open the door, I start talking, "Hey, I've been looking for you..." *Whoops!* I see him rearranging clothing and a thoroughly fucked blonde behind him doing the same. The sight stops me dead in my tracks. I should have known. This is exactly why Kate doesn't want to have anything to do with me.

Impatient, whatever Kate needs to say unable to wait any longer, she pushes past me irritably. "What's going on Dax? Move your big arse."

Oh Fuck. This is not going to be good. Kate's about to get another dose of visual proof of why a bloke like me is the absolute last thing she needs.

Kate

THE PHONE in my dormitory rings for the millionth time since I hightailed it out of the Viper Room last night.

Dax.

"Are you going to answer it?" My friend Abby is staring at me, an eyebrow arched expectantly, the end of her pen in her mouth.

"No."

"He's not going to stop calling until you do." She puts down her notebook and joins me on my bed. "What happened?"

"So much," I whisper. "It's all the same as it was back home, but somehow it's so different."

"What do you mean? The band? Dax?"

"Everything."

Visions of Adam with the blonde groupie last night are burned on the back of my eyeballs. The pictures in my head flash by so quickly I can hardly keep up—Adam and the blonde, Dax and Willa, the clusters of girls at the DK, the woman on her knees in the back room of the fight club...

"I'm sorry, Kate." Abby puts a hand on my arm. "For whatever is making you so sad."

"I just..." I hold in a sob. "My entire life has been about Dax Davies, getting him to notice me. Now that he has, I-I can't do it." Abby waits patiently for me to continue. "There will always be loads of girls, prettier girls than me, hanging around just waiting to give him a suck or a shag. Girls with more experience, or... I don't know. More *everything* than me!"

The scene from last night replays in my head again—Adam smirking, a sexed-out blonde girl fixing her inflated cleavage.

"You don't trust Dax?"

"He's never given me a reason not to trust him because we've never been together, but I've been there, Abby. I've seen what he does... what they *all* do with the groupies. I can't deal with it. I just can't. I don't have it in me to compete with them."

"Kate, you don't have to compete. If Dax didn't want you, he wouldn't pursue you." The phone rings again. "And right now, if that's who I think it is calling, my opinion is that he is definitely pursuing you."

I wipe away a tear that has run down my cheek and quickly right myself on the bed. Plain Kate versus a veritable horde of gorgeous, posh girls. *Yeah right.*

"Forget it. I can't deal with Dax right now. Let's study. There's no way I'll pass my test tomorrow if I don't learn this."

It's easy to avoid Dax after that night at the Viper Room. I'm so busy with school and traveling for football, I'm hardly ever at my flat. Not that he's ever stopped by. There's never a message on the whiteboard on my door and Lila's never mentioned Dax coming to see me, although she would be the crazy type to erase any messages he might have left.

The holidays come and go, with Abby being kind enough to invite me to her family's house for break. There isn't enough money for an airline ticket back to the U.K. for Christmas. Mateo has left me alone, finally realizing we'll only be friends. He's a good bloke, just not the bloke I want.

"Bollocks!" The phone is ringing as I try to balance a take-away cup of tea, my books, and my enormous footy bag while unlocking the door to my dorm. Somehow I manage to shove it open and get to the phone before it stops.

"Hello?"

"K-Kate?"

"Ellie?"

"Yes. It's me."

The door to the flat closes behind me. I drop my books and duffel to the floor. Right now, my only concern is my friend, a friend that has been through hell and back with no one there to support her. Tears flood my eyes, overflowing down my cheeks. My voice is already all choked up and my nose sniffling pathetically.

"Ellie," I sob, "where have you been?"

"Can I come visit?"

"You don't even have to ask."

As I lay back on my bed to catch up with Ellie I think that maybe a little bit of my life can be complete again.

∾

"So tell me about UCLA. Is it as much fun as we thought it would be?"

Ellie stares at me with wide eyes across the backseat of the cab we're taking from LAX. Two weeks after she called and she just landed, looking extremely tired. Worse than tired, she looks like she hasn't slept in weeks.

I don't answer her question immediately. Do I tell her how inadequate I feel here? Surrounded by posh homes, impossible beauty, and people who spend more money on one car than there is in all of Hackney? Or do I lie and tell her it's brilliant, that she could still transfer in next year?

"It's... it's keeping me busy." I give her what I know is a weak answer. Thankfully, Ellie is too knackered to realize how pathetic it is.

"That's brilliant, Kate. Really. I'm so happy for you."

She wants to know about all the glam parties I've been to, which doesn't take long since I've been to exactly zero. I tell her all about my coach and how great he is, and how he gets so much out of our team. Ellie laughs when I describe my wealthy flat-mate's very active social life.

I haven't told her about Dax yet, afraid I may open up old wounds with regards to Adam. I'm not hiding it, but I don't want to bring it up either. Calling him up and asking if I could meet up with them tonight was just about the hardest thing I've ever had to do. Ellie wants to see Adam, so I did it, but that doesn't mean it wasn't horribly awkward.

"*Davies.*"

"*Dax. It's Kate.*"

"*Oh.*"

God this is awkward. "*Um, so, I'm really sorry about ducking out of the club that night.*"

"*That was nearly five months ago, Kate. I think I'm over it.*" *His voice is harsh, cold. In other words, normal for Dax.*

"*Okay. Right. Well, I was hoping to meet up with you at one of your gigs.*"

Silence.

"*Dax?*"

"*You want to meet up at a gig? After vanishing and avoiding my calls you want to pop in and meet up?*" *Dax laughs sarcastically.*

"*Ellie is coming to visit. She wants to see Adam, but doesn't want us to tell him she's here.*"

"*Ellie? Here? Why the fuck can't we tell him?*"

"*She said she might not be able to go through with seeing him. She didn't want any expectations.*"

"*Right. So you're ringing for Ellie. Just like you visited the Viper Room for Ellie. Do you ever think about ringing or visiting me without a reason? We were friends once, weren't we?*"

Crap.

"*I'm sorry Dax. It's not you—*"

"Fuck it. It's not me it's you, right? Whatever. When will she be in town?"

THE THINGS I do for my best friend. That was the most awkward conversation of my life.

"Here we are." The cab pulls up in front of my dorm. We pile out of the car with her weekend bag.

"This is fab, Kate." Ellie shades her eyes to look up at the tall dormitory building. "This whole place, it's like…" she slowly spins in a circle, taking in the campus, the palm trees, the sunny weather, the students laughing and walking by, "it's like a movie in real life!"

I chuckle as I unlock the outer door. "I thought the same thing at first, El. You get used to it. It's not as posh as it seems, trust me."

We cram into the elevator with a few other students. "It's better than Hackney, that's for sure," she whispers.

"Yeah. It is."

I can't disagree. As insignificant as I feel in L.A., Hackney was bloody depressing. The misery and poverty pressed down heavily on your psyche, making you feel as if you carried the weight of the world around with you every single day. At least L.A. *looks* happy, even if it has a desperate, fake soul under that shiny surface.

"Let's get settled and get ready to go out. We've got big plans tonight!" I keep my voice light, trying to shed the dark mood that has fallen over us.

The lift doors open to my floor. Ellie grins, her face lighting up and for a moment she looks like the old Ellie again, the best mate who had a brilliant future ahead of her, not the shell of a girl who got off a plane an hour ago. "Big plans, huh?"

I grin back. "Yep. Big. Huge."

"Well, let's get to it then."

God, it feels so good to see her. "I'm glad you're here, El." I hug her, holding her tight. "I've missed you."

"Me too, Kate." She straightens up, breaking the embrace. "Now, take me to your flat. I want to meet this slag flatmate of yours."

I nearly choke in disbelief. Ellie never talks bad about someone. She meets my gaze and we burst out laughing.

"Right. C'mon then. The town bike's waiting to meet you. Be careful, she may try to chat you up as well. Her lust knows no bounds, I'm sure. She's some spoiled socialite or something."

We're overcome with laughter again, and just like that, it's as if we were never apart.

DAX

"C'MON! You lot are making us late." I barge into the backstage room of whatever club we're playing tonight to yell at my mates. Glancing around, I notice one of us is not where he's supposed to be. "Christ! He's gone missing again?"

Gavin looks up from his seat on the floor next to Hawke, pointing at the closed door on one side of the tiny space. The moaning and groaning I hear leaves no doubt what Adam's up to on the other side.

"We tried telling him. He doesn't listen to us." Hawke shrugs and returns his focus to his mobile, not caring one way or another if we're onstage when we're supposed to be. How in the fuck I became the dependable one of this lot, I have no bloody clue.

"Adam!" I bang my fist on the door, rattling it in its frame. "Get your sorry arse out here now!" I know I'm being a dick simply because I'm going to be seeing Kate tonight and it has me all wound up. After turning me down flat and then dodging me for five months she rings me out of nowhere, and not because she misses me, but because Ellie is in town and she wants to see Adam.

I'm angry with myself for caring, and even angrier with myself for trying to make things right with Kate after she shut me down. I don't know what's gotten into me, but I can't stand the thought of Kate thinking I'm a bastard. Even though I undoubtedly am.

Seconds later, the door to the room opens and out strolls a blonde tart, Adam trailing not too far behind. With a hand to the chest, I shove him back and slam the door, giving us privacy, although, I'm quite sure Gavin and Hawke will be able to hear every word I say, as I'm not planning on being quiet.

"You useless fucking tit!" My finger stabs into Adam's chest. "I didn't come to this bloody fucking hot, miserable, stuck up city to babysit your pathetic, whinging arse." My best mate's eyes go wide at my verbal explosion. I can only hope my words have finally hit their mark with him. "Get your shit together and do it fast, Reynolds. I'm not failing at this because you can't get over Ellie. Man the fuck up and stop being such a big girl's blouse. No more shags before gigs. I could give a fuck less what you do after, but we will get on stage on-fucking-time. Understand?"

Adam swallows and nods. In all the years I've known him, he's never been on the receiving end of my temper, precariously balanced on a knife's-edge at all times. He's bloody well seen what I can do with my fists when I'm angry and certainly doesn't want to go down that road.

Storming out of the room, I bellow at Gavin and Hawke. "Get your lazy arses up! It's show time and I'm going to have fucking fun if it kills me!"

Rule 2—Never let your emotions show.

Fuck you, dad. Despite my hate for him and his rules, I still force myself to wipe the hostility off my face as I was trained. I pause in the hall to calm down, clear my head, and carefully bottle everything up inside. The others brush past me as I lean my forehead into the wall and close my eyes. If Kate were back here she would have me set to rights in half a second. All she'd have to do is smile and I'd be ready to go.

Why am I thinking that? Because she's out in the crowd somewhere? She's not to see me. Why can't I just fucking let it go?

"Fuck me."

Sighing, I turn towards the stage area and meet up with the rest of the band as we're announced. At first, I have to force myself to play, but as the night goes on and the music flows from my fingers to the guitar, it becomes genuine. There's nothing I love more than our music and being on stage.

"Dax! I love you!"

I smirk at the screams that more than a few of the intoxicated ladies send my way. They're mostly harmless, and a little flirting makes the crowd more fun. So I peek at the girls shoved up against the stage as they give us moon-eyes and shoot lusty looks our way. Being up here reminds me of fighting, which always gets me anticipating my reward at the end. Some days, it takes quite a bit of concentration to keep from springing wood right on stage.

Adam works the audience like a maestro directing an orchestra, effortlessly pulling energy from the crowd and giving it back to them tenfold. By the third song he has every single person in the club eating out of his hand. It's a gift really, to charm, to instill passion, to make people feel special. Adam does it as well or better than the best in the business.

Our set ends on a brilliant high, the entire place going crazy for more. We stumble off stage, sweaty and smiling, riding the wave of endorphins that always follow a great performance. Using the hem of my shirt, I wipe off the sweat that's dripping down the side of my face. While the material is up over my eyes, a cool hand caresses my slick abs, making its way under the edge of my jeans.

"What the—?"

I immediately drop the shirt to see who's touching me.

Bloody fucking hell. It's Kate's crazy flatmate, Lila. A girl who for some reason can't get it out of her thick, spoiled skull that I'm not interested in shagging her.

"Lila," I deadpan, removing her hand from where it's trying to dig down into my briefs.

"Hey Dax." She leans into me in some sort of sad attempt at seduction, batting her eyelashes ridiculously. Five months of near stalker-like behavior with me turning her down every time and this girl still can't accept reality.

"Oi, Dax. We're goin' out. You coming?" Gavin is leaning out of one of the back rooms, ready to leave. I can't let him go, Ellie and Kate are here and we need to wait for them.

"Right. Yeah, don't leave yet." He disappears down the hall towards the back door of the club. I turn back to my number one fan. "Lila. What are you doing here?" I wiggle out of her grasp but she's much quicker, and more aggressive, than I expected.

"You're so big and muscular, Dax. I'd love to see what you could do with that body of yours." Lila purrs, wrapping her arms round my waist so I can't move. She actually fucking purrs at me! What the hell is wrong with her?

I reach behind me to unwind her octopus arms and the little shit uses the distraction to lean up on her toes and lick a line right across my neck as she takes a photo on her mobile.

"Jesus, Lila. Give it a bloody rest!" I snap, louder than intended. I'm just so fucking sick of this girl. She keeps turning up at my shows, throwing herself at me whenever she can.

Her eyes pop open in surprise at my rebuke, but only for a second. Then she's back all over me like a damn barnacle.

"You don't mean that, Dax. We could have so much fun together. I'm here with a bunch of my friends. Let's take this to the after party."

Lila's hands are everywhere at once—on my chest, my abs, my waist, my back. It's literally as if she has extra arms. I back up, knowing that my patience is reaching its breaking point. Being within striking distance of her isn't smart. I'd never hit a girl on purpose, but I've never been given a reason to either. I don't trust the beast inside me when provoked to this extent.

When Lila tries to move with me, the restraint I had over my frustration comes undone.

Rule 3—Women who act like slags can be treated like slags.

I grab her wrists, trapping them in one of my hands. "That's it. I've tried to be nice to you. I've tried being direct. Clearly, you have some sort of learning disability. Listen and listen good..." For the first time since I've met her, Lila's cocky attitude vanishes. *This is going to be ugly.* "I. Don't. Want. You. Got it? It's never going to happen. Never. Stop coming to my shows, stop coming back-stage, stop touching me, stop bloody talking to me. In fact, I don't want to see you at one of my shows ever again. Back the fuck off!" My last sentence comes out as a loud, menacing roar.

Without waiting for a response, I shove past her, not caring that I may have knocked into her a bit with my elbow. She shouldn't have been standing so close to someone as blatantly dangerous as myself. She shouldn't have been standing so close to me, period.

Gavin meets me at the back entrance. The smirk on his face makes it quite obvious he was waiting for me to finish disposing of Lila before heading for the car.

"Having issues with your fan club?"

I push Gavin out the door and he busts up laughing.

"Shut it, Walker. Just shut it." I turn to fetch Ellie and Kate inside, wondering what Gavin will say when he sees them. "Get Hawke and get the car. I'll be right out."

Now I'm all agitated and I have to face Kate.

Fucking Lila.

Kate

"ELLIE? Here. You look like you need this." I hand her another vodka tonic, noting how ill she looks, especially under these oddly colored club lights.

"Thanks." Ellie sips this one slower than her first, which she emptied in two gulps.

"C'mon. Let's mingle. The guys are done and told me to come backstage about fifteen minutes after the show. They need to pack up their gear or something. Come talk to the movie crew that's here tonight. They're really nice." I try to pull Ellie with me but she resists. "El," gently, I put an arm around her. "You need to relax. You can't chat with Adam if you look like you're scared to death. Let's make small talk, okay?"

"Sure. Right." Her body is stiff as a board.

"Some of them are pretty good-looking too." Dax told me that there was a big after party tonight at some Hollywood producer's house. The crew from one of the producer's films is here and the band has been invited to hang out with them.

When the guys had been on stage earlier, Ellie froze in place, unable to take her eyes off of Adam. My own gaze lingered a tad too long on Dax, greedily soaking in how every glorious ridge of his body looked in his tight-fitting shirt and jeans. It's been so long since I've seen him, even longer since I've spent any amount of time with him. In fact, it was about a year ago that we first started spending time together in Hackney.

"Let's go over there." I point at the rowdy group of actors and crewmembers.

She nods without speaking, her mind probably consumed with Adam. I miss Dax so much, and he was never even mine. If I had what Ellie had with Adam, only to have it ripped away? Hell, I'd never be the same again.

That's why it's better to not go down that road. Dax Davies is not cut out for a relationship and my heart's not cut out for the

kind of pain he would inflict. I remember all those times in
Hackney when I saw him chat up a girl. Always a different one,
always with the same result. Then I remember one time, right
before I actually got to know Dax, which stood out from all of the
others.

*"I'll see you in chemistry, Kate," Tasha calls out as she leaves world
geography.*

*"Right. Yeah, later," I reply, but Tasha's long gone. I sigh, trudging
to my locker slowly, not in any hurry to get to my next class. It's one I
have with Dax Davies—gorgeous, out of my league, and wholly
unaware of my existence. Knowing he's sharing space with me makes
me as nervous as a bloody bride on her wedding day.*

*After exchanging my books, I slam the locker door shut, determined
that today will be the day I don't let Dax get to me. Then, I spot him.*

*Before he can see me, I duck behind a group of younger students
loitering in the hall. A tall, stunning redhead with legs for miles is
standing with her back against the wall. Dax is leaning into her, one
arm propped up next to her head, the other gently toying with a lock of
her hair.*

*I squeeze my eyes shut, a familiar hurt gripping my heart. I
shouldn't listen. It only makes things worse. Yet, I'm unable to pull in a
breath let alone walk away.*

*I'm close enough so that Dax's deep bass rumbles in my chest. "So,
you have plans later?" He drops her hair and brushes his finger down
her arm.*

*The girl visibly shudders. "I do now," she purrs in what I assume is
supposed to be a sexy voice.*

"Good. Meet me in the art annex after final period."

*Then, as if he can feel me watching them, Dax's head tilts my way.
His dark eyes latch onto mine, unwavering. His hand drops from the
girl's arm. I'd swear I saw something flash across his face. Embarrass-*

ment? Nah. Dax Davies doesn't do emotions. Especially not embarrass-ment. The man literally has no shame. Or feelings.

Without ever turning back to the girl, Dax spins around and leaves.

I BLINK, wondering where that memory came from. I'd forgotten about it until now.

"Kate?"

Ellie's nervous voice brings me back to reality. Viper Room. Loud music. Musicians to confront. *Right.*

A cute bloke in the group of actors waves at me, inviting us over. Maybe there's hope for me yet. Then I think back at the six-foot plus display of power and strength that was on the stage tonight and realize any hope for me pulled out of the station a long time ago.

DAX

"I STILL CAN'T BELIEVE you're here," I say from where I'm sitting in the passenger seat of Hawke's huge SUV. Kate, Gavin, and Ellie are in the back. After meeting up at the club, the mood in the car has stayed tense, with Kate acting distant and Ellie looking quite ill.

"How was your flight?" Gavin asks, using his easygoing personality to try and break the heavy veil of anxiety emanating from the two women. I twist around to see Ellie's face, using it as an excuse to get a quick glance at Kate. Her emotions are shut-tered up tight, her mouth pressed into a line. Clearly, she doesn't want to be here with me. If she did, she'd have rung months ago.

"Long," Ellie says, giving Gavin a genuine smile. Those two always were thick as thieves together.

"Hope you're ready for this, El," Hawke says as he pulls into a long driveway. "The guy that owns this place is fucking loaded."

The SUV winds down the drive, pulling in front of the biggest house I've ever seen.

"Wow," Kate whispers. "Who lives here?"

Hawke shuts the car off and turns back to face Kate. "Some big movie producer. I forget his name, but he's huge. That part I remember."

A valet opens Hawke's door for him. He drops the keys into the man's hand as we all get out. I look up at the sheer opulence of the monstrosity, and then back at the lot of us. "We look like Tiny Tim and the rest of the Cratchets showing up at Scrooge's house for Christmas. Way out of our comfort zone," I joke.

Hawke laughs, a rare sound to hear. "Speak for yourself, man. This is normal for me."

"Right." I always forget that Hawke and Gavin grew up very different than those of us from Hackney. They're both from this area and are used to money, trust funds, stodgy rich people, and parties that cost more than the crown jewels.

"Come on, I'll be right here with you." Gavin calmly takes Ellie's hand and we follow them into a party filled to the brim with Hollywood elite.

I should be excited. This is what we're trying to achieve. Fame, fortune, recognition for our music... yet all I want is to duck out with Kate and find out why she refuses to give us a chance. I'm tempted to pull her aside right now, but we've entered the mansion and the noise crashes over us, making conversation all but impossible.

Next thing I know, Gavin and Ellie have disappeared into the thick crowd. I turn to ask Hawke where we should look for Adam, but he's gone too. It's just Kate and me and she looks as if she'd rather be anywhere but here.

I lean down so she can hear me over the thumping music. "Can we talk?"

Kate flinches back at my question. "Let's find Adam first, okay?" She crosses the room to a doorway on the right without saying another word. At least she didn't say no. Not having much of a choice, which I fucking hate, I follow, but at a much slower pace. I'm too big to slip through the sea of bodies as easily as Kate.

I find myself alone in a long hallway with doors up and down either side. No sign of Kate. I've lost her.

"Fuck!"

This is stupid. My hands dig into my hair, gripping it hard and pulling. The urge to throw Kate down, tie her up, and spank her until she admits we'd be great together nearly overwhelms me. Maddened, I check the rooms one at a time, opening the doors for a look before moving on to the next.

"Oh my god!" The loud screeching voice makes my entire body go tense. I brace for the unwanted physical contact that's sure to follow that hideous sound. Sure enough, Lila launches herself at me, wrapping her arms around my waist.

"Lila." I reach back and remove her hands. "What are you doing here?"

"Me? What are *you* doing here, silly? This is my dad's house. You came to the party after all!"

"What?" Her dad? The big producer is Lila's father? I'm so flustered, I don't notice Lila rubbing her body all over me like a cat.

"My dad. This is his house. Now, I didn't grow up here. My parents divorced so I only visited on weekends, but Daddy..."

I tune her out. Her dad. Shit. I wonder if Kate knows that Lila's dad owns this house?

"Dax? *Lila*? What the hell is going on?"

Slowly, I turn to face Kate. Her face is red and her eyes glossy with tears. I look down to see Lila is still pressed up against me, wearing the same microscopic red dress she had on at the club. I back up as if Lila burned me.

"No. Kate..."

Kate spins on her heel, hurrying down the hall.

"Fuck."

"Don't worry about her, Dax. She knows that she doesn't fit in with this crowd. I'm surprised you'd bring her." Lila smiles, reaching up to put her hand on my chest.

"Sod off, Lila." I take off after Kate, hoping she'll let me explain.

By the time I catch up to Kate, she's already talking to Ellie and Gavin. No one has found Adam yet. Hawke joins us and puts a beer in my hand. I've never been more thankful in my life to have a drink as I am right now.

Kate

GIGGLING. My dreadful, slutty, man-stealing flatmate is giggling from her side of the little suite we share.

I groan, pulling the duvet up over my head, too tired to deal with her this morning. Then last night comes back to me.

Dax, with Lila hanging all over him. Adam, shagging some bloke's girl. Ellie, leaving the party in tears, never returning to my dorm to get her things.

I nearly start crying when I think of Ellie's face when Adam shoved her. I grab my phone and dial the number she gave me. A lilting voice tells me that it's been disconnected.

Gone. She's gone. I feel ill, then the sick feeling morphs into fury.

On a mission, I throw off the covers and grab some clothes. Quickly, I shower, brush my teeth, and get ready to leave, more determined and angry than I've ever been in my life. I'm going to kick Adam's arse for being such a useless twat and destroying my best friend. Dax, the bastard, can be dealt with later.

When I step out of the bathroom, Lila is waiting for me.

"Did you have a good time last night, Kate?" She smirks, knowing I was upset to see her with Dax.

All right then. Adam can wait.

With my hands on my hips I step forward. A streak of satisfaction runs through me when Lila falters and is intimidated enough to step back.

"Let me tell you something, Lila. I am really not in the mood for your crap. In fact, I'd say I'm somewhere close to being quite unstable at this moment." Her eyes widen a fraction. I take another step forward and the backs of Lila's knees hit her bed. "You don't want to start something you can't see through. Do you?"

I cock my head and wait for her response to my veiled threat.

"I suppose not," she says.

"Good."

I grab my keys and head for the door.

One problem down, only about a thousand more to go.

Lila calls out after me. "Just one more thing before you leave."

I flinch, frozen in the doorway, one foot in the hall. Reluctantly, I turn around. Lila sashays over, her hips swaying as if she were strutting the catwalk at fashion week.

"What is it," I snap.

"Oh." Her eyes flutter as she feigns innocence. "I thought you might like to see a picture I took last night. You know, before my dad's party."

"Your dad? What?" Confused, I release the door, letting it close gently behind me.

"My dad. Oh no!" She acts embarrassed when it's obvious that she's enjoying every minute of torturing me. "That party last night was at my dad's house. Didn't you know?"

I swallow loudly. "No. I didn't."

"Well, no worries." Lila waves her hand as if it's no big deal.

"Here. Isn't this a great photo of me?" She whips out her phone, holding it in front of my face.

When I get a look at the screen, my knees nearly buckle. Somehow, I have no idea how, I manage hold in my reaction. Internally is another story. My heart flips around and stalls, plunging into my feet.

There, in all of her half-naked glory, is Lila, licking Dax backstage at the club last night. I know it's last night because I recognize the clothes they both are wearing.

"Where did you get this?" I snarl, snatching the phone out of her hand.

Lila deftly plucks the phone from my hand and walks over to her bed, sitting down gracefully.

"Oh, you know, just after the show last night. I go to all of Dax's shows." She sits up, all wide-eyed and childlike. "You do know that I meet up with Dax after all of his shows, don't you?"

Scorching heat floods my neck and face, burning me to the tips of my ears.

Lila smiles. "I guess you didn't. Well," she lies back on her bed, crossing her legs at the ankles and begins playing with her phone. *Is she texting Dax?* She doesn't look up as she dismisses me. "Have a nice day."

Humiliated, I spin and stumble as I reach for the doorknob. The last thing I hear as I fling it open and run down the hall is Lila's girly giggle.

Dax

"Dax? What are you doing here?"

I jump up from my seat on the concrete steps of the training facility at UCLA. I've been here for over an hour, waiting for the girls' footy practice to end. "Kate!"

Kate lets her hurt show for a brief moment before her face hardens. "I'm late for class." She slings a large duffel up on her shoulder, brushing past me.

"Wait! Don't do this again. Talk to me, Kate."

"Do what, exactly!" She whirls around so fast I stumble over my own feet. "Protect myself from getting my heart broken? Or distance myself from a highly dysfunctional group of slutty, immature men?" Her voice cracks on the last word, her full lower lip quivering.

My heart flinches from Kate's verbal slap down, but I manage to keep my face calm. She's right. We *are* a highly dysfunctional group of slutty, immature men. And I probably *will* break her heart. But the sadness behind her anger makes me even more determined to win her trust back.

"Nothing happened with Lila. You know I can't stand her. If you had stayed after talking to Adam yesterday at our flat—"

Kate cuts me off, her cheeks flushed red. "If nothing happened why have you been meeting up with Lila backstage after your gigs?"

How in the hell...?

"I don't meet her backstage."

"She's my flatmate, Dax! She showed me the bloody photo from the other night! Don't treat me like I'm stupid!"

"You're not stupid. She accosted me after our gig. Literally grabbed me, Kate. She took the photo before I could shove her off. I turned her down... blatantly. I know how much Lila upsets you, the way she's always chatting me up. We're fighting over nothing. You know I despise her."

"It's too hard, Dax." She shakes her head, her eyes glimmering with tears. I should let her go, let her think I'm the bastard that I am, but instead I push forward.

"Why don't you trust me? I told you I want to be with only you and that's not good enough. So what is it then?"

Kate harrumphs, crossing her arms over her chest to shield

her heart from my perceived betrayal. "You were snogging her in the hallway at that stupid bloody party Saturday night? As if it isn't bad enough what Adam did to Ellie..." a pained sob escapes.

And there it is, right there. She's afraid that what she saw happen between Ellie and Adam will happen to us. Kate's seen Adam and his parade of tarts and thinks I'll chuck her and do the same. The Lila situation has only made it worse.

"Kate..." I step forward, pulling her into my arms. "I would never do that to you. Ever." My body awakens at the contact, electrified sensations zipping through my veins.

"I don't know if I can believe that, Dax." Her body is stiff in my arms.

"Please. Give us a go. I'm not like that. Your flatmate is a total nutter, you know this. Once the term is over, you'll move and won't have to deal with her anymore. I told her off good this time, so hopefully I won't have to deal with her anymore either."

I can't believe I'm begging a girl to be with me, yet here I am.

Kate steps back, leaving a cold space where her warm body was pressed against me. "Why me? Huh, Dax? I'm nothing special, so tell me why?"

Reaching out, I take one of her hands in mine, threading our fingers together. I'm torn between keeping everything bottled up and hidden, and telling Kate everything I know to be true.

"You... you're different." I struggle to explain how I feel without giving away too much. How it felt knowing that we may have never gotten a chance to see how great we could be because of my past. My inability to let my emotions show, my belief that the post-fight rewards were not only deserved but that they were *owed* to me, those bloody rules—they fucked up everything.

Kate arches an eyebrow. "Different?" Her beautiful, full lips turn down in the corners. When she tries to tug her hand away, I hold on tight, refusing to lose the contact.

"Different is good, Kate. Bollocks. I'm not saying it right." Sighing, I rub my free hand over my unkempt hair. "I *respect* you.

That—well, it means something to me. You're better than some random shag in the backroom of my dad's club or Lila or a groupie." My dad's rules come roaring back to the forefront of my mind again, never far enough away to ignore.

Rule 4—Women who act like slags can be treated like slags.

Kate was never a slag and never will be.

I see her wince at the reminder of the women in my past and her stupid flatmate as I drag the knife over her wounds, bringing fresh blood to the surface. But there's something else shining there—behind the pain. Hope? Desire? *Hate?*

I swallow nervously. Fuck, I pray it's the first two. I couldn't live with the guilt of Kate hating me. For the millionth time, I wonder why I care, why I let this girl see my emotions, for her to see me stripped bare in a way I don't let anyone see.

She bites her lip, those white teeth sinking into the plump, pink flesh. The action makes my cock stir in my trousers. I say a silent thank you that I threw on baggy cargos instead of the tight, crotch-hugging jeans I usually wear.

My fate is in someone's hands other than my own and it's making me a nervous wreck. I hate it. The control I spent eighteen years wrestling back from my dad has now been handed over to this girl.

Sweat begins to bead up between my shoulder blades and on my temples. A lone drop trickles down my spine while the tension hangs between us.

Finally, right as I think I'm going to explode from anxiety, Kate releases her lip and smiles, wide and beautiful. Her perfection hits me like a shock of electricity to the heart, pushing it to work overtime to keep my blood flowing. She's fucking amazing when she smiles. All the dark shit from my past, all the things I've done, people I've hurt, women I've used—it all fades away until there's only me and her.

I gently squeeze her hand, which is still all tangled up with mine. "Does this mean I'm forgiven?"

Nodding shyly, she pulls her hand back, nervously scraping her long hair up into a high ponytail. A memory assaults me, hard enough to stun me for a moment. In school, Kate used to constantly fiddle with her hair, yanking it up whenever she was nervous or if it got in her way. She was always playing with it. Suddenly I want to bury my nose in those silky golden brown strands and inhale the sweet scent of her.

Fuck it.

Moving closer, I stand in front of Kate. She's watching every step I take, her eyes fixed on me, unblinking. Gently, my touch so light it barely brushes her skin, I move my hand up her neck to rest against the side of her face. Without realizing she's doing it, Kate leans her cheek into my touch, her mouth parting slightly.

That's the only sign I need to bring my other hand to the opposite side of her neck and pull her forward until our lips connect. Her taste explodes on my tongue, hot and sweet, with a hint of mint toothpaste mixed in. Using every bit of self-control I possess, I force myself to keep the kiss as short and chaste as possible. I don't want to ruin the moment when I've just gotten her to trust me with her heart.

"Wow," Kate whispers. I didn't think it was possible, but she's even more stunning now with her hair up, her eyes closed, and her lips swollen and red from our kiss than she was all put together at the club the other night.

Kate opens her eyes and I see it—she's lost in a haze of lust. It's a look I know well, having seen it on a woman's face more times than I can count. Only this time, it means something.

"I know. Wow." My thumbs brush over the skin in front of her ears, drawing small circles. "I'm not sure how many more rejections I can take, but I'm asking you again. Go out with me. On a proper date."

Kate's spine stiffens, and her head drops as she pulls away from my hands. She takes a few steps back but still doesn't say anything.

"Kate." She ignores me, still unmoving. "Kate!"

Her head jerks up, our eyes locking together. Closing her eyes, she presses her mouth into a hard line. She's changed her mind. Here it comes—the brush off. She's getting ready to wield the knife that will carve out my soul and leave me empty again.

Unconsciously, I rub the spot over my heart, as if I can soothe the sharp pain that's beginning to bloom. She can't say no, she's mine! Just the thought of anyone else touching her has me seeing red.

Another one of my dad's rules comes rushing back at me, blindsiding me with its strength.

Rule 5—Defend what's yours.

Inexplicably, all I can think about is how she's mine. The urge to throw her over my shoulder and hide her away nearly brings me to my knees. I struggle to keep it together while Kate decides our fate.

"Okay."

"What?" My hand drops to my side in shock. "Is that a yes?"

"Yes." Kate takes a deep breath, opening her eyes and giving me another one of her wide, brilliant grins.

For once in my life, I let my guard down, exhaling in relief. "Hell, I thought you were finished with me."

Seeing straight into my soul with those bright green eyes, her voice husky and sexy just like I remember, she steps closer. "I don't know if I'll ever be finished with you, Dax Davies."

Just like that, the glacial rock in my chest where my heart is supposed to be has a purpose. It can beat again.

7

K ate

SOMEHOW GOING on a proper date with Dax morphed into dinner then coming back to the flat to talk and get reacquainted after so much time apart. Making up for lost time.

Talking led to touching, which led to kissing. Once we realized all the other guys were out for the evening, words seemed unnecessary and things got intense... really intense. I've wanted him for so long, I can't resist his touch.

That's how I ended up in Dax's flat, lying on his bed, with his heavy body pressing me down to the mattress, snogging like there's no tomorrow.

"So gorgeous," Dax whispers, his large, rough hands sliding up and down my bare arms. My skin is so sensitive I can feel every single callous that has formed on his fingers from years of playing guitar and using his fists to earn money as they scrape over my exposed flesh.

Dax props himself up on his elbows so he can see right into my eyes—and I swear, right through me. I swallow loudly, my heart thrumming in my chest. Can he tell that I'm in love with him? That I've *been* in love with him for as long as I can remember? That I can see past that intimidating exterior he puts up to the man he really is?

Instead of voicing out loud whatever thoughts lie behind those expressive dark eyes, Dax lowers his head and kisses me—gently at first—light, barely there brushes of his lips on mine. It's enough to make my breath hitch with each pass of his mouth. He teases me like that for what feels like forever, minutes, hours... time seems to have stopped, everything collapsing in to focus on this one act.

Dax takes his time exploring me, his slow pace, his soft touches, the noises that we make growing louder and louder—it stokes a low burn inside that begs to be set free. I need *more*.

My body moves on instinct, attempting to get what it needs without my permission. I don't realize that my hips have arched off the bed, seeking contact with Dax's rigid length until I rub against his hard, denim-clad cock. He stops what he's doing immediately, but not before letting out a long, deep moan. The smoldering desire between us explodes into an inferno, turning us into panting, groaning animals in the blink of an eye.

Passion unlike any I've ever thought possible races through me unchecked. The scorching hot flames are burning my skin from the inside out, setting me on fire and boiling the blood in my veins. Unable to control his own reactions as I wantonly grind my hips against his, Dax shudders, giving in to his need for friction by dropping his weight down onto me for full body contact.

"Jesus, Kate." His voice is strained, his eyes wild. Dax's precious control is hanging on by a thread—one that I'm intent on unraveling.

I wrap my hands around his neck and yank him down for a deep, lingering kiss. My legs find their way around his waist, holding him close as we rock against each other, intense sensations jolting through me with each thrust of his hips.

Our mouths crash together again and again, sloppy, wet, and unbelievably perfect. Dax's tongue thrusts into my mouth, dominating mine. He tastes perfect. Like strength and security, with a bit of the chocolate trifle we shared for dessert. Needing more, I shove my hands up the back of his shirt, running them over smooth, hot skin wrapped over hard muscle.

Breaking the kiss with a ragged inhale, Dax slows down his rocking hips. "We shouldn't—I can't stop if we keep going, Kate."

My kind, gentle brute, concerned about taking advantage of me even when I all but attacked him. "Why do we have to stop?"

His eyes widen a fraction, the brown just a sliver behind his lust-blown pupils. "I-I..." Dax grinds his jaw, jealousy flashing across his face. "I thought you never...I didn't want your first... I guess I thought...*fuck*." He squeezes his eyes shut. "The thought of someone else touching you..."

"You thought this was my first time," I whisper, dragging a finger down his cheek. He's jealous. Holy crap, Dax is *jealous* at the thought of me being with someone else. The Iceman let his feelings be known! I nearly laugh out loud at his pointless jealousy, but hold back when I realize he's not using it as an excuse to behave like an unreasonable caveman. For a man like Dax, jealousy means he *cares*.

"Dax." He shakes his head and keeps his eyes shut tight, refusing to meet my stare or listen to my words. "Dax." I grab his head with both hands, pulling it down until our lips almost touch. "This *is* my first time."

That did it. His eyelids pop open, those damn dark irises of his showing me more than he'd ever want me to know—lust, protectiveness, concern, caring, power—all of his emotions exposed and available for me to read as if they were written out on his forehead.

"I want my first time with you, Dax. It's always been you."

Now we're even. My emotions are out there too, open and vulnerable for him to abuse should he desire. I don't mind. Against my better judgment, I trust Dax with my heart. I have no choice *but* to trust him.

I love him.

Dax gives me a slight nod of his head, a silent understanding passing between us, and his face relaxes from its hard set. We both understand the importance of this moment isn't to be taken lightly, me giving this to him.

Without looking away, he shuffles back, kneeling on the bed between my legs. Dax snags the hem of his shirt, whipping it off and tossing it somewhere on the floor. The sight in front of me —god, there are no words. I'm rendered immobile as my eyes greedily take in every single inch of Dax's torso. Each muscle is cut and defined, rippling under smooth, light skin, broken only by the occasional small scar. The long, perfect 'v' on his waist that leads down into his low-slung jeans makes my mouth water.

Hesitantly, I raise a hand between us, wanting to touch him more than anything. I get to touch this? Touch him? Wherever I want? Don't pinch me. I don't ever want to wake up.

"Wait." Dax grabs my hand before I get a single finger on him, drawing out a pathetic whimper. He grins, "If I have to be shirt-less..." Releasing my hand, he unbuttons my short-sleeved blouse faster than I would have thought his large fingers could manage. Dax pushes the silky material off my shoulders, exposing my blush-colored lace bra. He groans and squeezes his crotch, seemingly in pain.

"Jesus, Kate. California has been good to you. Your skin is so tan." Dax drags his huge, coarse hand down the center of my body from my collarbones to the edge of my shorts. It's so large he could probably span my waist with his hands and have room to spare. I shiver even though his touch leaves behind the heated ghost of a burn.

My body is becoming impatient. The need to touch him is overwhelming. "Get back down here."

Did I say that? When did I become so demanding? Probably when Dax got me all wound up then stopped.

The shocked look on his face is almost worth the near-crippling embarrassment I feel at being so bold. The corner of his mouth quirks up, his eyes devouring me without shame. "Oh baby, we're going to have so much fun, but you need to understand that the only one who gives orders around here is me."

Holy shit.

DAX

THIS IS what I've been waiting for. Kate Campbell, spread out beneath me, half-naked and waiting for me to tell her what to do. My baser needs, the selfish, demanding animal inside me is urging—no screaming—for me to tear off her clothes and sink into her wet pussy or stuff my cock in her hot little mouth. It's the only way I know. To use. To take. To demand.

But with Kate, I want it to be different—for this to be more than just a quick one-off with a nameless, faceless girl. I don't know if I'll be able to control myself to do make that happen. Hell, I'll probably *still* be a demanding bastard, maybe a tad less insensitive.

"Dax." Her husky, sex-laced voice whispering my name nearly undoes me right then. I look down to find her green eyes glazed over with desire, her body flushed and writhing beneath me, and I am awestruck by the trust she's giving me in this moment. Trusting me to take care of her, to make this good for her—for us. She's handing over the control I desperately need, even when I've given her no reason to do so.

Fuck. If that's not enough incentive to hold back the beast inside, then I don't know what is.

Quickly, I undo her shorts and whisk them away before doing the same with my jeans. When our bodies finally come together, skin on skin, with only our thin undergarments between us, I feel like I'm where I'm supposed to be. The rage inside is calm, the hatred I've harbored for years is gone, and all I can feel is *Kate.*

"I want you, Dax. I've waited for so long. Please..."

"Jesus, Kate." She twines her body around mine, arching up off the bed. Groaning, I take her mouth, forgetting to be gentle and attacking it roughly. I swallow her moans as my stiff cock grinds against her soft curves.

She bites at my lips, just enough to make it sting. Jerking back, I see a woman on the edge of losing her own control.

"Hmmmm, like it a little rough, do you?"

Kate lifts her hips, dragging them up and down on my rigid length. "I don't know. I suppose I'll like it any way as long as it's you," she rasps.

"I told you," I growl as I press her back down on the bed, "I promise it'll be good. But I'm in charge." I lick my way down the graceful slope of her neck, inhaling deeply as I go. "God you smell so bloody amazing." Her only response is to moan and tremble. I continue down her body, stopping when I reach her lace-covered breasts. Hooking a finger in each side, I pull the material down, tucking it underneath each perfect curve of flesh.

Kate jerks beneath me when I take a perfect pink nipple into my mouth, sucking it between my teeth.

"More, Dax..."

Holy fuck. She's going to kill me with her moaning and writhing. "Shhhhh, I'll give you more when you're ready." I move to the other breast, working it with my mouth and tongue until Kate is begging me for more.

"Dax, I can't wait any longer. Please!"

When I don't respond immediately, she thrashes her head

back and forth on the bed, struggling to keep from screaming in frustration. Hell, if Kate can't control herself then I have absolutely no chance. My body is always on a hair-trigger—primed to fight or fuck at any given moment.

Rising up from my thorough worshiping of Kate's breasts, I can see that her eyes are wild—dark black pools of lust—her neck and face flushed a glorious pink color. Kate's breathing is erratic and quick, as if she can't quite get enough air.

Mesmerized by her raw display of desire, my need to dominate roars back like an out of control freight train. I hurriedly strip out of my briefs, stopping only to grab a condom out of the bedside drawer. Once I'm sheathed, I turn back to the bed to find Kate has shed her own lacy knickers and is spread out and ready for me. Her hand is dipping between her legs, her head thrown back as she shamelessly touches herself. My eyes nearly bulge out of their sockets when I see that she's waxed almost completely bare.

Gone is the hesitant, unsure girl I know. "Christ, Kate. You're fucking amazing."

And she *is* amazing. Most girls are either fake, playing it up like porn stars or they're like limp rags during sex, thinking all they have to do is lay there. Sometimes, the second is true. I just want to bust a nut and do it quick with whoever is handy. But a partner that takes her sexuality and embraces it, whether it's to take what she wants or to turn her pleasure over to me—the result is the same. The scene in front of me is nothing short of a wet dream come true.

Kate's loud groan, combined with a full body tremor, breaks me from my gawking. I climb up on the bed, using my knees to push her legs apart until I'm situated between them. She reaches up to hold onto my shoulders, smoothing her hands all over my skin.

Feeling my restraint spiraling out of reach, I grip her hands and hold them over her head to get it back. If I don't calm down and take over, I'll go too far, too fast, and hurt her. Lowering my body down, I let my weight settle on top of Kate, using care to keep my heavy bulk from crushing her beneath me.

Moving both of her wrists into one of my hands, I reach down between us with the other, lining up my cock with her entrance. Her wet heat against me feels beyond incredible. Kate shifts, tearing a deep, rumbling growl from my throat as she drags herself across the sensitive head.

"Dax. I'm ready," she whispers.

I kiss her gently and slowly press forward, straining from the effort it takes to hold back when all I want to do is bury myself balls deep and claim her as mine. Our hands are intertwined above Kate's head again, her fingers gripping me hard enough to cause my knuckles to ache.

She feels so good I have to break the kiss, dropping my head into the hollow between her neck and shoulder. "Holy... my god, you're so fucking tight. You feel even better than I imagined." I push in further, meeting firm resistance. Kate lets out a small cry. Alarmed, my head pops up to see her face. "Are you okay?"

Kate nods, so I drop my head back down to her shoulder. Her rapid breaths caress my neck. "I-I'm okay. Just get it over with. Please."

Fuck. Hurting her goes against everything I believe, but god, the need to take her, to sink all the way into her gripping heat and be the first—the only—to have her, is overtaking every other instinct.

Gritting my teeth, I snap my hips hard, breaking through the taut barrier. Kate flinches beneath me, her body going stiff, her hands jerking in mine. I know it's normal for it to hurt the first time, but damn if I don't feel like the world's biggest bastard and fucking invincible at the same time.

I'm not the kindest bloke. In fact, I'm a miserable, selfish asshole who wants nothing more than to pound her into the mattress. But surprisingly, if it were possible in this moment, I'd take every bit of Kate's pain on as my own.

Kate

DAX FULLY DRESSED IS GORGEOUS, stunningly so. Naked, I want to drop to my knees and worship at his feet. I've seen him shirtless before, so I know how cut and muscular he is, I just didn't know how *big* he'd be in other places.

When Dax enters my body, tearing away the final shred of my virginity, I can't help but cry out at the pain. It hurts. *A lot.* Then, before he can say anything to mollify me, the sharp agony turns to pleasure—a deep, burning, twisting pleasure that begins to build upon itself, growing more intense with each thrust of Dax's narrow hips.

"More."

Dax responds to my whispered plea immediately, roaring up and releasing my bound wrists so he has room to move. And holy hell does he move. Balanced on his hands above me, Dax pounds away at an impossible pace. I have to brace my hands on his shoulders so we don't slide across the sheets with each powerful thrust. With the rapid pistoning of his hips and the intense plea-sure vibrating through me, it's nearly impossible to keep my eyes focused on his. Somehow I manage to stay locked on those dark, shimmering pools.

"Kate, I..." His face contorts with ecstasy, and I realize that I'm doing that to him. *Me.* Boring Kate Campbell is sending the cold and unapproachable Dax Davies flying into unrestrained bliss.

My entire body starts to shudder, waves of pleasure rippling out from the place where our bodies join together. I can't breathe as it crashes over me, drawing my muscles tight in ecstasy then leaving me boneless as the incredible feeling recedes. I'm float-ing, and Dax is right there with me.

He lets out a string of unintelligible curses (Gaelic maybe?) and thrusts one final time before collapsing in a heavy, comforting heap on my chest.

Somehow, I manage to move my hands, running them up and down Dax's sweaty back, feeling every dip and ridge beneath my fingers, trying to get my fill of touching everything he denied me earlier. After a few minutes, Dax shifts, causing me to wince when he pulls free of my body. It doesn't detract from the moment though. Everything is perfect. My eyelids grow heavy and I'm vaguely aware of Dax moving around the room. Then I'm wrapped up in his arms, my back pressed against his large, warm chest.

I'm drifting off to sleep, on the edge of reality and dreams when I hear a soft whisper. "M'aingeal."

8

K ate

"THIS IS THE LAST ONE." Dax drops a box on the floor of the bedroom in my new flat.

"We're taking off, Kate!" Gavin calls out from the lounge.

"You guys are so great to help me move. Honestly, I couldn't have done it without you." I tell them as I walk down the tiny hall to say goodbye.

"No worries, love. Happy to do it," Adam says. I wrap him up in a big hug.

I buss his cheek before I pull back to give Adam a quick once over. He looks much better than he did a few months ago when Ellie was in town. Not great, but better. He was completely devastated when I told him what he said to Ellie at that stupid party. He was so plastered he didn't even remember seeing her. Having to tell him what happened with her was one of the worst moments of my life.

"Gotta split, Kate. Give me some love." Hawke leans in to give me one of his bone-crushing hugs. He's so open with me and the other guys, but around everyone else, he's quiet and withdrawn.

"You know I live to be smashed to pieces in your arms, Hawke," I laugh when he lets me go.

"I count on it." He winks at me and disappears out the front door.

"Ugh! This is the last of my stuff too." Abby staggers in, throwing a pile of clothes onto the second-hand sofa her parents gave us. "I'm beat!" She flops on top of the clothing, sweaty and exhausted.

"Coming with?" Adam turns to Dax.

"Nah. I'll find my way back later." He throws an arm around my neck, pulling me back against his chest. "I'll stay here with my woman for a little bit."

I roll my eyes, which makes Adam laugh, something he doesn't do enough of these days. "Right. Cheers mate."

The door shuts, leaving the flat blessedly quiet.

"Oh shit! Is that the time?" Abby jumps up from the sofa. "I have to be at work in thirty minutes," she calls out from her room. Less than five minutes later, she's saying goodbye and is out the door for her summer job working at a camp for low-income city kids.

I giggle, leaning back against Dax so I can rub my ass across the front of his athletic shorts.

"Naughty," he laughs, gently spanking me. Dax whispers in my ear, his hot breath giving me goose bumps. "No more Lila."

"No more Lila," I agree. "And, I have my own bedroom now."

Dax spins me around to face him, grinding his erection into my hip. "That's my favorite part about this place."

"So," I say coyly, "want to go workout?"

He kisses me long and deep, and then slings me over his shoulder, giving my butt a playful slap as he strides toward the bedroom.

"I'll show you a workout," Dax grumbles under his breath.

Yeah, this is my favorite part. This summer is going to be brilliant.

DAX

"REALLY? ARE YOU HAVING A LAUGH?" Adam asks Ross Evans, our manager.

I scan the room, checking the face of each one of my band mates. They all have the same shocked look that I'm sure I have on mine.

Ross smiles. "No Adam, I'm quite serious."

I turn to Ross. "So, you're saying that Underground Records wants us to sign us and have us go on tour with U2? The real U2, not some basement band cover rendition?" My expression must be comical because Ross starts laughing.

"Yes, that's exactly what I'm saying," he answers once he's finally stopped making fun. "Just the U.S. part of the tour, not the European or other countries... yet. If they like what they see, who knows?"

None of us say a word. Gavin and Hawke are eyeing Ross dubiously, as if waiting for him to shout out "just kidding!" and claim the entire thing is a joke. Adam is staring intently at his shoes, his fingers scratching back and forth across his unshaven jaw.

I guess it's up to me to break the silence. Standing, I hold my hand out to Hawke's uncle, a man who has done everything in his power to get us noticed and apparently, it's just paid off.

He shakes my hand, pulling me into a hug. "Thanks mate." I slap his back a few times. "We couldn't have done this without you."

Ross releases me, the excitement on his face evident. "You guys are great. I've told you that before. It was only a matter of time until someone important noticed. Now they have and the only direction you can go is up. They want you in the studio right away to get an album released in time for the tour."

The others finally get to their feet, excited and congratulating Ross and each other. I accept my handshakes and pats on the back with a smile. A bottle of champagne is produced, doled out to each of us in real crystal flutes. God, Kate's going to freak out when she hears we'll be touring with bloody Bono.

This is it. What we've been working for. Over a year slogging in tiny clubs up and down the California coast has turned into our dream.

I want to call Kate, but it's better to do this face to face. I want to see the excitement on her face when I tell her. Adam and Hawke are chatting with Ross about the studio space we'll be recording in while Gavin is on his own mobile speaking to someone.

"So, tomorrow, I'll send out the recording schedule and give you guys all the information you'll need. The phone number at the studio, your new producer's phone and email, your contact at the studio, you'll need that email as well..." Ross goes on and on about minute details when really I could care less. We'll be making an album, going on tour, and living our dream—that's what I care about.

Kate

"I CANNOT BELIEVE IT!" My face is splitting in half I'm grinning so big. "You're going on tour? With U2?"

Dax nods, his smile larger than any I've ever seen on his handsome face. I'm so proud of him and the other guys I could just burst.

"We are, angel. I want you to come with." Dax pulls me into his arms, nuzzling his mouth and nose against my neck.

"Dax." He places kisses up and down the sensitive skin, sucking my earlobe into his mouth. "God, Dax. I want to, but I can't go on tour with you." My breath is coming faster and heavier. I can't think when he's doing that.

"What?" Dax stops, pulling back to face me. "Why not? I want you there."

"I want to be there. But you said it's in four months. I have school, Dax. And it's footy season. If I don't keep my grades up and continue football, they'll pull my scholarship." My hands find their way under his shirt, using my thumbs to caress the skin on either side of his waist just above his low-slung jeans.

"But... I'll be gone for six weeks." His brows pull together and his beautiful lips turn into a frown.

I laugh. "You're being silly, Dax. I'm not going anywhere. It's good timing actually. I'll be so busy with my studies and traveling to matches, we wouldn't be seeing each other much either way."

Still sulking, Dax thinks about it for a minute. "I don't like it. I want you with me, Kate."

Really?

Removing my hands from his skin, I cross my arms. "I'm not quitting school to go on tour with a rock band, Dax. So you'll have to adjust. We have all summer, and then when you're gone, we'll talk every night and you can send me photos and text. Good thing you got me that mobile, yeah?"

Dax nods, but it's stiff. He doesn't like this at all. Stubborn, bossy Dax isn't getting his way and he doesn't know what to do. Did he really think I'd just give up my life to follow him around the country?

Taking another look at my sullen boyfriend I realize that yes, yes he did.

9

Four months later

"This is un-fucking-believable!" Hawke exclaims as we head inside Madison Square Garden in New York City to start the U.S. leg of our tour opening for U2.

Adam walks right out onstage, stopping in the center. He looks out over the arena, bustling with the crew that is putting everything together for tonight's show. I have to say, he belongs there. The gloom and doom mood that's been over him for the last year seems to lift while he's on the massive stage.

He turns to me and grins, waving me over. Once there, Adam slings an arm around my shoulders. "Can you believe this? A couple of years ago we were playing in dusty old an abandoned basement. Now—" he releases me, spreading his arms wide, "we're in New York fucking City and we're going to play to a sold out crowd."

"Yeah, who woulda thought two blokes from Hackney could ever get here?" I look around at everything, the lights, the massive, four-story telly behind us, the twenty thousand empty seats that will have people in them tonight. "It's bloody over-whelming, Adam."

Adam's grin dissolves into a frown. "If only—"

"Don't do it mate. You can only go forward." I give him the same advice I've been repeating since Ellie broke up with him a little over a year ago. Adam and I turned that advice into a song of the same name that has become an instant hit from our new album, *You Can Only Go Forward*.

"Right. I know. Forward."

"Alrighty!" The tour manager, Aaron Shiftley, claps his hands to get us to gather around. "Your instruments are still being brought in so sound check won't be for an hour. After that you have a pre-concert fan meet and greet, then wardrobe. Okay?" We all nod, not having any clue what to do except what we're told. Ross is just off stage on the phone. He usually conveys the infor-mation to us as to what to do and where to be, but this bloke is in charge of everything, so if he wants to tell us directly, then he will.

We all nod and grunt in understanding.

"Then get backstage and rest up. I'll see you out here in one hour. Do not be late. U2 has their sound check after yours and I will not have them held up, got it?" Satisfied we all understand, like we're small children or something, he shoos us away.

"Well, that guy is something else," Hawke whispers.

"Yeah. Real charmer, he is," I agree.

We get to our dressing room, which is really just a large room with a few chairs and a sofa with a big rack of clothing in the center, and flop down to wait. Adam wanders over to a side table loaded down with snacks while Gavin and Hawke fire up some sort of gaming console.

I figure I should ring Kate now, since it doesn't seem as if there will be time later. Slipping out quietly, I find an empty room right across the hall.

"Dax?"

"Hello, angel. I wanted to ring you before it got too crazy."

"I wish I could be there tonight, Dax. You're going to be amazing."

Kate's praise makes my skin warm and my heart soar. It's nice to hear good things about yourself that don't involve your ability to smash someone's nose in with your elbow.

"Thanks. I wish you were here too." Ross had said he could arrange for Kate to fly out for tonight's concert, courtesy of our label, but, to my extreme displeasure, Kate has a football match tonight and an exam tomorrow so it was impossible.

"It's going to be a long six weeks, isn't it?" she says sadly.

Sighing, I flop down on a nearby sofa. "Yeah. It is. You can still join me in our next city."

"Dax, I can't. You know this. Let's not have another row."

I grunt, unhappy with her decision. "All right. I'll leave it be."

"Just, don't forget about me." The melancholy in her voice is evident.

"I'm not going to shag a bunch of groupies, angel. I'm not Adam." She's so insecure and she has no reason to be. She's gorgeous, fun, fit, everything I could want. Everything I *do* want.

"Right, you never shag groupies, Dax." Kate's sarcastic tone can't be missed. She's alluding to my previous hookups. And she's right. Before her, I played around a lot and didn't care who it was.

"If we're together I don't shag anyone but you. You know that. There's no comparison."

"It's—"

"There you are!" A piercing squeal interrupts our conversation. I look up and am horrified to see a familiar figure in the doorway.

"Lila?" I'm so shocked, I can't help but say her name.

"Lila? Lila's there with you?" Kate asks, sounding alarmed.

I can't respond to Kate, I'm too bloody surprised to see her former flatmate flinging herself at me, landing solidly in my lap.

"What the fuck, Lila?" I struggle to move her off as she winds her arms around my neck, locking on tight.

"Dax! What the hell is going on?" Kate is shouting through the phone while I remove Lila and dump her on the sofa.

"Dax, honey, stop pretending to be surprised to see me here," Lila says, plastering her body against me again. Angrier than I've been in a while, I shove her back with complete disregard to the fact that she's a girl. She stumbles, nearly going arse over tit on her bloody high heels.

"Stay the fuck away from me! You're mental!" I hiss, taking a step back. "Hello? Kate?" There's no response from my mobile. When I look at the screen, I see that the call has been disconnected.

Putting my back to Lila, I grind my teeth, warring between two different rules at the same time.

Rule 2—Never let your emotions show.

Rule 3—Women who act like slags can be treated like slags.

I'll hit her if I don't get it under control and I can't have that. She's a cow, but she is a girl. Plus, she'd have me tossed in jail. Rule 2 wins. Breathing slowly, I put my mobile in my pocket, uncurling my fists. Turning slowly, I face the girl who has caused me more problems than I can count.

"Why. Are. You. Here." I keep my cold, hard mask up, determined not to let her see how much she affects me.

"Oh Daxey, my daddy is the producer for your latest album. Didn't you know that? I asked if I could have a job on this tour and he made me the assistant to the tour publicist. Isn't that great?"

Daxey? Job on tour? Publicist? Isn't she in school?

Lila is smiling, but her eyes aren't. They're cruel, cunning, and full of secrets. She knows exactly what she's doing.

I shove past her before I do something stupid. Storming into the dressing room, I spot Ross in the corner chatting with who-the-fuck-knows and who-the-fuck-cares.

"Ross, I need to have a chat."

He looks up and does a double take when he sees me. Shit. I must not be hiding my anger very well. I'm out of practice, used to being free to feel however I want around Kate and not care that she knows.

"Sound check is in thirty minutes," he says to the others after dismissing the two blokes. "Let's go to the other room." Ross directs me towards a door to the right. Once it's closed behind us, he whirls around, concern on his face. "What's going on? You look like you're ready to kill someone."

"I might just do that," I growl, cursing under my breath as I once again try to manage my building anger. "Fuck, Ross. Why didn't you tell us that Lila was going to be on tour with us?"

Ross jerks back in surprise. "Lila? Who's Lila?" He is genuinely baffled.

"You didn't know?"

"I have no idea what you're talking about," he admits.

I pinch the bridge of my nose. "Sebastian Griffin."

"The producer of your album?" Ross asks.

"Yeah. Does he have a daughter?"

"What?" Ross seems uncertain where this conversation is headed. "Well, yes..." He presses his mouth into a tight line. "Tell me you didn't fuck the boss' daughter, Dax."

That's it. I snap and Ross has the unfortunate luck of being the closest one to me when it happens. Ross stumbles as I surge forward. He ends up with his back pressed against the door. I get as close as I can without actually touching his ridiculous thousand-dollar suit.

"No I didn't fuck her! She's been trying to fuck *me* for the past year and a half!" I roar. "She's Kate's old flatmate, Ross!"

His eyes widen further than I would have thought possible. "The one who stalks you at the clubs?"

"Yes, that one! I didn't know her last name! I can't have her on tour with me, Ross. She's fucking mental!" I back up, pacing the room while I concentrate on not punching the wall or something else that would injure my hand and make me miss the show.

Ross steps forward, shaking his head, genuine remorse in his eyes. "I'm sorry, Dax. But she's literally is the boss's daughter. I can't fire her."

"What the hell am I supposed to do?"

Ross's gaze hardens and he straightens out his suit, tugging at his shirtsleeves. He turns from Hawke's kind uncle into the professional Hollywood manager in the blink of an eye. The one who doesn't tolerate rock stars who have temper tantrums.

"I suggest you ignore her. She's a ninety-pound girl, Dax. She can't force you to do anything. You'll figure something out."

With that, he turns and exits the room, leaving me with the raging urge to punch someone and a near crippling desire to throw Lila Griffin over a cliff.

"Dax! Sound check!" Someone calls for me from the other room. I storm off, hoping the music will take my mind off of Lila and her bloody fucking shit.

It's not until we're getting back to our hotel, early in the morning, after one of the biggest moments of my life that I realize I never rung Kate back.

Fuck me.

Kate

"So what? You're just never going to talk to your stony boyfriend again? That's ridiculous and immature, Kate." Abby is glaring at me from the opposite side of our table at a tiny Mexican restaurant near our flat.

"No. I didn't say that. I... I need to figure out what I'm going to do, that's all. And why are you calling him stony?"

Abby laughs. "You know, because he's always so... composed."

"You only notice things like that because you're obsessed with trying to figure people out, Miss Psychologist." He is stony and composed, but I won't give Abby the satisfaction of being right. I drag my fork through my chile relleno, not interested in actually eating it. In fact, I've probably lost a half stone since hearing Dax with Lila at the New York concert.

Lila. On tour with Dax. My slutty ex-flatmate around my boyfriend twenty-four hours a day for the next six... well, now five, weeks.

"Have you decided?"

I stare at her blankly, having missed the question. "What you're going to do about Dax. Have you decided?" Abby asks again.

"No. It's just," I take in a deep breath, willing myself not to cry. I've cried more than enough over the last week. "I can't compete, Abby."

She wrinkles her nose. "Compete? What does that mean?"

I huff. What would Abby know about feeling invisible? She always looks like she's ready to pose for a swimsuit magazine, all tall, tan, and skinny, with beach-ready blonde waves cascading down her back and big blue eyes.

"What am I, Abby? Honestly? I'm nothing special. I'm not gorgeous, I'm not rich, I'm not posh... I'm just some plain girl from the East End. Why *wouldn't* my boyfriend go on the pull while he's on tour? He'll have girls like Lila flashing their tits at him every chance they get."

Abby sits back in her chair with her arms crossed, looking bored. "Are you done?"

Heat fills my cheeks in embarrassment.

"Now, look at me and listen up." Her harsh tone gets my attention right quick. "You are not," she puts up her fingers and makes quotes, "'some plain girl from the East End'. You're beautiful, smart, and one of the most talented soccer players I've ever seen. You have to stop putting yourself down all the time, Kate. If Dax didn't want you, he wouldn't be with you. It's as simple as that." She finishes drinking her lemonade and fishes out an ice cube to munch on. "And what makes him so much better than you anyway?"

I shrug, not knowing what she's looking for me to say.

"Hmph. He's *not* better than you, that's why." She swallows down the remainder of the ice. "Money, fame, good looks... those things don't make anyone better than you. Some of the most attractive people I've ever met are actually quite hideous on the inside."

I roll my eyes. "Don't use your psychology crap on me, Abby."

"It's not crap. It's true. God, you *need* a shrink to help with that low self-esteem of yours. You have to trust that Dax loves you. If he doesn't, then you'll find out." Abby pushes her plate away and signals for our server.

"He's never even told me he loves me, Abby. It's just that..." I sigh. "I've loved him for so long. He was always unattainable to me. I guess I'm afraid it won't last."

"He's not a guy who lays his feeling out there, Kate. You're looking for reasons to end things so you don't have to be hurt if he's the one to end it."

"I hate that you're so smart." I throw some money down on top of Abby's when the check comes.

"It's the psychology major in me," she giggles. "So, will you answer when he calls?"

Abby bumps my hip with hers as we exit onto the crowded sidewalk. "Yeah, I will."

"Awesome. Now, let's go work on our tans. The beach is calling." She flips down her sunglasses and I do the same. Arms linked, we begin the three-block walk to the nearest beach.

As much as I want to believe Abby, the insecure girl inside is begging me to end things with Dax so he can't hurt me. I have to swallow down the bile that threatens to rise at the thought of never seeing him again. From that reaction, I'd say there's a big part of me doesn't want to let him go.

DAX

"DAXEY! I NEED YOU!"

Fuck!

I cringe at the sound of that squeaky, high-pitched voice. It's like nails on a chalkboard. Avoiding her is exhausting and it's only been two weeks.

"Daxey! I need you!" Adam mocks in a singsong voice, strumming his guitar along with. Hawke and Gavin crack up—at my expense, naturally.

"Sod off, Reynolds." I give him a quick punch in the arm, earning a loud *"ouch"* for my effort.

I've only just gotten Kate to start speaking to me again after we found out Lila is going to be on the tour. I don't want to have to deal with any more of Lila's bullshit that could cock up my relationship again. One week of the cold shoulder from Kate was plenty.

With quick knock on the door of our dressing room, Lila enters without waiting for an invite.

"Fuck, Lila. What if one of us was changing in here?" I snarl.

She rolls her eyes, teetering on her ridiculous heels as she crosses the room towards me. "You don't have anything I haven't seen before, Daxey. Not that I wouldn't mind seeing what you're packing." Lila licks her lips and stares at my crotch. My damn traitorous dick twitches from the scrutiny of a hot woman. It doesn't seem to care that I despise her.

Son of a bitch!

"Whatever." I turn my back to her and pick up my guitar plucking on it randomly, determined to do what Ross suggested and ignore her.

"Can we help you, Lila?" Hawke asks, thankfully coming to my rescue.

Lila starts to sneer at him, but fixes a plastic smile on her face. There's something more going on between Hawke and Lila, some history I don't know. Not that I'd ask, but they truly despise each other, and it seems to go further back than just this tour.

"Rachel wanted you to know that there's a mandatory appearance tonight after the show at a club ten minutes from here."

"Kind of late notice, don't you think?" Adam growls from where he's slumped on one of the plush recliners backstage at the United Center in Chicago.

Rachel is in charge of promotions for the band, appearances, media events, interviews... all the crap that comes with celebrity. I continue ignoring Lila as she argues with Adam, thankful for the stupid bastard. I'm lucky to have him running interference for me.

After a minute of everyone ignoring her, she huffs in annoyance. "You have to be there. That's all I can say. You don't like it, take it up with Rachel." I can hear the impatience in her voice, waiting for me to acknowledge her. When I don't, she huffs again and stomps out the door.

I wait until I hear the door slam shut before I speak to Adam. "You got her to leave you fucking brilliant bastard!" We burst out laughing, so overcome with hilarity at Lila's fury that even Gavin and Hawke join in the fun. Suddenly it feels like we're back in the U.K. hanging in a dark, dusty basement, just a bunch of kids with a dream.

"I gotta look out for my best mate," Adam quips.

We exchange a look and I know that in his own way, he's thanking me for being there after the whole Ellie thing happened and he fell to pieces. I nod, smiling before returning to my guitar.

The concert is a blast and after a quick check-in with Kate, we're whisked away in a massive SUV to a party at some club called Whipped.

"Ever been to Chicago before?" Lila asks everyone while she directs her unwavering gaze at me—well, at my crotch.

"Can't say I have," Adam answers, once again playing defense for me.

Lila purses her lips, annoyed by Adam as usual.

"I have," Gavin quips. A quick glance shows the bass player hiding his mouth with his hand. Even though it's dark in here, I can still see him squelching a laugh.

Bloody arseholes. They think Lila's obsession with me is so fucking hilarious. Adam doesn't, but Gavin and Hawke... they have a laugh at my expense whenever they can.

"Here we are!" Lila chirps in that damn screechy voice.

One look out the window and I'm flabbergasted. Paparazzi line the sidewalk in front of the club, swarming the car as we pull up. I am not ready for this.

"What the fuck, Lila!" I snap.

"Daxey, you're a star now. This is how it is." She flutters her eyelashes and acts all innocent, but I know her. There's evil shining in those soulless eyes of hers. Something isn't right with this situation.

"C'mon Dax." Adam tugs at my arm, pulling me back in my seat. I hadn't realized how close I had gotten to Lila, snarling right in her face.

Jesus. I have got to control my temper around this girl. I find it so easy to fall back on dad's rules around everyone but Lila and Kate. Breaking them for good reasons... and bad reasons.

"Fine." I unclench my hand and breathe deep, returning to

my icy exterior. Adam looks at me oddly. "I'm fine," I snarl. "Let's go."

"You look like you're going to pop a blood vessel," he mutters.

Lila grins. "Your fans await boys!"

The driver hops out and opens the door, holding back the paparazzi as he helps Lila down to the walkway. The rest of us pile out behind her, Adam, Gavin, and Hawke smiling and chatting with the fans who line the sidewalk in front of the club.

Me? I remain unapproachable. I've been bottling it up for so long, it's second nature. I'm not about to let these parasites see me lose it.

Lila trips and I smack into her back, grabbing her arm to keep from flat out knocking her arse over tit in front of the media.

"Thanks Daxey." She grins like I hung the moon and I have to refrain from rolling my eyes.

"Let's get inside, okay?"

"Sure thing, Daxey." She pats my chest with her free arm.

Fuck it. The second we get past the cameras, I roll my eyes and damned if it doesn't feel great.

Kate

"Shannon, can you grab my gloves?"

My teammate slams the locker next to mine, tossing a pair of thick gloves over my head to Bridget, our keeper.

The locker room is in complete chaos as I lace up my own shoes and pull my socks over my shin guards. Quickly, I whip my hair up into a ponytail to keep it out of my face. Today's game is pivotal. We're playing Oregon, one of our biggest rivals, and it's our first conference game this year.

"Kate! Get your butt out here!"

Whoops! Coach's angry shout from the locker room door has

me moving. I must have been lost in thought longer than I realized.

"Sorry Coach Russo." I jog past him to join the team at the entrance to the pitch.

"As long as your head's in the game out there," he points towards the stadium, "I don't care what you do otherwise. You ready?"

I nod.

"Alright ladies! Let's get out there and kick some ass!"

Amid the hollers and cheers of my teammates and the fans, we run out onto the pitch. After the preliminaries, everyone gets into place. I inhale the scent of fresh cut grass, loving the cool breeze, the clapping from the stands... everything about this game. With Dax gone and my parents far away, this is what keeps me grounded. I'd be lost without the sport I love.

I catch the sight of Mateo and some of the other men's footy players in the stands. They're standing up cheering for us. We support each other when we can, the men's and women's teams. When we can, a bunch of us girls go to their matches. Football doesn't get the same massive crowds that the American gridiron team pulls in.

The referee blows her whistle, I tense up for the drop, and the game begins.

"GET UP!"

My head is so groggy with sleep it takes me a minute to realize that Abby is in my bedroom.

"Go away!" I pull the covers over my head to block out the bright morning sun.

"Kate. Get up."

The impatience in my flatmate's voice is obvious, but I'm shattered. "Abby. I've had a late night. We went to a frat party to celebrate after our win and I didn't get home until three. I'm having a lie-in, so sod off."

Of course, the men's footy team joined us at the party, since some of them are members of the frat. I chatted with blokes when appropriate and got a few lustful stares from several of them. They left me alone for the most part. I must have been giving off unapproachable vibes or something.

One or two of my teammates were caught snogging a few of the blokes in different back corners of the frat house. That's par for the course at university. Especially around a bunch of horny athletes.

My duvet is suddenly ripped off of the bed, exposing me to both the chill of the room and the ever-present L.A. sun.

"Christ, Abby! What the hell is it?" I snap, rubbing the sleep out of my eyes.

"This! That's what!" A magazine lands on my lap, the pages fanning open.

"So? What is it? A gossip mag?" I glance at the cover. Hmmm, that Andrew Forrester bloke from that new movie. I run my finger down hi picture. "He's quite the hottie, yeah?" Frowning, I feel as if he looks familiar, but can't remember where I've seen him before.

Abby huffs. "Not him." She flicks the pages to one that is folded down and stabs at a picture with her finger. "Right here."

My brain hasn't woken up yet, so I process the information slowly. But once I figure out exactly what I'm looking at, I'm most definitely awake.

"What in the bloody fucking hell is this?"

"That's what I want to know," Abby says. She flops down on my bed next to me, waiting for me to say something.

My mouth opens and closes like a fish, unable to come up with anything more than a few creative curses. "I knew it! That stupid cow and that lying, cheating bastard!"

"You don't know that he's cheating, Kate. It's only a picture."

I stare at Abby in disbelief. "You're the one who brought me the sodding magazine, Abby! It's right here in print, plain as day!"

On the "Who's Out and About" page of *CelebWeekly* is a large color photo of Dax and Lila, looking quite cozy at a dance club in Chicago where they went to a party a few days ago. Dax's usual icy expression is gone, and in its place is someone who is laughing and smiling and having a fantastic time.

Lila, the whore, is wearing the skimpiest white dress I've ever laid eyes on and has her arm threaded through Dax's elbow, her pouty face looking right at the camera.

Abby reads the caption out loud. "Lila Griffin, gorgeous socialite daughter of Sebastian Griffin, Hollywood mogul and producer for *Sphere of Irony's* first album, is seen out on the town with Dax Davies, lead guitarist for the band. The couple has been spotted together on various stops along the band's U.S. tour with *U2*, which kicked off last month in New York City."

One photo. Two sentences. That's how little it took to rip away every shred of confidence I had built over the last five months with Dax.

10

D ax

"I'M NOT KIDDING, Liam. There's a fucking international cunt circus following around us all the time now."

My brother's chuckle comes through the phone, reminding me of home and family. I never thought I'd miss them, but I do—even Shaun, the mean bastard.

"Gotta be fun though, touring with such a popular band. The crowds must be amazing!"

"It is amazing, Liam. It's unreal. Like every night is the biggest fight of your life, on a stage in front of the entire world. It's such a fucking rush." I catch myself, holding back on the gushing. "Sorry. Didn't mean to prattle on."

"Dax, I'm not dad. You can be excited, yeah? Don't hide your feelings. It's not healthy. The old goat was wrong about a lot of stuff."

I sigh, knowing Liam is right. "I know. It's just hard to

change, you know? I—fuck, I hate talking about this shit." Cringing, I rub a hand over my scruffy chin. Randomly, I think about how I'll have to shave before tonight's show. "All those rules he forced on us, my mind and body react automatically. I can't help it."

"You mean shutting down into an emotionally stunted ape? Or do you mean getting a stiffy whenever you're about to do something huge? Like going on stage, maybe?"

My mouth hangs open. "How did you know? Do you—?"

"No. Not me. Shaun. It happens to him all the time. Although, he really *is* an emotionally stunted ape," Liam jokes.

A knock on my hotel room door interrupts our laughing. "Look, I gotta go."

"Anytime, Dax."

"Give my love to mum. Cheers."

I open the door to a, thankfully, sober Adam. He pushes past me and flops down on my sofa.

"Why don't you just make yourself at home?" I quip.

"Heard from Kate?"

"Huh?" I narrow my eyes. "Why are you asking about Kate?"

When Adam's face turns bright red, I know I'm not going to like the answer.

"Adam—" I say threateningly.

"Here mate. Don't get all puffed up. We know it's bollocks. But, ummmm—"

He tosses me a magazine, which I snatch mid-air. "What's this?" I growl, not sure I like whatever is going on here.

"Fuck, just remember mate... like I said, it's complete crap."

I open the magazine to where it's been folded back and skim the page. What. The. Fuck.

My first instinct is to punch the hell out of something... anything, whatever will make the sharp pain in my chest go away. Adam must notice, because he jumps up from his seat and guides me to a chair, pushing me back into it.

"Don't fuck up your hand, Dax. Not over this. It's not worth it."

"Not worth it?" I snarl, staring up at him. "Kate's gonna—" I suck in a sharp breath, "She's gonna see this and think. Oh no. Fuck no. That bitch isn't doing this to me again. Bloody Lila Griffin!"

Leaping to my feet, I shove him out of the way and head for the door.

"Dax! Don't!" he calls out. Adam grabs my arm and I instinctually swing, grazing his chin with the edge of my fist.

He stumbles back, stunned, while I stand there horrified.

"Jesus, mate. I'm sorry." The blinding rage takes a backseat to the fact that I just punched my best mate.

"No worries." Adam rubs his jaw. "Huh. Honestly, I always wondered what it was like to fight you. I thought you'd hit much harder than that, actually."

I'm shocked into silence for a moment, then burst out laughing. "If I had actually hit you, like full-on for real hit you, you'd have a broken jaw, mate."

"No doubt. No doubt," he chuckles. "So. Let's go grab a cold one before we have to be at the arena, like the good old days."

My eyebrows fly up. "The good old days? We're only twenty. Do we even have good old days yet?"

"Yeah. We do. Feels much older sometimes, doesn't it?"

I take a good look at Adam, a man I've known for most of my life. He's right. He does seem older, worn down by life and its never-ending bullshit. The booze doesn't do him any favors either. Yet despite all that, his public persona is captivating. People fucking love him.

"Yeah, sometimes it does," I admit. Growing up in Hackney won't keep you youthful looking, that's for damn sure. "Fine." I chuck the magazine on the sofa. "Let's go. But I'm not going to forget what Lila's done."

Adam puts his arm around my shoulders and gives me a

brotherly squeeze. Grinning, he opens the door, waiting for me to grab my wallet. "That's all bullshit, Dax. We're fucking rock stars, mate. Let's go live like it!"

I glance over at the magazine and realize I'm too tired and too angry to deal with it right now. Maybe Adam is right. I need to loosen up.

"Let's go. Lead the way, Mr. Reynolds."

WHY I THOUGHT DOING anything Adam suggested would be a good idea, I have no bloody clue. The bloke is a walking disaster of epic proportions. Yeah he's great and brilliant musician, but Adam's judgment, especially post-Ellie, is total crap.

One thing I have to credit him with, he knows how to have a good time. We ducked out of the hotel without telling anyone and asked the cabbie to bring us to the nearest college bar. Women and alcohol are Adam's answer to everything.

"That's sooooo interesting," a too-skinny redhead says, brushing her tits up against my arm as I try to scoot away on my barstool.

"Right, Dax. Sooooo interesting, isn't it?" Adam copies with a smirk. He's lucky we're in public, or I'd smack that look right off his face. Okay, so I wouldn't. He is my best mate, after all.

"What's it like living in Seattle?" Adam asks a gorgeous blonde that has made herself quite comfortable on his lap. Huh, I guess we're in Seattle. It gets confusing after a while. Too many cities. Even on a piss up Adam always knows where we are. It's a talent.

"It's not as fun as it must be in London," she squeals. "Oh! Have you met Prince Harry?"

The redhead chirps in. "Yeah, he's hot!"

"Ummmm, no. I haven't," Adam says, hiding his impending

laughter behind his pint glass, his shoulders shaking in amusement.

These girls are idiots. Pretty to look at, but dumb as doornails. Perfect for a quick shag or suck in the loo. I blink hard, wondering why that though popped into my head. I have Kate. Smart, kind, brilliant Kate. I won't ruin what we have for a name-less shag, no matter how hard my dick is right now.

"Dax, right?" the redhead asks, throwing her arms around my neck.

"Right." I motion to the bartender who comes over straight away. "Can I have another pint?"

The dark lager slides across the bar into my waiting hand. I need it if I'm expected to deal with Red here grinding on me and no relief anywhere in my near future.

"You're hot," she says, dragging her painted fingernail down my pecs.

"Thanks," I say blandly, keeping my ever-present composure up while my cock hardens in my briefs.

"Be right back, mate," Adam says cheerfully, pulling the blonde towards the back of the bar. Fucker. The thought of him getting sucked off while I sit here drinking is depressing. And it makes my cock even harder from frustration.

Luckily, I'm an expert in self-denial. After years of having my urges controlled by my dad's schedule, I know how to go without sex for extended periods of time. Six weeks is rough, but I can do it. I *have* to do it. I'll do whatever it takes to keep Kate.

❧

"Chop chop boys!" Lila's grating voice burrows right under my skin and starts crawling around like an army of ants.

I yank up my trousers, spinning around to see her smirking.

"Fucking hell, Lila! I've told you to bloody knock on the fucking door before coming in." I am so sick to death of her shit.

Because I won't speak to her most of the time, she's taken to trying to catch me naked or semi-naked before or after shows while I'm changing.

"Sorry, Daxey," she pouts, her eyes shining with lust and her skin flushed pink.

"Lila, get out!" Adam takes her shoulders and spins her towards the door.

"No. Wait!" I walk over and put myself between Lila and the exit, giving her my best angry scowl.

"Need something, Daxey? You know what I can give you," she purrs, sliding closer.

I hold a hand out to keep her from advancing. Over her shoulder I see Adam's eyes widen. He knows me well enough to predict what's about to go down, and he knows it isn't going to be pretty.

"Gavin, hand me the magazine." My hard gaze never leaves Lila's. She shifts uncomfortably, the dents in her armor showing.

"Here you are," Gavin says gleefully, smacking the rolled up magazine into my outstretched hand.

"Daxey, I really need to get going," Lila cries in that whingy voice of hers.

"You're not going anywhere until you explain this." I hold out the magazine article from the club in Chicago. "Girlfriend, Lila? Really?"

She blanches, but holds her ground. "They put whatever they want in those things, Dax. That's not my fault."

It doesn't escape me that she didn't call me Daxey. "This shit is going to stop, Lila. I'm not your boyfriend. You're not my girl-friend. I don't want the media thinking it, photographing it, or reporting on it. Do you understand what I'm saying?"

Lila's face twists into a sneer so powerful that it would be intimidating to most people. I'm not most people.

"This is the game, Dax. I'm in promotions and getting you and the others recognized and talked about is my job. Tell Kate to get over her jealous whining and that this is the way it is in the big show. You too *Daxey*. Public perception is everything. Your fans don't want to see a hot stud like you hanging out with boring Miss Nobody. You'll thank me when you see your album sales increase."

Lila pushes past me and stalks out of the room leaving me wondering what the hell just happened.

Kate

THREE WEEKS later

"GOOD JOB EVERYONE!" Coach Russo high fives us as we leave the pitch, giddy after another win at home.

"Thanks Coach," I say as I slap his hand.

"Great game, Campbell. Great game."

Smiling, I hit the locker room to change out of my kit and grab a shower. Dax is back from his tour and supposed to come over later. I took Abby's advice and gave in, finally speaking to Dax on the phone. He confirmed that Lila set the pictures and article up for promotional reasons. He claims he had no idea she was standing next to him when the photos were taken.

I have no reason not to believe him, but my low self-esteem rears it's ugly head. Why wouldn't he prefer Lila to me? She's rich and blonde and drop-dead gorgeous, with a famous father to boot. Even I was convinced that the photographs were real. They look perfect together.

Then there were pictures of Dax and some ginger slag cozying up in a pub in Seattle. After getting hysterical, eating an entire sleeve of Oreos, and getting ready to call Dax screaming, Abby talked me down by pointing out that there are going to be loads of similar photos in the future, and I'd either have to trust Dax to be faithful, or break up with him now.

Once again, Abby was right. I don't have to like the photos, but they are going to happen. Plus, Dax promising he'd try harder not to be caught unawares by the paparazzi helped soothe things over.

Reaching into my locker for my mobile, I bring up a picture I took of Dax and me before he left for the tour. He's as handsome as ever, gorgeous smile, angled jaw, and rugged good looks. Then there's me, plain, no makeup, wearing athletic gear and a ponytail.

I drag my finger down the picture of Dax's face.

"What's got you all mooney-eyed?" my teammate Brittany asks as she tosses her filthy cleats into her bag. I quickly lock the screen and toss the mobile onto the bench.

"I am most certainly not mooney-eyed!"

Brittany rolls her eyes. "You are so mooney-eyed I'm surprised that you aren't humming cheesy love songs, Kate." She chuckles at herself.

"Ok fine. I might be in a good mood," I admit, pulling my hair up into my customary high ponytail, which, in light of my recent thoughts, makes me frown. I'm so predictable.

"So...?"

I look at Brittany, confused. "So... what?"

"Who's got you so giddy? A man? You've never mentioned anyone." She hikes her bag on her shoulder and we walk out of the locker room together. I shoot her a look to which she responds, "Please. I can tell it's a man. No one gets like that unless love is involved."

Trying to act casual, I play it off like no big deal. I haven't mentioned Dax to my teammates because we only started dating this summer and by the time school started, the band was on tour. Plus, I'm not sure I want to share my semi-famous boyfriend with anyone else yet.

"Just a bloke I know." I shrug casually as if it's no big deal that I'm finally in a relationship with a man I've been in love with for the last fourteen years.

Brittany laughs loudly, following me out of the locker room. "Yeah right. *'Just a bloke'*," she says in the worst British accent I've ever heard.

I laugh with her and push open the door to exit the athletic building. We must walk through a black hole that takes us to hell, because no sooner have we stepped foot outside than we are completely surrounded by screaming, pushing, loud reporters. Men with enormous cameras jostle for position amongst the journalists that shove microphones and recorders under my nose.

"Jesus! What the hell?" Brittany shouts as an overzealous paparazzo shoves her aside.

Brittany, being a brilliant defender for our team, kicks the man in the shin, eliciting a loud complaint.

"Kate, what the fuck is going on?" she asks, threading our arms together so we won't get separated again.

I don't want to explain it to her, and don't get a chance. The questions have already begun.

"*KATE! Is it true you're dating Dax Davies from Sphere of Irony?*"
   "*Kate! Kate! Did you cause a break up between Dax and Lila?*"
   "*Kate! What's it like being the other woman?*"
   "*Kate! Are you dropping out of school to join Dax on his next tour?*"

HOLY HELL.

The pack gets closer and closer until Brittany and I can no longer move. I resort to being polite so I won't break down crying in front of them.

"Please. Let us through. We just want to get home."

It doesn't help. The extremely personal, and mostly untrue,

questions keep hitting me rapid-fire like bullets sprayed from a machine gun. It's been less than two minutes since we've stepped out of the building and I'm nearly in tears from the stress. The blood pulsing behind my ears is so loud I can barely hear Brittany threatening the reporters with bodily harm if they don't let us through.

"Get out of here!" A thunderous voice booms across the quad. "This is completely out of line!" Muffled curses erupt from the direction of the bellowing. Coach Russo pushes his way into the tight inner circle amid a sea of protests.

He stands directly in front of Brittany and me and addresses the reporters in his loudest *'don't fuck with me'* voice. "You are harassing my players and causing a disturbance on campus. I will call the police if you don't allow us through!" He puts one hand on the back of each of our necks, guiding us through the crowd towards the safety of the athletic building.

Once the door is shut and the frenzy locked out, Coach turns to speak. "They're not allowed inside the buildings on campus without permission, but the public areas are fair game." He gives me a strange look and turns to Brittany. "Miss Cavanaugh, you may go out the back entrance. Miss Campbell," his piercing gaze hits me again, "come with me to my office."

Brittany stares at me as if silently asking if I'm okay.

Nodding, I let her know it's fine. "Go ahead, Brit. I'll talk to you later."

She's hesitant, I can see dozens of questions in her eyes, but eventually she turns and goes down the hallway in the opposite direction. Inhaling deep, I follow Coach Russo to his cramped, messy office.

"Sit." He points at a chair covered with equipment. I move each item to the other one, now overflowing, and drop down heavily once it's clear. He is a terrible slob.

Coach sits behind his desk, clasping his fingers in front of his mouth in a steeple. "So. Want to explain whatever that was I just saved you from?"

I stare at my hands, *so* not wanting to discuss Dax or my private life with my coach.

"Kate," he says in a softer tone. "What is going on? Are you in trouble or something?"

My head snaps up to meet his concerned face, his dark eyes shining transparently with his desire to help.

"I'm not in trouble, Coach."

He sighs, sitting back in his chair, which emits a loud squeak as it bears more of his weight. "You're not going to tell me, are you?"

I shake my head, my eyes filling with tears.

"Alright. But I can't have reporters accosting my players. If you need something, ask."

"Right, Coach."

"I'll walk you out the back to make sure there's no one there waiting for you." He stands up and joins me on the other side of his desk. Coach Russo isn't a large man, just an inch or so taller than me. His skin is a dark olive and his hair jet black and curly, giving away his Italian heritage almost as much as his last name.

"Thanks," I whisper, my voice cracking.

He nods, opening the door to his office so I can exit first. We walk to the back of the building in silence and I relax my tense muscles when I see that the only people outside are a few members of the track and field team, warming up for practice.

"It's clear. Go home, rest, and remember, Kate, you can talk to me about anything. You girls are my responsibility." His dark eyes shine with concern.

"Yeah, thanks Coach."

I hurry back to my flat to call Dax. When I get there, I find over thirty messages on the answering machine. After playing the first two and realizing they're all from nosy reporters, I delete the rest without listening.

Sitting on my bed, a bed Dax and I have made love in count-less times, I wonder how long this thing with him can possibly last. Dax and the other guys are becoming more and more famous every day. Their first album is a huge success, debuting at number thirty on the Billboard list. As the tour progressed and singles were released, it now rests comfortably in the top ten.

Tired and still freaked out by the incident on campus, I kick off my shoes and lay back, arranging my pillow beneath my head. Without thinking, I turn and inhale the other pillow, the one Dax uses when he stays over. His scent is long gone, having been six weeks since he was last here.

Depressed, I close my eyes, willing the rock that's sitting in my stomach to go away. I must fall asleep, because the next thing I know, someone is dragging a hand down my cheek. My eyes fly open and my heart begins to pound.

"Dax!"

He gives me a crooked grin, yet his eyes look wary, as if he's waiting for me to scream or yell at him. I fling myself at him, wrapping my arms around his broad shoulders and tucking my face against his neck.

"You scared me half to death!"

His large arms surround me, squeezing me into his chest.

"Sorry angel. You didn't answer the door, so I let myself in," he whispers into my hair. I gave him a key a while back so he could come over after a late gig or recording session and not bother Abby.

"I missed you so much." I try not to choke up or cry. I don't want to ruin this moment with my tales of horror with the media.

"Me too, angel. Me too." Dax leans back, cupping my face in his hands. Despite his determination to keep everything shut-tered up behind a strong front, he seems on the verge of breaking down as well. I'm about to ask what's wrong when his mouth crushes against mine and all rational thoughts fly right out of my mind.

DAX

I DIDN'T REALIZE how worried I was that Kate would never talk to me again until I had her in my arms, my tongue sweeping into her mouth for that familiar taste. After six weeks of tense phone calls and moments where I thought she'd get sick of the bullshit with Lila and the other photos and chuck me for good, I've got my girl where she belongs. With me.

Mine. I won't let Lila or any of my shit hurt her.

Rule 5—Defend what's yours.

The thought of losing Kate sends fear skittering down my spine. Desperation takes over and I push her back on the bed, covering her with my body as I devour her sweet mouth. In between moaning, sloppy kisses, and frantic pawing, we manage to strip off our clothes.

"Jesus, I missed this," I groan into her mouth as our naked skin comes together. We grind against each other, reveling in the reconnection after time apart.

"Dax."

It's a whisper from her lips. Just a quiet sigh. Yet the sound of it kicks my instincts into overdrive, sending molten desire coursing through my veins. My skin feels so hot, I wonder if I'll end up burned from the inside out.

"Need you," I mumble back, trailing small bites and licks down the side of Kate's neck to her breasts.

"Me too," she says breathlessly, obviously feeling the same urgent need.

I fumble to get a condom out of the nightstand and on as quickly as possible. Once ready, we waste no time. It's been so long that foreplay is not on today's menu. Thrusting in deep and hard, I hiss from the tight heat of Kate's body as she moans loud and long.

"Fuck. Feels so good." The groans and curses fall out of my mouth unconsciously as she lifts her hips to meet mine.

"Faster, Dax. Harder." Kate is panting loudly, her hands pulling at my shoulders in a bid to get me to give her more.

I know my self-control is shit, but with Kate, I try even harder so I'm not the selfish asshole that hurts her. I always worry about freaking her out with the power I want to unleash when fucking. Kate's begging for it though. *Fucking begging me to go harder.* My willpower will only hold up for just so long.

Propping up on my knees, I take one of those long, toned, legs and throw it over my shoulder. I get a tight grip on her hips, my fingers pressing in so hard she might end up with bruises. Then, I fuck her as requested. Hard.

After the first solid thrust, Kate's hands shoot up above her head, landing flat against the headboard to keep her from hitting it as I pound into her over and over. The sound of skin slapping on skin is drowned out by her loud keening and my vicious snarling. All I can think of is "mine" as I lay claim to her gorgeous body.

Sweat trickles down my temples, dripping off and rolling down my chest but I don't stop. I can't stop. Watching Kate's face contort with ecstasy as she takes every bit of my brutal fucking is one of the most erotic things I've ever seen. My name falls from her lips like both a curse and a prayer as she comes, sending me over the edge. With one final, ruthless drive, intense heat explodes from the base of my spine and I roar with my release.

"Christ." I collapse over her in a heap, forgetting to hold up my considerable weight. "Fuck, sorry." As I start to roll off in fear of squashing her, Kate wraps her arms and legs around me, locking me in place.

"No. Don't move yet. This is... it's perfect."

"I don't want to hurt you, Kate." My lips find hers, brushing over them lightly. I use one hand to push her tangled hair back from her face.

Kate's green eyes trap me in place, the honesty in them stunning to see. "You would never hurt me, Dax. Not physically anyway."

I'm about to ask what she means when the front door slams shut and her flatmate Abby calls out, "Hey Kate! Want to grab a bite?"

Kate squeals and I yank the duvet up as the bedroom door swings open. "Whoa! Sorry!" The door closes and Abby starts giggling from the other side. "I forgot you were coming back today, Dax. I'll just... ummmm, change up and leave you two alone. 'K?"

Laughing, Kate answers. "No. Don't worry, Abby. We'll have something to eat with you." She glances at me to see if this is okay. I nod, willing to do whatever she wants as long as we're together.

"I'd rather spend the rest of the week in bed, but we will have to eat at some point," I say. Kate shoves my arm jokingly, apparently thinking that I'm kidding.

I'm not.

She hops out of bed to clean up, moving to throw on some clothes and somehow the strange comment Kate made is forgotten. My eyes are glued to that lithe, naked body, effectively wiping every other coherent thought right out of my head.

Kate

"So, how's uni, Kate?" Adam asks, talking with his mouth full of hamburger.

We got takeaway and invited the band over so we could catch up without interruptions. I couldn't be more thankful. Watching gorgeous women hit on my boyfriend in a crowded restaurant isn't very high on my list of things I'd like to experience. The guys are definitely becoming more recognizable.

"Gross, Adam," Abby mock-whines, shoving against his shoulder playfully.

Ever so slightly, but enough that I notice, Hawke's posture stiffens when Abby flirts with Adam. She's *so* Adam's type, gorgeous, blonde, and very Ellie-like. Abby is only teasing though. She's told me Adam is not even close to what she likes in a man. Too bad for Adam, I guess, but good for me. I don't need him shagging and ditching the best mate I have in California. She's turned him down enough times that he's given up trying.

"Classes are good. We're a definite for the tournament this year. Now we just have to see if we win the PAC-10." I take a big sip of my drink as Adam half-listens to me while ogling my flatmate.

"Hey," Dax says playfully, reaching across the coffee table to lightly punch Adam on the arm. "When my girl is talking, you could at least look at her. You *did* ask her a question."

"Don't get your knickers in a twist, Davies. I'm listening." Adam swings his gaze over to me. "When's your next game? I'd like to watch you play. All this time knowing you and I've never seen you on the pitch."

"That's a great idea," Gavin adds with one of his killer smiles. The kind that makes me think the man should be modeling posh watches or expensive men's wear. He's bloody gorgeous. Literally achingly beautiful.

"Dax?" I turn to see what he thinks of going to my last regular season game. It's a big one, against California, one of our big rivals.

"I thought you'd never ask, angel. I'd love to see you play." He leans in for a quick kiss, his hand skimming over my knee.

"Dirty, dirty, boy," I whisper in his ear as his hand moves up my thigh.

"So are we going?" Gavin asks.

I glance around the room. Adam and Gavin are excited, Abby is smiling like crazy, Hawke is, well, being Hawke—staring at his food with a blank look on his face. Dax, the sexy thing, he's moving his hand higher and higher up my leg and pretty soon we'll have to kick everyone out so we can get naked again. Six whole weeks without sex has my hormones on a hair-trigger.

"I'll have five tickets left at the box office," I tell them. "Unless..." I pointedly look at each of the guys, "you want to bring someone with you."

Hawke's head snaps up, the disinterested pouty look replaced by a sly smile. "Maybe." His eyes betray him when they flick over to Abby for the briefest of seconds. *Is he trying to make her jealous?*

"Right, okay. Adam? Gavin? Either of you need an extra?"

"Nah, I like to keep my options open," Adam laughs.

"Of course," I answer, my tone dry.

"Gav?"

His cheeks redden slightly. "No. I just want to see you play, no distractions."

Poor Gav. The stupid promotions team at their label, including that cow Lila, has told him not to *flaunt* his sexuality because it detracts from female fans' fantasy of him. God forbid he be seen with a man in public.

I would have told them to bugger off, but it's not my call to make.

"Okay, so six tickets. It's Saturday at three. I'll leave them under my name."

Everyone agrees to meet out front before entering the stadium. I'm excited. None of my non-footy playing friends except Abby have seen one of my games. Now I'll have my own cheering section.

Dax is back and all of the freaking out I've done over the last six weeks seems like an overreaction. The paparazzi, the pictures with Lila, feeling inadequate... it falls to the wayside as long as he's with me. The guys are like family to me, and I can't wait to show them what I can do on the pitch.

DAX

"HELL, it's too early for someone to be calling." I tuck my head under my pillow, trying to block out the shrill sound of my phone.

"It's ten, Dax," Kate mumbles sleepily, wrapping herself tighter around my waist, burying her head into my chest.

"Bloody hell." The phone stops, then immediately kicks in again. Several texts ping in at the same time.

Trying to shed the heavy layer of sleep that is making my body sluggish, I throw my legs over the side of the bed and promptly fall arse over tits when the duvet refuses to release my feet. "Shit!"

"Are you alright?" Kate's face pops over the edge of the mattress, imprints from the sheets still on her cheek.

"Yeah, angel. Just not quite awake yet." I manage a smile so Kate rolls away, probably to go back to sleep. Then *her* mobile starts to ring.

"What's going on, Dax?" It takes me a minute to find my own phone as it's still tucked away in last night's jeans. Kate's rings *again*, and now I'm beginning to get worried.

Eighteen missed calls—three from Rachel, two from Ross, one from Gavin, and eleven unknown. "What the—?" Flicking through the texts, there's more of the same, Rachel asking me to call, Ross demanding that I call, and Gavin asking if I'm okay.

Okay? Why wouldn't I be okay?

"Dax?" Kate is standing next to me, her mobile in her hand. She's fully awake now and she looks very unhappy. Kate's normally bright expression is sullen, brows knitted tightly and that perfect mouth turned down. "I forgot to tell you something," she whispers, sinking down onto the edge of the bed.

"Huh?" I don't quite catch what Kate says with my head all up with horrific scenarios that would cause both of our mobiles to blow up simultaneously.

"Dax."

"Yeah?" Turning, I see the absolute misery on Kate's face. Fear drops into my stomach like a lead brick. I sit next to her on the bed, pulling her into my arms. "What's going on? Do you know about these calls? I was about to ring Gavin."

"It's just that... well, yesterday before I saw you..."

Kate is biting into her lip, nervously twisting her hair into a knot over and over. She jumps up, hurrying into the bathroom. When she returns, her hair is in a perfect ponytail. She's freaking out.

"Kate, you're scaring me. What happened?" My heart is racing and that damn instinct to hurt someone floods my body.

Rule 5—Defend what's yours.

The urge to protect Kate, to shield her from whatever she's frightened of is so strong I nearly yell just to get her to tell me who it is I'll have to kill.

"When I left my match yesterday, the media..." She lets the sentence hang unfinished because the rest is obvious.

"Fuck," I breathe out, "they found you."

"Yeah."

"Shit. Tell me everything."

Once Kate is done explaining her run in with a mob of journalists that for the most part assaulted her, I'm seeing red. We've been so careful, not wanting Kate's name to get out to the press. In interviews I say I'm in a relationship if asked, but that's the most I'll disclose. Neither Kate nor myself wanted the shitstorm that would descend if they found out who she was. Now it's too late.

"C'mon," I say to Kate, pulling her to her feet.

"Where? What are we doing?"

"Get dressed. We're going to my flat. I want to use my laptop to see what is being said. Yours is too slow, angel."

I hurry into my jeans and yank my shirt on, impatient for Kate to do the same. After a few minutes, she gets tired of me following her around the room, nagging her to move faster, and explodes.

"Dax, stop rushing me! I have to get my bloody clothes on. Go call Gavin."

"No." I shake my head. "I want to read it myself first. I don't want to hear second-hand. It will only make me angry with whoever is telling me."

Kate pulls a face, but finishes brushing her teeth and puts her shoes on. "I'm ready."

"Right, let's go."

Kate

Dax Davies.

A man of so many contradictions. With the rare exception being the guys in the band and myself—and even then it's only occasionally—he keeps his emotions shuttered in so tight it'd take a freaking crowbar and a sledgehammer to chip away at that stoic façade. Yet when upset, thrown headfirst into that protective fight mode from his days in the cage, anyone can read the pure, lethal fury on his face. Even when it's hidden behind that blank stare.

Like right now.

"Fucking bastard cunts," he hisses along with a slew of other shocking profanities that fall from his lips as he pulls up website after website detailing my encounter with the paparazzi yesterday.

As Dax skims each one, I read over his shoulder, my hands trembling, tears pressing at the back of my eyes. I can feel the shame flooding my skin, prickling hot up my neck as I see each headline.

"Is Dax Davies Cheating on Lila Griffin with Co-Ed?"

"Love Triangle Involving Rock Star, Hollywood Heiress, and UCLA Student."

"Soccer Standout Breaks Up Couple on the Verge of Stardom."

SWALLOWING down the bile that's crept up my dry throat, I manage to croak out a few words. "So... *I'm* the other woman."

Dax stiffens, sitting up straight from where he's hunched in front of his laptop. "Fuck no. We know it's not true. I don't give a rat's arse what these shit for brains write."

Only, I know that's not true. He cares. And even if he didn't, *I care*. I don't want to be involved in this part of Dax's life, the part that is getting more and more famous with each passing day. Especially not painted as the villain in this scenario—vs. that cow Lila of all people!

Dax continues flicking through the articles, grumbling under his breath the entire time. The front door of the flat opens. "Hey guys!" Gavin calls out. He's got his surfboard under his arm, deftly swinging the long board into the room and leaning it on the wall. His hair is all mussed from the ocean, stiff in places from the dried salt. He takes one look at my face and frowns. "So I take it you heard?"

I glance at Dax's back, coiled with tension, muscles ready to strike out at anyone who so much as looks at him wrong, then flick my gaze back to Gavin. The sympathetic look he gives me is so heartfelt and honest the tears I had been holding back fill my eyes.

I move away quickly, not letting Dax see how upset I am. He's on edge enough to act first and think later—not a good combination with someone as volatile as Dax. Add in seeing me cry? Well, you may as well roll out the hearse for whoever pisses him off and happens to be within striking distance.

"I-I have to go. Practice starts soon." I nearly trip on my own feet, stumbling towards the door. Gavin catches me before I end up smacking my head on the wall.

"Careful, Kate." One blonde eyebrow goes up, asking a silent question. *Are you all right?*

I'm far from all right, but I can't let Dax know. Looking over my shoulder, I see that Dax has rung someone and is busy shouting into his mobile.

"I'll see you later," I mumble. Gavin doesn't look happy, but he lets me go.

Somehow, I manage to wait until the door closes behind me before I freak out.

I saw some of the comments on those articles, confirming everything I already knew.

"*WHY WOULD Dax Davies hook up with that girl?*"
   "*Who is that nobody? She's nothing special.*"
   "*God! I'm better looking than that! What is he thinking?*"
   "*Who would cheat on Lila Griffin? She's smoking hot!*"

INSTEAD OF HOPPING the bus to practice, I walk, needing the time alone to process how my life is about to change. I don't skip footy practice, *ever*, but I can't bring myself to deal with it today. The fear of encountering another mob of paparazzi is enough to keep me away. Let alone what my teammates will think about the articles.

My mobile rings several times in a row, texts pinging every few minutes. I know it's Dax, so I turn it off, not ready to discuss anything while it's so raw. While *I'm* so raw.

Hours later, after wandering the city, I trudge down the hall to my flat, shoving the key in and more or less collapsing inside.

Part of me—okay, a *huge* part of me—expected Dax to be waiting for me at my flat, overcome with worry, wrapping me in those massive arms and letting me know he was going to fix everything. Instead, I come home to a dark, empty space.

Why would Dax be here? He's probably realized how embarrassing it is for him to be caught "philandering" with a nobody footy player from Hackney. I mean, he's never even told me he loves me.

It seems that no matter how close I get to Dax, he'll always be just out of reach.

11

D^{ax}

"THIS IS BULLSHIT, Ross. It's fucking manipulative and I won't be a part of it." I've jumped up from my seat on one of the plush leather chairs in my manager's office. "Everyone at the label, and you as well," I point at Ross behind his massive desk, "knows that this is all fucking Lila's doing!"

After seeing the ridiculous lies all over the Internet, I immediately called Ross to get this mess under control.

"Dax, we don't know that." Rachel Whatley, head of marketing and promotions for our band, bravely puts a kind hand on my arm in an attempt to be reassuring. And fails miserably.

"Rachel, you're brilliant at what you do," I say honestly, "but that little bitch you have working for you is devious and border-line psychotic." My voice turns into a snarl by the time I've spit out the last word.

Rachel frowns, almost looking hurt, but I know her better than that. She's beautiful and charming yet tough as nails. She has to be to put up with spoiled rock stars and pompous men in power suits all day.

"Dax, my hands are tied." She holds her hands together as if they're bound in a gesture meant to prove her point. "Lila's dad is huge at the label. Hell, he's huge in Los Angeles. I can't fire her and I've tried to reassign her. She wants your account."

"This is crap! She wants it because she's trying to ruin my life!" I roar, standing up to pace the back of the room.

Rule 2—Never let your emotions show.

Fuck that! I don't know if I've ever been this angry. I know it's because I've been rendered helpless and that pisses me off more than anything. Nothing I do will stop Lila and her campaign to stalk her way into my life. Even worse, this entire thing makes *me* look like a whinging crybaby, which makes me want to punch something until it bleeds.

"Calm down," Ross says in an even tone, but his eyes betray him. Wide and fixed on my clenching hands, I can tell he's nervous to be around me when I'm this murderously angry.

He should be afraid. Maybe a smack to his head will get my point across?

"Dax." Rachel has turned in her seat to watch me as I struggle to rein in my emotions. "I'll talk to her again, okay? I promise."

My fists are balled so tight that I can feel the pressure in my knuckles.

"What about Kate?" I growl.

"What about her?" Ross asks.

I leap over to him, slamming my hands down on his desk with a loud bang, leaning over far enough that he scoots his chair back to get out of reach.

"They know who she is. She was fucking surrounded by paparazzi at her school, Ross! What are you going to do to get the attention off of her and keep her safe?" I bare my teeth, breathing heavily through my nose, knowing I probably look demented. Ross's eyes get even wider, shocked that I'd direct my fury at him. He's never seen me in the cage, doesn't know what I'm capable of. Now, maybe he has an idea.

Once again, Rachel plays with fire by touching me while I'm a hair's breadth from exploding. She pulls on my arm until I sit back down in my chair.

"Let's come up with a plan, okay?" she says calmly. "I'll call a team together and we'll meet in the conference room."

Mashing my lips together, I cross my arms over my chest to keep my fists under control. "Fine. You better not think I'll be placated by some pathetic, hollow words and a pat on my back."

She smiles. "I'd expect nothing less."

Six and a half hours of 'emergency meetings' later and I'm so shattered my eyes are blurry. Who knew how much complete bullshit was involved in publicity? It's all fucking smoke and mirrors with paparazzi set up to 'catch' you doing all sorts of things, from holding specific products to promote or being seen with specific people in specific places.

The only thing we could actually agree on was leaving Kate out of everything—refusing to acknowledge her, any of the rumors, or draw attention to her by association. No way am I going to let this mess affect her anymore than it has already.

While waiting for the lift, I pull out my mobile to call Kate only to realize it's after midnight. Fuck. Kate's big game is tomorrow. I can't wake her up only to upset her with this load of bollocks. Frustrated, I shove the phone back in my pocket. Kate ducked out of my flat earlier without telling me, and when I tried to follow, Gavin said to give her time. I hadn't meant to wait this long.

"Hey, you can catch a ride home with me," Rachel says as she reaches the bank of lifts and stops next to me. "I have a driver outside." There's a quiet ding and a set of doors slide open.

"Thanks." I let Rachel enter first before I follow, sagging against the wall with my eyes closed.

"It gets easier to ignore."

I keep my eyes closed. "What gets easier to ignore, Rachel?"

"The lies, the stories, the made up crap... it's meant to sell magazines or to sell you. It's not personal. You're a product, a commodity. Eventually you'll stop caring."

The lift stops on the ground floor. I don't say anything until we're settled in the back seat of a comfortable sedan, shrouded by darkness. My features are carefully blank, more out of habit than anything else since Rachel certainly can't see my face.

"Rachel, let me be perfectly clear." I let the calm, even, yet very threatening tone of my voice say more than my actual words. "Anything, and I mean bloody anything, that upsets Kate isn't something I'll *ever* stop caring about. Do you understand me?"

"Yeah, Dax. I understand. Unfortunately, the media doesn't."

"Then they can fucking deal with me."

I leave it at that, too tired to think anymore tonight.

Kate

"KATE!" I cringe at the sound of my name, worried that the media bloodhounds have found me again. Footsteps pound the ground behind me and as much as I don't want to face them again, I can't let them sneak up on me. I turn around and exhale in relief.

"Bloody hell, Jenna!" It's only my teammate and soon to be kicked to death midfielder. "You scared me!"

"Sorry, Kate. So, is it true?" She slings a friendly arm around my shoulders. I know she doesn't understand that I don't want to talk about Dax. That doesn't stop the urge to tell her and everyone else on earth to piss off from catching in my throat.

Sighing, I gently extract myself from her embrace, using the excuse of opening the athletic center doors. "I'm not discussing it, Jenna. I'm sorry, but it's not something I talk about."

"What?" she shrieks. "You're dating Dax from *Sphere of Irony* and you don't want to talk about it? Hell, I'd be wearing a t-shirt or take out an ad describing everything I've done to his hot body! Yummy!"

I must be scowling, because Jenna's eyes widen and her mouth drops. "I didn't mean that in a bad way, Kate. You should be proud if it's true, that's all."

At least Jenna left out the bit where I'm too homely and poor for someone as perfect as Dax.

We reach the locker room and I hesitate, not wanting everyone else to overhear and think they're welcome to join the conversation. "That's the problem, Jenna. I'm a real person. Dax is a real person. He's not an object to brag about. I have actual feelings that shouldn't be laid out just to be trod upon by everyone and anyone."

"I guess I didn't think..." Jenna trails off. I can't tell if she's contrite or secretly rolling her eyes at me in her mind.

Before I can respond, Coach Russo barks at me from down the hall. "Campbell! My office!"

Jenna slips away while I'm looking at Coach. Wonderful.

"Yes?"

"Come in. Close the door, Kate."

I comply quietly, not meeting his stern gaze.

"Sit."

The chair is still cleaned off from the other day, so I sink down into it.

"Why did you miss practice yesterday?"

Oh.

"Sorry, Coach." I can't bring myself to look up, afraid to see the disappointment in his eyes.

"Kate, I'm not mad, though I should be. Honestly, it's good you skipped." That gets my attention. Coach Russo doesn't look angry, but weary, like me. "Those reporters were here again looking for you." He lets out a big sigh. "I'm not going to ask, Kate. It's not my business. But I need you dedicated to the team. We have a better than average chance of winning the Division I cup this year. I need all of my players focused on soccer without any distractions. Am I making myself clear?"

Nodding, my eyes drop back to my hands, which are shaking. *I'm* a distraction. At least, the pack of hungry paparazzi following me is.

"Go get changed. I'll see you in a bit."

Without saying a word, I bolt out of Coach's office, not wanting to break down in front of him. He laid it out there in no uncertain terms—football has to come first—no distractions, no excuses. That means no paparazzi, no gossip, no private life interfering with the team.

Can I keep Dax separate from football? It would be beyond difficult but I think I can do it. Without footy, and my scholarship, I'll be back in Hackney. Then I'll really have nothing.

My breath hitches in my chest as I force the growing knot of anxiety out of my throat to settle uncomfortably in my stomach. I can do this. I can talk to Dax about keeping things hidden better from now on. He'll understand that I have to have my priorities right. Without footy, I can't afford school. Without school, I'm back in my parents' dismal flat in Hackney. No way am I going back there.

By the time I hit the locker room, everyone's already kitted up and down by the doors leading to the pitch. I hurry to get changed, rushing out to meet up with the rest of the team. I pretend not to notice every single head turn my way as I approach.

No distractions.

"Okay, okay," Coach Russo claps his hands to get our attention. Better they stare at him than me.

"Ladies! This is it, the big game! Win this and we win the

PAC-10 and are most likely a number one seed in the West for the tournament. Don't let them get to you out there. I expect the best out of each one of you."

Everyone cheers in excitement while I think about how I never turned my mobile on this morning and haven't talked to Dax since I bolted from his flat yesterday.

"Kate!"

Crap!

I look up from my daydreaming to find the doors open and my team running onto the pitch without me. Coach is staring curiously, disappointment clear in his dark eyes.

"I'm here, Coach. One hundred percent." I manage to project confidence while on the inside I'm wilting into a useless mess.

He pulls a face but says nothing else. I take advantage of Coach's silence and trot out the path that leads to the pitch.

Madness.

That's the only way to describe the scene at the stadium. Utter madness. It almost feels as if I've stepped onto the set of an action film. The noise alone is enough to make me want to cover my ears.

"What's going on?" I yell into a group of my teammates.

"Not sure," Brittany shouts back. "Some kind of commotion in the stands." I follow her pointing finger to a section of seats. She's right. A mob of people is surging in one area, whatever is at the center causing a near panic amongst the spectators.

"Reckon David Beckham stopped by to watch us?" I joke.

Brittany giggles, but Coach shoots me a perturbed frown.

Properly chastised, we turn our backs to the chaos as the referees start the match. Somehow, I manage to block out everything—the horrors of the tabloids, Dax blowing me off last night, the caterwauling that is still going on in the stands—and play without a single misstep.

As for the rest of my team... I can only say they aren't doing as well ignoring the noise. Players continually lose focus, making amateur mistake after amateur mistake. Fortunately, the other team is having the same problem, letting the distraction in the stadium break their concentration.

Coach motions for me to sub out and take a rest. I shake my head, not wanting to lose my momentum or break my good fortune. The uncharacteristic anger on his features sends a shiver down my spine, pooling like ice in my veins. I head for the sidelines only to notice that the screaming gets louder. That's when I realize they're screaming at me.

"You whore!"

"Ugly bitch!"

"You're not good enough for Dax!"

I blanch, the blood in my body rushes to my feet. Jenna must notice me sagging, because she rushes over, shoving her shoulder under my arm and her hand around my waist to keep me from hitting the ground. She lowers me onto the bench and I can feel the eyes of the entire stadium burning into my back. Even my teammates are staring, hell... everyone from the other team is staring as well. Coach can't stop mid-game or else he'd certainly be staring at me too.

"Do you have anything to say about your affair with Dax Davies, Kate?"

"Kate! A quote?"

"Kate! Kate! Did you know Dax was already seeing someone?"

"Is Dax here to see you play?"

"What about Lila Griffin? Do you feel bad for stealing her boyfriend?"

Shit! I forgot the band was coming to watch the game. How stupid am I to not think about how recognizable they would be! That's what's going on in the stands!

Naturally, the paparazzi are here for me as well, making everything ten times worse. They jostle the spectators and shove at the haters that are lined up along the edge of the pitch to hurl insults at me.

"Kate," our assistant coach, a former player named Paige, crouches down in front of me. "You can go get showered up."

"What?" I can't believe what I'm hearing. "You...you want me to go? Miss the game? I'm the only one playing out there!"

Paige gives me a look so sad it could break hearts, and it does, I can feel mine shattering in my chest. "Kate, right now you're too much of a distraction. This..." she waves at the psychotic group of girls that are still screaming at me, "is too much. We can't play like this and neither can the other team. They've asked to have you removed and Coach agreed."

"That's not fair!" I protest. "None of this is my fault." I swipe at a stray tear.

"I know. We all know that. But we're here to play and we can't do that with all this going on. Campus security doesn't have enough guards to contain the crowd."

"So *I* have to be the one to go," I growl, not wanting to admit defeat.

A very loud, very agitated, *very* familiar voice rises above the screeching crowd of women. "Kate!"

I shoot up from the bench, looking over the sea of people to find the source. "Dax?"

I should know better. I do know better. As usual, I wasn't thinking when I called out his name. The rabid girls hear it and turn, jumping on Dax like wolves descending on a steak dinner. Our gazes meet for a brief second. I see enough in those angry, dark brown eyes to know what's about to happen, and I watch helplessly as my life flies apart at the seams.

12

D ax

"DAVIES! YOU'RE OUT."

The loud clank of a bolt turning followed by the screech of metal on metal rouses me from a half-sleep. My entire body aches, my back, my face, and especially my hands.

Fuck. I look down at them, red and swollen, and pray I haven't broken anything. The guys will have a go at me if I can't play guitar.

"Follow me."

As exhausted and angry as I am, I manage to restrain my emotions. Yesterday proved to me exactly what happens when I lose that precious control.

Another lock opens, this one with the whirring sound of automation. I ignore several pairs of eyes that are fixed on me. Yeah, yeah, get your fill assholes. Everything I do is a walking three-ring fucking circus these days. Why should this be any different?

Finally, we arrive in the lobby, crowded, hot, and smelling like month old tube socks.

"In there," my escort says crisply, pointing towards a small office. "Your friend was causing a near riot in the lobby, so they put him out of sight."

I wonder who is here to pick me up. Not Adam, certainly? Guaranteed he's either still drunk from whatever he did last night after the incident, or frightfully hung over this morning. Plus, he's too recognizable.

When I enter the dingy, fluorescent-lit room, I see Ross staring at a wall of accolades and awards that must belong to the occupant of this office. I expected Ross. I didn't expect to see Gavin, but it shouldn't surprise me. He's one of the most caring people I've ever known. The one person who is noticeably absent, causing a nauseating cramp to grip my stomach, is Kate.

Gavin smiles, rising from a tattered chair to embrace me, whispering in my ear so Ross can't hear, "Got your back, man. Don't worry about it."

Ross doesn't seem as chuffed to see me. His face looks years older, even with his clean shave and expensive suit. Mouth down-turned, Ross gives me a thorough, disparaging look before speaking. "Well. They've dropped the charges, so we can go."

I'm stunned. "Dropped them? Completely?"

He walks over, narrowing his eyes. "Why? Do you want to stay in jail, Dax? Did you have fun in lockup overnight with the drunks and petty criminals? Make a few friends?" His voice is hostile, on the verge of a shout. But he wouldn't do that, not here. Not in listening distance of a half-dozen coppers and another dozen random people in the lobby of the precinct.

"What's your problem?" I keep my tone low and even, knowing it's even more important now than ever to keep my temper.

"My problem?" Ross asks incredulously. "My problem is that you went completely batshit crazy at a college sporting event, punched three security guards hard enough that they may sue you for damages, caused a near riot, and destroyed property on the UCLA campus. And you're asking what *my* problem is?"

"You weren't arrested, so what the fuck is it to you?" I fist my hands at my sides, itching to give Ross a piece of my mind.

Gavin must feel the stress radiating off of me, because he steps between us to talk me down off from a rapidly approaching cliff.

"Not here. Let's get going." He looks directly in my eyes, pleading with me to listen. "Everyone is tired, Adam and Hawke are worried, and I'm fucking starving. So can we leave this shit-hole and deal with this later?"

The tension in my jaw aches, but I nod. He's right. This isn't the place to do this. Plus, I'm on the fucking edge of going mental again, and after yesterday that's not something I'm particularly eager to repeat.

"Let's go then," Ross says, tamping down his own irritation. For now. From the look on his face I'm certain to be getting a proper ass reaming later.

We leave the cramped office only to be stopped by a copper in full uniform. Thankfully, it's not the same one that helped bring me in last night. The guy was a wanker. Kept mentioning how celebrities expect special treatment or some other bollocks. I didn't expect anything, stupid twat.

"Where are you parked?" he asks, glancing at each of us.

Ross steps forward. "We have a car waiting, why?"

"You'll need to call your driver and have him pull up front as close as he can. The media is here and there's a lot of them," the cop explains.

Shit.

I can't handle anymore of that crap today. It was bad enough that we couldn't watch my girlfriend's fucking football match without being spotted and swarmed with fans. Now I can't leave a building without a police escort?

"It's okay," Gavin says quietly. "Your arrest is big news. It's just the way things are."

I drag my hand down my face, scratching at the stubble and wincing when I pass over a sore spot on my chin where I hit the ground. "Yeah, but after yesterday..."

"I know. Let's just have the cops keep them back and jump in the car." Gavin turns to Ross. "He doesn't have to make a statement, does he?"

"Hell no!" Ross' eyebrows shoot skyward. "Rachel will get a press release out later today. Don't say a word." Ross looks at the cop. "Can you keep the media back?" Ross eyes me cautiously. Likely considering what would happen if one of those reporters were to bump into me or got in my face. After yesterday's outburst, I can't say I blame him.

"We can keep them back. No problem," he says with a wicked smile. "Let me get a few friends. Be back in two. Don't move."

It seems Mr. Copper dislikes the media almost as much as me.

Seconds later, six uniformed officers are at the ready, whisking us out of the office towards the front doors. I can hear the murmuring of the bystanders as recognition hits them. It's a ripple effect, spreading outward from the center of the room to the edges until the entire police station knows we're here.

The two cops in front open the doors and move directly in front of us, caging us in and the media out. And it's a good thing, because outside, it is a shitstorm of epic proportions.

"Dax! Dax! Are you going to jail?"

"Dax! Has Lila dumped you for your cheating?"

"Dax! Care to comment on the destruction of property at UCLA?"

"Dax! Is it true that you attacked security because Kate was pulled from the game?"

What? I try to turn to whoever asked the last question, but Gavin is right behind me, shoving me into the backseat of the waiting limo.

"Don't even think about it," he hisses. Gavin's harsh tone shocks me right out of my fury. He's never angry. Never. Gavin is the epitome of the laid back, California surfer. Sometimes, I wonder if he's more like me than one would think at first glance —burying his emotions under a thick layer of stereotypical 'whatever dude' instead of the stone façade I prefer to use.

Our eyes stay locked for a moment longer before I relent, deflating back into the leather seat.

"Fine. You're right. I'd be proper fucked if I punched someone outside the police precinct."

Ross glares at me from the seat opposite us. "That would be an impossible sell, Dax. I can see it now." He holds his hands up as if highlighting a glowing marquee, "Rock star jailed for assault as he's released from jail...for assault."

Gavin's lips twitch. Then Ross's do the same. I can't help it. As shitty as the last twenty-four hours have been, the laughter bubbles out of me, my sour face broken by a grin. Soon enough, we're all choking from our demented senses of humor.

As I wipe the tears of laughter from my eyes, I pray that this won't be the last bit of enjoyment I get for a while. Even with the confusion and Gavin's distraction, that jouno's words are stuck in my head, hanging over me like a guillotine ready to fall.

"Dax! Is it true that you attacked everyone because Kate was pulled from the game?"

If she was kicked out of one of the most important games she's ever played in because of me? The shitstorm has only just begun.

Kate

"Hullo."

Dax's quiet greeting when I open the door to my flat isn't what I expected. It's not even close. He's wearing baggy cargos and a pullover with the hood up, partially obscuring his face.

"Hey," I respond stupidly, thrown off by his cold demeanor and his strange choice of clothing.

What did I expect? For Dax to come in here ranting and pissed off? For him to sweep me into his arms and crush his mouth down onto mine letting me know everything will be all right? For Dax to stand stony and silent like he does with everyone else? I don't know. All I know is that this... *subdued, defeated* Dax isn't someone I recognize at all.

Dax says nothing, so I fill the awkward silence. "I called Gavin. He said it was better for me to stay home. I wanted to come to see you at the jail, Dax. I did. The media... well, you know."

He nods, his dark eyes evading mine, landing on everything in the room except for me. A trickle of fear slithers down my neck, making the fine hairs stand up. Something is very wrong.

"Your face—" I move to touch the swollen skin of his jaw, stunned when Dax steps out of reach.

I swallow thickly. The tiny thread of fear has now blossomed into a huge knot of pure panic. My heart races in my chest, my pulse thudding loudly in my ears.

"Dax?"

"We can't do this anymore," he says harshly, still looking everywhere but at my face.

My mouth is dry, my tongue thick. "Can't do what?"

No, no, no, no. He can't. He wouldn't. He promised!

"This." He points back and forth between us. "I can't do this. Us. A relationship. Whatever."

My entire body burns from the sting of his words, my gut cramping with anxiety. "Why?" I whisper, already knowing the answer. He's famous, gorgeous, and going to be massively successful. I'm me. A student. A tomboy. A nobody footy player from Hackney.

"You know why," he growls. "Don't make me say it."

A flood of anger temporarily replaces the feeling that I'm worthless and inadequate. It rushes in like a freight train, giving me the strength to pretend I'm not affected by his words.

"Fucking say it, Dax! Don't be shy. Spit it out," I hiss. "Is it so you can fuck Lila? Or revert back to your whoring ways? Or maybe you never stopped whoring and I'm the fool who believed you?"

He turns away and I can see his jaw clenching, the muscles in his cheek pulsing under the bruised skin.

"Fine! Don't tell me. You're a fucking heartless wanker, just like always, Dax. Hide behind your macho bullshit, keeping everything bottled up inside like a real man, yeah? Why would I expect you to be any different now?"

A flicker of remorse crosses Dax's face for a split second. It would seem my tirade has hurt him. In the blink of an eye, it's gone. He's back to being the man of stone.

"Don't act all hysterical, Kate. We knew this wasn't going to last. Yesterday proved that we aren't meant to be together. You're too—"

"Fuck you!" I spit out. How dare he think he's going to stand in my flat and tell me I'm not good enough for him? "Fuck you, Dax Davies!" I shove at his chest, trying to push him towards the door. His ginormous frame doesn't move an inch, so I shove again, harder. "Go!" I scream in frustration, my hands trembling from the physical effort of holding in the tears that threaten to fall.

I glance up to find Dax staring at me. If he weren't here breaking up with me, I would swear I see something else in those dark eyes—heartbreak of his own? But no, *he's* the one destroying what we have, shredding my soul and letting the bits fly away in the wind.

He doesn't deserve to look so miserable when he's the one being so cruel.

"Just go," I beg, my vision blurry. I turn my back to him, unable to watch him walk out of my life. A tiny part of me thinks this is some sort of joke, that any minute, Dax's hand will land on my shoulder and spin me around kissing me senseless while holding me in those strong arms.

The soft click of the door closing tells me that it's done. *We're* done. As I sink down to the carpet, sobbing, my life crumbles to the ground. I always knew Dax Davies would destroy me.

I hate being right.

DAX

"WOW, YOU LOOK LIKE SHIT."

"Sod off, Walker," I snap from my seat in the kitchen. Annoyed, I pour another lowball of single malt scotch, downing it quickly.

"Whoa! What's with the whisky?" Gavin asks.

I feel my lip curl up in response.

"Forget I asked, man. If it's about getting arrested, don't worry about it. Your record is clean."

"Like I could give a fuck about my record." I snag the bottle and tip more into the glass, splashing some on the countertop. "Fuck."

Gavin puts his hand over mine, gently extracting the bottle. He places it out of reach, knowing full well I can easily get it back if I want it.

He snorts. "I know that's not true. If you were arrested and found guilty, you could lose your visa. You could lose your ability to travel to the U.S. and other countries. So I know you care."

"Whatever." I throw back the rest of the scotch, slamming the glass down on the table.

"Now, what's going on with you?"

"Are we this fucking annoying when Adam is on the piss?" I ask with a humorless chuckle. I can't believe I feel bad for getting on Adam's case all those times, but right now, I do.

"Yeah, we are," Gavin responds, smiling.

"Shit." I rub my hand over my eyes. "I broke it off with Kate."

"You did what?" he yells. "Why? What the hell—?"

Scowling, I glare at Gavin. He's killing my buzz and I plan on getting good and rat-arsed. "Piss off, Walker. I had no choice in the matter. It's not like I'm not gutted over it! It was for her own good. I'll just fuck up her life. Now, give me the fucking bottle back."

"Not until you tell me why you did it." Gavin moves the scotch behind his body.

I narrow my eyes at him. "I can get that back you know. Don't make me hurt you."

The little shit smirks. "You wouldn't hurt me. You're a fluffy kitten underneath all that muscle."

"Walker, you have no idea what I'm capable of," I warn. "Now give me the bottle."

Gavin pushes back from the table and stands to his full height, the whisky still behind his back. "I was at the game, Dax. I saw *exactly* what you're capable of. It took four security guards to get you down on the ground and you still managed to hurt a few of them." Unexpectedly, he slams the bottle down in front of me, making me flinch.

Bastard.

I reach out, curling my hand around the neck, but he doesn't let go. Our eyes meet. I don't think I've ever seen Gavin this angry. It's subtle, but the fire in his eyes is unmistakable.

I don't know if it's because I'm half-pissed, or because I never saw it coming, or because, you know, it's bloody *Gavin*, but before I can blink he has me down on the floor, pinned in some sort of fucked up ninja hold. One of my arms is wrenched behind my back, my shoulder joint screaming for relief. Gavin's other hand is wrapped round my neck, doing it's best to stop the flow of blood to my head. A sharp knee presses down on my lower back.

"What the fuck, Walker," I hiss, struggling to pull in a breath.

"Go ahead and get drunk. Be a fucking pussy that won't fight to keep Kate. But hear what I'm saying, Dax," he leans over, his mouth inches from my ear. "You hurt her again and you'll have to go through me to do it. I might be just a *fag,* but trust me when I say that I know how to fight." He releases his hold and storms out of the kitchen.

What. The. Fuck.

Jesus. I need my mates angry with me like I need a hole in my head. Honestly, Gavin would understand why I broke up with Kate if I told him. But he's right, I'd rather bury all my shit underneath the tough guy mask I wear everyday than discuss feelings and shit.

Rule 2—Never let your emotions show.

Fuck you dad. Fuck you for fucking me up so much I can't have a normal relationship with a woman.

I rub my shoulder while I think of all the ways she's better off without me, even if I *could* open up to her. Kate's future is in school, playing football and getting her degree. She should settle down with some wanker accountant and have children and a house and a dog.

Being with me would lead her straight to heartbreak—tabloids, traveling, fame, paparazzi, bloody Lila—Kate's better than all that crap. Subjecting her to it is cruel. I already made her miss the opportunity to play in an important game on Saturday. I can't take any more of her future away.

As much as I want to go straight to Kate's flat and beg her to take me back, I won't. I've always been a self-centered tosser, only interested in my own pleasure. Just this once, I'm not going to be selfish and stay until I've cost Kate every single thing she has. Unfortunately, this is the one time it will cost *me* everything.

13

K ate

"CHEERS EVERYONE!" I raise my red plastic cup, tapping it against those of my teammates'.

Everyone in the frat house whistles and whoops at our victory toast. The house of Sigma Kappa Theta, a frat made up mostly of student athletes, is hosting a party for our NCAA Division I Championship slash holiday party since winter break started today. My entire team is here, along with most of the men's team and a bunch of other jocks.

"To victory!" Myriah, our team captain yells out as a couple of enormous blokes lift her up on their shoulders.

"Having fun?"

I turn to find Wes, one of the few non-footy playing fraternity brothers right next to me, leaning in so I can hear him over the loud cheers and thumping music. We've met once or twice before at different parties at the house.

"I am," I shout back, swaying a little on my feet. Frowning, I hold up my cup. "What is this?"

Wes laughs, throwing an arm around my shoulders. "It's grain, babe." I pull my brow down, so he explains further. "Grain alcohol, you know, like Everclear? With fruit juice."

"Oh." I giggle, leaning into him. "I have no idea what that is."

Wes takes my cup, refilling it from a nearby pitcher. "As long as it tastes good, who cares?" He hands it to me, smiling.

I grin back, happy to be free of my worries for a night. I take a big swig of the bright blue drink. "You're right. Who cares?"

Dax certainly doesn't care, and the thought makes me want to lose myself for once, be reckless for a change. Stop being the good girl and have a good time.

In the three weeks since Dax dumped me, this is the first time I've socialized outside of practice and classes and I plan on making it count.

Myriah barges into the kitchen, wedging herself between Wes and me. "C'mon, Kate! Be my beer pong partner!" She grabs my wrist without waiting for an answer, tugging me into the living area. Glancing over my shoulder I see Wes with a dark look on his face. It sends chills down my spine. But Myriah doesn't stop pulling me, so I turn away from Wes and focus on my teammate.

All of the furniture has been pushed to the edges of the room, lining the walls and filled with students who are sitting and talking and laughing. In the center of the space is a large folding table with red plastic cups lined up on each side.

"We're here," Myriah says, leading me to our end of the table. I sway for a moment when we stop, having to concentrate hard to keep from falling down. The thought of going tits up in front of everyone makes me giggle.

"What's so funny, Campbell?"

I look across the table to see two of the men's footy players smirking at us. Our challengers I'm guessing. I've met them both many times before.

A rude noise catches my attention. Wes is standing nearby, glaring at the man who just spoke to me. His hands are clenched at his sides.

What's his problem?

I focus back on the handsome bloke opposite me. "Nothing's funny, Chad. Don't get all cocky. Us girls are going to thrash you."

Chad winks, holding up a small white ball. Tossing it, it arcs across the table, landing in a cup of beer on our side. Chad's partner Brent, who everyone calls Bud because of some sordid incident involving beer bottles that no one will explain, high-fives Chad, both of them cheering and dancing.

Myriah snatches the cup, draining it in a few long swallows. She slams it down and wipes her mouth, yelling, "It's on!" Laughing, I hug my partner, noticing Wes behind her, staring at me. His mouth is pinched and his body seems stiff.

Unsettled, I let go of Myriah, focusing back on the game. All too quickly, I forget about Wes, letting the blissful numbness of the alcohol wash over me. Soon, I have no worries, not Dax, not Ellie, not Wes. There's only this moment, having fun with friends.

We play until the four of us have had way too much beer and I finally have to admit defeat. Myriah and I just can't match Chad and Bud drink for drink. Stumbling around the table, I get a touchy-feely, too-long hug from Chad and a fist bump and a belch in the face from Bud.

Shattered, I fall back onto an empty sofa, groaning. The entire room is tilting side to side which makes my stomach queasy. When the cushion next to me sags, I look over to see Wes watching me through narrowed eyes.

My sluggish, drunk brain fails to recognize that something is wrong with Wes's behavior tonight, not that I know him well enough to distinguish it from his normal behavior. Instead of asking what's wrong, I give him a weak smile and let my head fall back onto the sofa.

"I'll take you home," he says stiffly.

Before I can answer, his arms are around me and I'm being pulled to my feet. "Wha—?"

"You can't stay here, Kate. Move your feet. I'll do the rest of the work." Wes's tone is clipped, harsh, yet I do as he says putting one foot in front of the other.

"Are you mad at me?" I ask once we're outside. It's late, but it's Saturday night, so there are loads of students walking by on a regular basis.

"We'll talk about it once you're in your apartment," he snaps.

Well what the hell?

I want to be cross with Wes, but the alcohol has me feeling fuzzy, like my body is heavy and my mind is in a fog. I like it and hate it at the same time.

Wes stops to unlock his car doors, then guides me into the passenger seat, pulling the seatbelt across my body. He hops in the other side and starts the car.

"Where do you live?"

"Huh?"

"Kate, you have to tell me where to go," Wes says. I hear him sigh and rustle through my purse. "Is this right?" He holds up my I.D. with my address on it.

I stare at the small card in his hand, my brain struggling to make sense. "Yeah. That's it."

I must fall asleep because the next thing I know, we're in front of my building.

"Are we there? I'm knackered." It takes most of my effort to open my eyes.

Wes pulls my key out of my purse before coming round to my side and pulling me out of the car. I lean on him heavily as we make our way up to the flat I share with Abby. It feels as if my head is stuffed full of cotton wool.

Once the door is open, I stumble inside, nearly landing on my arse. Wes moves to lift me up, but I stagger to my feet, suddenly adamant in my independence. "I don't need your help!"

"Kate!" He follows me to my bedroom, trying to help me walk when I find my coordination lacking. "Christ, let me help you!" he barks rudely.

"Why are you so cross? I hardly know you," I slur, staggering into the tiny space. I flop down on my bed. "S'not my fault I can't make my legs work right." A fit of the giggles overtakes me. I laugh until the room starts to spin.

"Kate," the bed dips beside me and I feel a warm hand slide up my thigh. "I *was* mad at you. I didn't like seeing you with the other guys."

Fear tingles down my spine. Something is wrong. The way Wes is looking at me, the way he's looked at me all night. Hostile, possessive, lustful... I remember that Abby is home with her family for the holidays and the fear spreads into my heavy limbs, turning into full-fledged panic.

I'm so bloody stupid!

My eyes feel fuzzy. I want to respond, but I can't. My tongue is dry and too big for my mouth. Apparently there's plenty of room in there, because Wes's tongue has joined mine, the weight of his body pressing me down on the bed. His hands skim down my sides, kneading my breasts before moving to the button on my jeans.

No, this isn't happening. This happens to other people, not me!

The urge to scream wells up inside my throat, but Wes's mouth swallows any noise I make. He moans, grinding on top of me. I want to fight, to run, to do *something, anything,* yet all I can do is lie there as I descend into a nightmare.

He shoves my shirt up, exposing my bright purple bra.

"Wes, don't—"

"Kate, you're so sexy." His mouth devours mine again before I can say anything else. I can feel him fumbling for the button on his jeans and my panic ratchets up another notch.

"Wes! Get off!"

He ignores my protests, pushing down his jeans. Suddenly his hands are back, holding my arms over my head. When I feel his hard length against my bare stomach, I begin to cry.

"You feel so good."

"Please, Wes. Don't do this."

Wes doesn't answer. His grip gets tighter on my hands and his head drops between my neck and shoulder. He thrusts against me again and again as tears run down the sides of my temples.

I can't move. I can't think. The alcohol has completely stripped me of my defenses. I'm totally helpless. As Wes grunts and collapses on top of me, I slip away. A wave of darkness washes over me, taking me from this unspeakable horror. I go somewhere where Dax and I are happy and I'm not cold, alone, and left discarded on my bed like the piece of rubbish that I am.

DAX

"WHERE'S ADAM?"

The woman passing by shrugs her shoulders, not bothering to say a word.

All right, then.

I glance around the massive room at Ross's house. *House.* I scoff. Right. It's more like a mansion or an estate. Why I agreed to come to this holiday party, I have no idea. Rachel said it was good for the band to be seen socially with the executives, and since Ross invited them all, it made sense to pop by.

Then my mates went and ditched me.

A loud fuss in the foyer has everyone in the room turning towards the front door.

"Holy fuck." I am struck dumb at the sight before me.

In sashays Lila Griffin, barely dressed per her usual, with a full fucking camera crew following close. One has a boom mike hovering over her head as she walks, a second is trailing behind with a camera, and yet another is filming while walking backwards in front of her, making certain to catch her at her finest.

Murmurs quickly spread amongst the guests, everyone curious and looking to each other for answers no one seems to have—until a nearby man speaks to himself, or to me, I'm not sure which.

"I heard she started filming, but I had no idea she'd be here tonight." I glance over at the man and then force myself to focus back on Lila.

It's annoying that I have bother with asking about bloody Lila and her insanity. "What do you mean? Filming what?"

The well-dressed man, who I believe is one of the other talent executives at Ross's talent agency, huffs out a fake laugh, swirling some sort of expensive whisky in a lowball glass. "Her reality show, of course. Paid for by good old dad. He's somewhere around here as well."

Not much can pull a reaction out of me, but *that* sure does. My mouth drops open in shock. While I gather my thoughts, Lila weaves through the party, chatting with various guests, her ridiculous fucking entourage sticking to her like glue.

"Reality show?"

"Yeah. She always wanted to be famous." He points at Lila. "Now she'll get her wish." As if she knew we were talking about her, Lila's eyes meet mine. They narrow slyly and her mouth quirks up in a wicked smirk.

"Fuck." The curse slips out before I can think.

"Gotta go, big guy." The man slaps my back, downing his entire drink in one gulp and placing it on a nearby table. "Don't want to end up on that hot mess of a show and she's coming this way." Before I can say a word, he's gone, leaving me to face Lila Griffin alone.

Fucking cowardly corporate twat!

"Daxey! How are you?" Lila saunters up, swinging her hips so far to either side, I'm left wondering how she stays upright. Especially considering the utterly ridiculous shoes she's wearing. They must be five inches high and still, she's only about as tall as Kate is in her bare feet.

I swallow down the lump that forms in my throat. It's only been three weeks since I called us quits, so it's not surprising that I still think of Kate constantly. What messes with my mind is that it actually *hurts*. I broke all of my dad's rules and look where it got me—alone and fucked in the head. I'm actually fucking *feeling* shit.

Now I know why he thinks emotions are total crap.

Leaning closer than the safe distance I normally keep from Lila, I snarl in her face. "Leave me alone. I'm not in the mood for your bloody shite." When I make a move to get around her, Lila wraps her claw-like red nails around my arm, nearly spilling my beer.

"Don't be such a sour puss, Daxey."

She runs those damned fingernails up and down my bicep, making me shudder in revulsion. I'm reminded of the days back in school when girls would try to lay claim to me. It didn't work then, and it sure as hell won't work now.

"I heard you're not tied to that pathetic ex-roommate of mine anymore. Let's get out of here and find something fun to do." She eyes me up and down, licking her lips.

I don't belong to anyone. Not anymore. Not ever again.

"Get your hand off of me right now unless you want me to make a scene in front of your cameras." The glare I shoot her way doesn't phase Lila's cool exterior, but each of her cameramen take a few steps back. "And don't ever mention Kate to me again. She's too good for the likes of you."

Lila flinches. It's subtle, but enough that I can tell I've rattled her.

Good.

She fake pouts, batting her eyelashes and putting on a damn good show for the cameras. "I can see that you're no fun tonight.

I'll catch you later, Daxey." Lila winks, blows me a kiss, and spins around. "Come on boys," she says to her crew. "Let's find someone who wants to party."

Rubbing a hand across the back of my neck, I mutter under my breath. "Bloody fucking hell."

I really need to find Adam. He despises Lila and her psychotic bullshit nearly as much as I do. It takes me a while to spot him. I'm stopped by several label executives who want to introduce me to their spouses or make me promise to sign something for their kids who are such big fans.

When I finally do find him, Adam is outside, sitting across the pool on the furthest side from the house, alone with his mobile to his ear.

"Hey." I drop into the chaise next to his. Adam turns his back to me, whispering into the phone.

What the hell? Has everyone lost their bloody minds tonight?

Adam disconnects the call almost immediately after I turn up, but makes no move to speak or turn around. I watch my best mate carefully, staring at his back...waiting. He's all hunched over, shoulders rounded forward. His legs are spread wide with his elbows propped on his knees. Adam's head of dark hair hangs down while one shaky hand rakes through it.

"Adam? You okay?" For a moment I wonder if he's on the piss. He's been doing really well the last few weeks, keeping sober, avoiding nameless slags. It would be difficult to see him backslide again.

Adam's shoulders go up as he takes in a deep breath then they collapse in as he lets it out slowly. After what feels like ages, he turns his head so I can see his face. It's blotchy and red and, I swear, I think he's been crying.

"Fuck. What happened?" I jump to my feet, circling the chaise until I'm in front of him. "What the fuck, Adam? Who was on the phone just now? Did something happen to Ellie?"

My mate, who I've known for my entire life, who has had

some really really shitty things happen to him in the past, has always tried to never let the pain show on his face. The man who's always smiling, is honest-to-god fucking crying.

Hell, the only other time I've known him to shed a tear is when Kate told him about how he was smashed and he chased Ellie away at a party in L.A. a couple years back.

Adam doesn't say a word. He simply wipes his eyes and leans back on the chaise, kicking his feet up onto the cushion. I watch, speechless, while he stares up into the night sky.

Unable to stand the tension, I throw back the rest of my beer and put the glass on a nearby table.

"Adam...?" I croak, afraid that perhaps Ellie has... No, she couldn't be dead. He'd be headed straight for the bar to get rat-arsed if that were the case.

When he finally speaks, he carefully avoids any sort of eye contact. Instead choosing to stare out at the pool, the water lit up in the darkness.

"Life really sucks sometimes, yeah? I mean, you try to be a good person, try to do right by people, but shit just follows you around wherever you go."

I'm not sure if I'm meant to answer or if it's rhetorical, so I stay silent. This is how Adam's brain works. It's what makes him such a brilliant songwriter—his deep emotions, his caring soul, his heavy burdens. They clog up his mind, filling it with unwavering devotion to all things, both good and bad.

"Maybe good things aren't meant to happen to good people," he says despondently.

What on earth is he going on about?

"That's not true. Look at us. We came from nothing—fuck, less than nothing—and here we are." I hold my hands up, indicating the posh surroundings.

Adam turns towards me, his brows knitted together in a twisted grimace. "Yeah mate, look at us. You really think all this... this fucking shite is what makes us happy?" His voice is rising in volume, hostility radiating off of him. Adam gets to his feet, towering over my chair. "You're no happier than I am! I've got bloody nothing, Dax! Nothing! And neither do you. We've both lost the only things that matter to us, and no amount of money will ever make up for it!"

He flips a nearby chair, sending it flying into a nearby flowerbed. Adam twists back towards me, his finger pointing accusingly. "You had it all, you bastard! You had what I fucked up and lost! And what did you do?" Adam's lip curls up in disgust. "You tossed it in with the rubbish—tossed Kate as if she were nothing!"

I stand up to try and calm him down, but he explodes.

"Fuck this! Fuck everything! I can't take it anymore! It's nothing but fucking misery, every single fucking day!" Adam's voice cracks as he chokes down a sob.

My arms reach out to grab his shoulders, to talk some sense into him. I have no bloody clue what this is about but I have to do something. Adam is self-destructing again.

He bats my hands away. "Don't fucking try to tell me every-thing is okay you wanker, because it's not!" he shouts. "You think pretending shit isn't happening is going to make everything alright? How's that working for you, Dax? Hmmm? Is bottling everything up making you fucking happy? Because I'm not seeing it! Your actions have consequences whether they affect you or not!"

I get in his face, good and angry now. "I have no bloody clue what's got you so pissed! You haven't told me what the hell you're going on about! And leave me the fuck out of your crap! I'll deal with my own shit however I want! It's none of your concern. At least I'm not buried in booze and whores!"

His furious expression dissolves into utter despair. Lively hazel eyes turn glassy. "If you knew what you did, you'd want to..." he pauses, the fight draining out of him as if someone pulled the plug on a tub full of water. He swipes the back of his hand across his eyes. "Forget it. Fuck you. I need a fucking drink."

Adam turns and storms off, leaving me shocked and gaping, my arms still reaching out towards where he was standing. I drop them to my sides and fall down back into a chair.

Not much gets Adam going like that. We haven't had a proper row in a long time. I have no clue who he was talking to on the phone or what happened. I do know that it's pointless to wonder. Adam won't tell me until he's good and ready. If I'm the expert in burying my emotions and locking them up tight, Adam is the expert at putting on a happy face and going through the motions.

For something to affect him this deeply, to have him lose it like that, hell... he'll be drinking himself back into oblivion in no time. Just like me, he's learned that the mask only stays in place for just so long. When it cracks and your true self is revealed, the result isn't always pretty.

I lean over and pinch the bridge of my nose, a pounding headache coming on. *Bloody hell.* Between Lila's shit and Adam's drinking, I'm going to have my hands full.

I slump back, feeling ages older than my nearly twenty-one years. Maybe Adam is right. Maybe we'll both be miserable forever. Maybe dealing with Lila's obsession and Adam's addiction is penance for being such a violent, unfeeling bastard all my life.

Fuck knows I deserve whatever suffering is thrown at me, if for no other reason than breaking Kate's heart.

Kate

"KATE? I'M HOME!" I hear Abby enter the flat, the noise of her luggage rolling across the hardwood floor. "Kate? You here?"

I can't bring myself to answer. I've hardly moved in the two weeks since... since... A whimper escapes my throat. The panicked feelings I've been having spread out from the pit of my stomach, worming their way into my limbs. I breathe slowly, in and out, focusing on holding myself together like I read on the Internet.

Using the Internet as a psychologist when I have a flatmate who has a degree in psychology. That's what I've resorted to.

A knock on my bedroom door startles me. "Kate?" It swings open a crack, revealing my flatmate. "There you are." She gets a good look at me and her brow crumples. "Why's it dark in here? You're still in bed. Are you sick?"

"No." My voice is raspy, tired sounding. "Just having a lie-in, that's all."

Abby stares at me, the psychologist in her trying to piece together the picture she's seeing. I pull the duvet up higher, trying to hide my swollen, red face. "Are you sure? Do you want to talk?"

I shiver. The last thing I want to do is discuss that night with my psychologist flatmate. She'll have me in therapy in no time, reliving it over and over until I'm *empowered* or some bloody crap. All I want to do is forget. The Internet doesn't ask questions.

"No. I'm fine, really."

She presses me again. I know if I can't get it together she'll be dissecting every little thing I do in that analytical brain of hers.

"I-I..." I burst into tears, sobbing uncontrollably.

"Kate, what's going on?" The bed dips down where Abby has sat next to me.

Still, all I can do is snuffle into the duvet, soaking it with tears.

"Hey," Abby rubs a kind hand over my back, speaking in calm, soothing tones. "Kate. Tell me what happened while I was gone. You know I won't judge you. Does it have to do with Dax?"

I shudder, inhaling a snotty, loud breath. "No. Not Dax."

"All right," she murmurs, her hand still making small circles on my back. "Then who?"

"I don't want to say," I admit. Knowing Abby, she's march right over to the frat house and knock on the door, demanding to speak to Wes.

"That's fine. So what did he do? I've never seen you this upset." Abby hands me a box of tissues off of my desk.

"Thanks." I mop up the mess of tears and snot, my sobs weakening to a silent clench in my heart. Steeling myself, I tell Abby about the party, how I drank too much, how I let Wes bring me home, and what he did.

Abby takes my hand, squeezing it tight. "I hope to god you reported it," she says icily.

"I didn't want to." I fiddle with the used tissue. "But I did."

"What did the police say?"

I shrug. "I had already cleaned up. He didn't actually, you know," my face burns with shame, "put it in me. There was no evidence. They spoke to him and that was it."

"I hate this," Abby whispers.

"What?" I look over at her, surprised to see the pure, undiluted loathing on her normally serene face.

"I hate that he'll get away with it." She scowls, turning to me. "Even if you saved your clothes, really, it would just be your word against his. What's the point?" Her voice rises until she's shrieking. "They always get away with it, Kate! I fucking hate it!"

My mouth falls open in shock. Abby swore. Sweet, easy-going, laid back Abby.

"I'm sorry," I whisper.

"Don't be sorry. He's the sick bastard that did it, not you. You have nothing to be sorry about," she snaps.

"I don't really want to talk about it anymore." There's nothing left to say. I'm drained. Completely drained.

"Well, you know I'm here if you need me." Abby stands up. "Are you hungry? Want to order a pizza?"

"Sure. Let me clean up." I haven't eaten properly since she left for the holidays. I'm sure I'll have to force the food down. Brilliant. Hopefully I don't gag.

I turn the shower up as hot as it will go and step in, letting the water scald my skin. I've had dozens of showers since that night, but I never really feel clean. It's as if I'm dirty all the time, tainted somehow. Even though Wes technically didn't rape me, what he did makes me sick to my stomach every time I think of it.

Tears start flowing, mixing in with the water and washing down the drain. Each drop that falls represents something I've lost—trust, hope, my soul, Dax—the pain is so powerful it nearly doubles me over.

Dax is no longer the only man that's touched me. I think that's what hurts most of all.

Once I've stopped sobbing in the shower, I clean up and get dressed. It takes all of my energy to put on a pathetic sort-of smile as I head for the lounge. Abby already has the pizza open on the small table in front of the sofa and is dishing out pieces onto plates.

"Did you get out on Christmas at least? Or New Year's?" she asks through a mouthful of pepperoni and cheese. I can tell by the pinched look on her face that my story affected Abby more than she's letting on.

"Nah. I spent both days watching the telly. Loads of holiday movies on."

I actually spent Christmas and New Year's in bed. First, crying over Dax, then crying over Wes and what he did. The day after it happened, I broke down and rang Adam, letting him calm me down with his comforting voice. I don't know why I called him.

Was it a subconscious way of reaching out to Dax? Maybe because he's a tie to my home and that makes me feel safer somehow? I couldn't ring up my parents and tell them. They'd never get over it. They'd make it their fault somehow. By letting me come to uni here.

Whatever my reasoning was, Adam was incredibly emotional over the whole thing. He's a great listener, always has been. Adam is a very sensitive person.

It helps that both have our demons so we're able to speak freely with one another. He still laments the loss of Ellie, trying to work through the guilt he feels for running her away after that posh party almost two years ago. I'm quite certain he'll never be over that moment, never be over her.

I confided in Adam about the assault I suffered. He let me use him to vent my anger at Wes and at myself for getting so drunk that my judgment was impaired. Adam was the one who begged me to call the police, but by the time I did, several days had passed, any evidence long gone.

When I hung up I cried some more—not that I'll be telling Abby any of that. She doesn't need to know that I'm speaking to Adam.

"I really wish I had pushed you to come home with me. My parents would have loved to have you."

She frowns and wipes her hands with a napkin. "I could have used someone there with me. My brothers were just awful. Jace is in those moody teenage years where all he wants to do is hide in his room and play X-Box or text his friends. Evan has been accepted to Columbia, in New York, so his girlfriend was all over him dropping hints about how she's always wanted to live on the East Coast."

I smile for the first time in two weeks. Abby's family is perfect, even if her brothers are annoying sometimes. "Is she going to go then? With your brother to New York?"

Abby laughs so hard she chokes on her drink. "No! Christ, no. My mom and dad would kill him. School always comes first with them. They wouldn't let Evan screw up his future with the distraction of having his girlfriend tag along." Abby makes a face, as if she thinks her parents are being ridiculous.

Unfortunately, I do know about difficult choices. Just like her brother and his girlfriend. My choice to be with the one I loved was taken away from me. Only, the decision to split us up didn't come from a parent doing what they thought was in my best interest. No, it came from the person I trusted with my heart, only to watch him crush it to bits.

So what? I'm not the only one to lose someone. Is that supposed to make me feel better? Misery loves company? That's rubbish, because right now, my miserable self wants to be left completely and totally alone.

14

D^{ax}

THREE MONTHS LATER.

"CHRIST YOU'RE BEING a miserable bastard today," Adam says, glaring at me from across the tiny sound studio. "What do you have to complain about?"

"Fuck off, Reynolds," I growl.

Adam's eyes flash with anger. "We're never going to get this done if you don't man up and bloody concentrate!"

Hawke and Gavin are watching us carefully, their eyes bouncing back and forth between the two of us as we argue.

"Don't fucking talk to me about responsibility, Reynolds! Half the time we're due for studio time you're either rat-arsed or coming off the piss, so sod the fuck off!" I roar.

Adam's eyes go wider than I've ever seen. I'm normally

sympathetic to his issues with alcohol. Even more so now that I know what it's like to love someone and lose her. Today is just not the day to fuck with me. I'm confused and angry and ready for the closest target to let loose all of that negative energy on.

Adam just made himself the obvious choice.

He yanks off his guitar strap, placing the instrument on its stand. "Fuck you, Davies!" he snarls before turning on his heel and storming out of the booth.

"Well, that went wonderfully," Hawke says. "I guess we're taking a break?"

A voice booms over the speakers "Jesus. Yes, take a ten-minute break. Davies, in here. Now." Our sound engineer Gary is in the booth on the other side of the glass, his expression stormy.

Gavin pats my shoulder and follows Hawke out of the room. I put my guitar down and count to three before entering the control room. Gary is scowling, ready to explode in anger.

"What the fuck, Dax?" He leans back in his chair, staring me down with hard, grey eyes.

"Reckon I'm not feeling it today." I say it unapologetically. Sue me, I feel like being a whinging bastard today. I'm entitled after the dream I had last night.

"Too bad. You're booked in here through the rest of the week and Griffin expects it all to be laid down by then." Gary narrows his eyes, challenging me to defy him.

A challenge? That, I can do.

"Griffin can go fuck himself," I snarl, storming out of the booth. Gary tosses out threats that bounce harmlessly off my back. I'm too busy fuming to pay attention.

Of course, since today seems to be the day that karma kicks my ass, I run right into Lila and that bloody film crew that follows her everywhere. She always manages to get her schedule to coincide with mine.

She's either a bloody psychic or she's stalking me. I know which one I think it is.

"Daxey babe, there you are." I duck aside before she can get her octopus arms around me. Lila is flat out barmy. Nearly three fucking *years* of me dodging her, ignoring her, and even yelling obscenities at her and she still thinks we're a couple. She's completely demented.

Three months ago, daddy got her a reality TV show and her number one goal is to prove to the world that she and I are madly in love.

Never going to happen.

Unfortunately for me, being a complete wanker to her hasn't worked. The first episode aired a few weeks back and they edited all that shit out, making it look like my sole purpose in life is to hang around Lila. I threatened to sue her for misrepresenting me, but Ross said something about an appendix on television appearances in our contract. It's worded so broadly that he says there's nothing I can do except try to avoid getting caught on camera.

Easier said than done when you have a five foot one, hundred pound, bleach blonde stalker who happens to be the daughter of your boss, a very important man in the entertainment industry.

"Let's not have a repeat of last week, Lila." I smirk at one of her cameramen who swallows nervously.

"Oh Daxey, you wouldn't hit Kirk again, right?" She turns to Kirk, his camera shaking in his hand. "He's kidding, Kirk."

"No, I'm not." I shoot him a lethal glare.

Kirk made the mistake of getting way too close while trying to capture a shot of Lila attempting to wrestle a kiss out of me.

"It's not my fault you're learning impaired, Lila. I'll do it again in a heartbeat if you or him ever gets that close to me again." I stab a finger in Kirk's direction, causing the man to go ghostly pale.

Lila's mouth flattens into a line, then she smiles wickedly. "Don't be such a grouch, Daxey." She leans in to my side, trying to get a few shots that make us look like a cozy couple.

"Sod off." Without a second thought, I walk away, leaving Lila to stumble without my shoulder supporting her. I ignore her pleas for me to come back, grateful when I turn a corner and can't hear her annoying voice anymore.

"Dax!"

I stop, looking into one of the small rooms that are used for 'talent' to rest up between recording sessions to see who's shouting. I find Adam leaning just inside the door. "Get your stupid arse in here." He motions for me to enter.

"Adam," I rub the back of my neck. "I'm in a really really shitty mood right now, yeah? It's probably not a good idea—"

He steps into the hall and yanks me inside the room by the wrist, slamming the door behind us.

"Too bad. I was never in the mood for *your* harassing when I was hung over or acting like a wanker, but you never let up on me. And I have to tell you, I'm grateful for it."

My eyebrows must shoot up into my hairline I'm so surprised. Adam has never once let on that he appreciates my efforts to keep him sober. All he ever does is call me and the other blokes nags while he starts his whinging.

"You're grateful?"

Adam folds his arms across his chest, leaning against the wall. "Yep. So, now you know. I actually do hear you when you tell me to get my head together, to man up and quit burying my head in a bottle. I don't always do what you want, but I know you're there for me. To pay you back, you're going to tell me what the hell is going on and let me be there for you."

My best mate, the one person in the entire world who knows me better than I know myself, is staring at me hopefully, waiting for me to do the one thing I never, ever do... let someone in.

I hate to admit it, but I'm exhausted. Years of being a rock, ignoring my own needs and feelings, putting up a strong front for everyone—it's fucking killing me. Maybe it's time to let someone else share the burden. Since it can't be Kate, it may as well be Adam.

"Fine." I move past Adam and sit on the small sofa tucked to one side of the room. "It's about Kate."

Adam rolls his eyes. "Of course it is. I'm not stupid you know. What happened with her?"

"How did you—?"

"Dax. I've known you a long time. Years. More than a decade actually. The only time you get emotional in any way is when you're thinking about Kate or your dad."

"I'm not emotional," I say defensively.

He snorts. "Not in a touchy-feely way, no. More like an *I'm so angry I'm going to beat the absolute shite out of you'* way. You only have two settings, icy cold and erupting volcano."

I bristle at his apt description. "Whatever."

"Don't be a big girl's blouse. We all have our weaknesses." Adam is grinning. "What happened?"

I tell him what I dreamt this morning. "Kate was being attacked. I couldn't get to her. Fuck! It was awful mate. To see it, to feel so helpless."

He nods, swallowing loudly. "Yeah. That would be awful." His voice wavers as he speaks. I scowl at Adam's odd response.

"Anyway," I continue, "I woke up sweating with my heart racing so fast, it was as if it were going to explode in my chest. It felt so real." I lean over and put my elbows on my knees, running my hands through my hair. "You know my dad and his rules."

"Yeah. I remember."

"I refused to break any of them in the dream. I refused to get upset. I let her think I didn't give a shit that she was being hurt. It was as if *I* was the one hurting her. I..." I breathe deeply, wincing when it hitches in my chest. "I didn't fight for her, defend her. She's... she's like fucking family, Adam. And I did nothing."

Neither of us speaks for a few minutes, digesting what my dream means, if it even means anything.

"Well," Adam says, nervously rubbing the back of his head, "I'm sure it means that you think you let her down somehow.

That you think of yourself as her protector..." he stops, tears welling up in his eyes. *Goddamn tears over my dream!*

"What is this about?" I snap, standing up to pace the tiny room. The stress has me so wound up I'm ready to burst out of my own skin. The room feels smaller all of a sudden, like I'm being squeezed from all sides.

This must be what the Hulk feels like right before he rips his clothes and turns green. "Why are you all touchy and sensitive? It was *my* fucking dream! *My* fucking girl, Adam!"

He turns, snarling at me, his hands gripping his hair in frustration. "She's not *your* girl, Dax! You dumped her, or have you forgotten? You had *everything* and you tossed it, you stupid sod!"

I glare at him, clenching my fists. "Are you trying to pick a fight with me?"

"'I'm not trying to pick a fight. But...fuck." Adam lets out a huge breath. "There's something you should know. About Kate." He sits on the sofa, leaning forward with his hands covering his face. "Shit. I promised I wouldn't say anything, but..."

A chill wracks my body, putting goose bumps down my arms. The temperature in the room just dropped ten degrees. Adam's behavior has an ominous feeling hanging over me, as if the floor is about to fall out and I'll find myself hanging by an invisible noose that has somehow slipped around my neck.

If Adam doesn't tell me what's going on in the next ten seconds, I'm going to flatten him into a smudge on the floor. As strong as I think I am, as much control as I think I have over my actions, it's seems to be that when it comes to Kate, I have very little choice in the matter as to what I do next.

Then, he speaks and my world fucking shatters.

⁓

"Dax! Let go! You're choking him!"

Hawke and Gary are trying to pull my hands off of Adam, who I have shoved against the wall by his throat.

"He fucking knew and didn't tell me!"

"What are you talking about?" Hawke yells, tugging uselessly on my left arm.

The rage I feel is so overwhelming, so all encompassing, that I have no way to stop it. It's as if time lapsed, skipping over parts like a bad stop motion film. One second Adam was telling me that Kate was sexually assaulted at uni, the next, I have him up on his toes with my hand wrapped around my neck and my mates trying to pull me off.

"Dax..." Adam gasps, his face turning red.

I'm about to let Adam go when electrified pain shoots down my body. I drop to the ground, my hands flying up to my neck to stop the source of the agony.

"Don't move," someone says from behind where I'm writhing on my knees.

"Gavin?" I should have known it was him. After the way he fucking dropped me when I broke up with Kate, I've been more cautious around him since that day. But not today. All I saw was red.

I claw at Gavin's hand, his long fingers deep in the hollow on one side of my collarbone.

"Stay still," he commands in a firm, very un-Gavin like tone.

Still on fire from the crippling pain, I lower my hands in defeat.

"I'm going to let you go but you have to promise you'll calm down." Gavin sounds like an entirely different person. Gone is the sweet, playful man I'm familiar with. Replaced by a cold, ruthless soldier.

"I won't." My chest is heaving. Not from exertion, not from pain, but from the pure physical anguish of my heart breaking.

Gavin releases his grip, slowly removing his hand. Without it, the pain stops instantly and I fold over onto my hands and knees.

I can hear Adam in the background, apologizing over and over, "I'm sorry mate. So sorry. "

I can't listen. All of my attention is on the voices in my head screaming at how I've failed. Failed Kate. Failed the band. Failed myself.

The control I so desperately seek is always just out of reach. Everything is falling apart around me and there's not a goddamn thing I can do about it.

I fist my hands in my hair and for the first time in my life, I *willingly* set my emotions free. I welcome them. I deserve every single painful lash of the mental whipping I torture myself with. I'd take more if I could. As it is, my suffering pales in comparison to what Kate's been through.

After I've let it all out and am crumpled, spent, on the floor, someone's arms come around me, helping me stagger to my feet.

"Let's go home, yeah?"

"Adam? I-I'm sorry mate." I lean heavily on my best friend, letting him share the burden. Fuck, he already *does* share the burden. Add him to the long list of people whose life has been fucked up by Dax Davies.

Kate

"OH MY GOD, no you didn't!" Myriah squeals from her perch on the sofa in the house she rents with three other girls from the footy team.

"She totally did," Bridget giggles. "Brittany made out with Bud after last week's frat party!"

I cringe at the mention of the frat, unwelcome memories assaulting me. None of them know what happened after that party, and none of them ever will.

"Kate, you should have been there. It was a really good time."

Myriah throws her arm over my shoulder, hugging me to her side.

"Right. Sorry. I had loads to do with classes and midterms and what not." I squirm uncomfortably at my teammates' scrutiny. Or maybe it's my imagination and they're not looking at me oddly at all. This is my first outing since... *it* happened, and what little self-confidence I had built up, evaporated like an oasis in the desert.

"Well. Midterms are over, so you'll have plenty of time to hang out with us now." Brittany smiles at me from across the cozy living room. "And I did *not* make out with Bud," she insists. Everyone starts chattering, refuting her claim. Brittany holds up a hand to silence them. "I got a piece of his hot ass!"

The room erupts into giggles and girlish squeals, the sounds of friends having a laugh. I force a smile on my face, pretending to fit in when I know deep down I'll never fit in with this crowd again. I won't drink, I won't date, and I sure as hell won't ever set foot inside a frat house again.

I get up and escape to the tiny kitchen, desperate to stop trembling before anyone can notice that I'm falling apart.

"Hey."

I startle, knocking over a half-full glass of something pink.

"Sorry Kate. I didn't mean to frighten you." Myriah grabs a kitchen roll and starts to mop up the mess.

"No worries," I lie, crouching down to help.

"What's been going on with you?" Myriah asks as she tosses the soggy towels in the bin. "You've been avoiding us lately."

"Have I?" I concentrate on wiping up the now non-existent spill to avoid looking at my friend. "Just busy with classes, that's all."

"Kate."

Noise and laughter from the other room breaks the uncomfortable silence. Myriah's pause is long enough that I can't get away with any more fake cleaning, the spill already gone. I stand up, leaning back on the counter to face my team captain.

"I've just..." My eyes begin to fill with tears. "Crap. Sorry." I wipe them away with the back of my hand. "I'm going through some stuff, okay?"

Myriah's concerned gaze meets mine, her face slightly blurry through my tears.

"Is this about that guy you used to see? The famous one? Because of the new T.V. show?"

My heart stutters, skipping a beat. "The what?"

"The reality show. You know, *Life With Lila*?"

"Life with—what? No. What are you talking about?" *Lila?* She can't be talking about Lila Griffin, my psycho ex-flatmate. Can she?

"The new show on the CelebCast channel. *Life With Lila*. It's all about that rich socialite from around here, Lila Griffin."

At the mention of her name, my throat begins to close up.

"I thought maybe you saw it and got upset. Because Dax Davies is with her now."

"No way!" I say louder than I intended.

Myriah shrinks back, surprised by the vehemence of my words. She holds her hands up. "If you say so, Kate. Just, if you're going through a rough time, call me. We can hang out."

"Yeah, I will," I choke out.

No. I won't.

As soon as it's possible to escape without anyone noticing, I hurry back to my flat and boot up my laptop, trembling all over. While I wait for it to go through it's painfully slow process, my mind begins to wander.

Dax and Lila aren't really together, are they? He said he hated her—*despised* her. I believed him when he told me that all of those photos of them together on tour were set up. But then... why did he break up with me? Was it to be with her? Was he with her while we were together?

My head begins to hurt from the possibilities.

The home screen finally pops up. I choose a search engine and type

CelebCast Lila Griffin Reality Show

THE LITTLE SPINNING hourglass that appears has me sitting on the edge of my seat—literally—drumming my fingers on the corner of my desk. Then finally, the results are in.

I click the first one. It links directly to CelebCast's website where you can watch the episodes for free.

EPISODE I

ONLY ONE EPISODE has aired so far. Holding my breath, I hit play. The scenes begin to unfold, each one more horrific than the last.

People actually watch this?

That's my first thought as cameras follow Lila as she shops, gets her nails done, and does more shopping. My second thought is to wish for a lightning bolt to come out of the sky and strike Lila dead because there it is.

Lila and Dax. On the screen. Together.

The clips of them are short, never more than a few seconds here and there. Dax hardly says more than a word or two. Yet there they are, arm in arm in one scene, Lila cuddled up to his side in another where she honest to god blows Dax a kiss as she leaves his recording studio.

The rush of emotions that flood my system are near paralyzing. Not because I'm sad. I should be, but I'm not. No. This time, I'm good and fucking pissed off.

I slam the lid of the computer shut, fuming with anger. Fuck Dax Davies and fuck Lila Griffin! They can have each other. And fuck Adam Reynolds for not telling me about it while I was pouring my shattered, broken heart out to him.

First thing tomorrow, I'm getting a new mobile number. Maybe Ellie was onto something when she disappeared. Those sodding Hackney arseholes just aren't worth the pain.

DAX

I GRAB my leather jacket and the keys to my bike, a custom built Ducati Monster I bought with our first big paycheck. L.A. is no place for a car, but with the Ducati, I can slip through even the worst traffic jam in no time.

"Oi! Where are you going?"

My back stiffens at the sound of Adam's voice. Using an extraordinary amount of control, I school my face and turn to face him. Then, I lose my composure.

"Fuck, Adam. Your neck."

Adam winces when he gently touches the dark bruises that wrap around his throat. Bruises *I* put there yesterday.

"No worries, yeah? I'll be fine." As usual, Adam brushes off his own health, giving me a weak smile. "But you, you look like you feel worse than me, mate."

"I'm just brilliant," I say sarcastically, glaring at Adam.

"You're going to see her, aren't you?"

Adam looks... tired. Twenty-one years old and he looks like he's been to hell and back. That still doesn't give him the right to ask me questions.

"Can we skip the interrogation? I don't answer to you." I grip the keys tightly in my fist, the jagged edges digging into my palm. I have to find Kate. I need to see with my own eyes that she's okay.

Adam drops down into one of the hotel chairs. Both of us have been living in hotels since Gavin and Hawke each moved out and got their own places. Neither of us could bring ourselves to put down permanent roots—most likely for the same reason.

Adam brought me to his room last night to crash since I was in no shape to be alone.

"Go. You should," Adam says, nodding. "I didn't fight hard enough to win Ellie back. At least you still have a chance."

My mate's eyes go vacant, the way they do when he's thinking about having a drink. I know that the minute I step out of the room, he'll either clean out the minibar or head straight for the nearest bar for an all day-all night piss up.

Sighing, I drop my keys on a table in the foyer and slide onto the chair next to Adam. I can't leave him like this. Hell, I don't even know if Kate would want to talk to me. For all I know, I'll make everything worse.

What's best for Kate? I realize I don't have a bloody clue. Instead of barreling ahead with my own actions—actions that are purely selfish—I make a suggestion.

"Maybe...maybe we should *use* this."

Adam looks at me warily. "Use this? What's that supposed to mean?"

"You know, our..." I swallow down the revulsion that's trying to choke me. "Our emotions and feelings and shit. We're both raw, yeah? Let's use that to make a fucking brilliant song."

Adam's solemn expression perks up then deflates again. "But we're only in the studio for three more days. There isn't time for a new song."

I reach down and pull a stack of Adam's notebooks from under the coffee table, dropping them loudly on top. "I guess we better get started then."

Adam dials Ross to let him know we need a couple of days off before we get back into the studio. Ross is angry, but with the promise of a record-breaking song coming out of the deal, he relents.

"Two days," Adam says. "Bloody wanker only gave us two

days." He rubs his eyes and tosses his pencil on the dining room table. We have our notebooks open and spread out all over the surface, lyrics haphazardly written here and there.

"Relax." I can tell Adam is back to thinking about having a drink. His eyes keep flicking towards the bar. "We've got this. Haven't we done this before? Fuck, we wrote a song in two hours once."

He laughs, his dark mood lightening just a bit. "Yeah. That was brilliant, wasn't it?" Adam picks up his pencil, snagging the nearest notebook and dragging it in front of him. "Reckon I can write a sadder fucking song than you in less than an hour?" He cocks his head as one eyebrow lifts with the challenge.

It's not funny, writing about all the shit that has crushed your soul. Yet I can't help but chuckle. It's Adam's way of dealing with stuff, making a joke or putting on an ill-timed smile. It's what makes him so damn charming.

"I'll have the audience blubbering in no time, Reynolds. Challenge accepted."

Turns out, Adam's a bloody genius. I mean, I already knew he was a genius with music—guitars and singing and what not. But he's some sort of back room psychiatrist or something. Letting the blackness in my heart pour out of my hand and onto paper, releasing all of that negative energy and hate and helplessness... it felt fucking great.

Twenty-one years worth of our hatred, frustration, love, and loss mash together to create some of the most brilliant songs we've ever written. When we finish two days later, we don't have a record-breaking song for *Sphere of Irony*. We have an entire bloody album of award winning songs and a two lifetimes worth of suffering set free.

15

Dax

Two years later

"Does she know you're here?"

I flinch from the sudden closeness of a voice. Someone sneaking up on me has caused me to splash some of my drink onto my jeans.

"Bollocks." I turn to see who spotted me, wiping my hand on my sweatshirt.

Bloody hell, it's Kate's flatmate.

"Abby. Didn't think anyone would know who I was."

The oversized hoodie I have pulled up over a cap and sunglasses would fool most people. Not having shaved in two weeks and sporting a fairly decent beard, *that's* the bit that lets me walk around L.A. without being recognized at all.

"I didn't recognize you. A little bird may have told me you'd be here." She holds up her mobile, as if that's supposed to answer my question.

"Who—? Hawke? You still chat with Hawke?"

I didn't know she kept in touch with him, but it seems obvious now that I see Abby smirking. Hawke, that little shit. I'll have to have a chat with Hawke. Something about learning to mind his own business and not tell people where I'll be.

"We haven't been speaking, per se." Abby blushes. "Only recently. Anyway," she waves her hand dismissively. "Enough about that. Why are you here, Dax?"

She's quite beautiful, Kate's friend. Reminds me a lot of Ellie. Blonde, blue eyes, sweet—but Abby doesn't have the same naiveté that was so endearing on Ellie. I can't explain it except to say Abby seems to realize the world isn't all butterflies and unicorns. Something that Ellie, who used to think the best of everyone, has certainly found to be untrue by now.

"I heard about her joining the team." My eyes are focused on the football pitch. I chose a seat all the way at the top of the outdoor stadium. I didn't want Kate to spot me and definitely didn't want to be seen by any fans. Not after what happened the last time I went to one of Kate's games.

I shudder just thinking about it.

Kate graduated university a year and a half ago. I know this because I went to the ceremony courtesy of the Dean. He let me sit in a private box at the school's massive indoor sports pavilion where the ceremony took place without even asking a single question as to why I wanted to be there. Sometimes it pays to be famous. You can get away with things that other people can't.

"You just *happened* to hear about her joining the team?" Abby asks incredulously. "Do you normally follow professional women's soccer?"

Abby has a gleam in her eye that lets me know she's torturing me on purpose. "I just," I drop my head and rub a hand through my hair. "I wanted to make sure she was alright. You know, that she was doing okay. I've been checking up on her here and there ever since she was assaulted."

"What?"

Abby's sharp tone makes me whip my head away from the game to find her shocked expression.

Okaaay. I'm confused by her reaction. "What do you mean, *what*? That bastard who sexually assaulted Kate two years ago. I've been looking out—"

"Oh my god." Abby goes pale, her mouth hanging open. "You know?"

I suck in a sharp breath and a knot forms in my stomach.

Oh shit.

"Fuck. I'm not supposed to know." Christ, I'm such a fucking prick. "I'm sorry. I... shit."

Abby glares at me, which loses some of its potency due to the fact that she's still gaping like a fish. "Come to think of it, how did *you* find out? I sure as hell know she didn't call you up to talk about it."

Fuck me, again! I'm really putting my foot in it today.

The referee's whistle catches my attention. I spot Kate running onto the pitch. Number eight. Same as it's been since we lived in Hackney.

"Dax." Abby pesters. "Who told you about Kate? I mean, she didn't even want to tell me. Oh my god, don't tell me that Hawke knows. I'll kill him if he does."

"No. Stop, Abby. Hawke doesn't know anything. Shit. *I'm* not supposed to know. Kate called *Adam*, if you can believe that." I huff in annoyance.

It still stings that Kate turned to Adam instead of me. But hell, why would she turn to me? I'm the bloke who had just broken her heart.

"*Adam*? Adam Reynolds? All this time, she's been talking to Adam?" Abby is talking to me, but her gaze is far off. Almost like she's taking apart everything Kate's done over the past two years and fitting the pieces back together with the knowledge of the assault.

"Yeah. Adam. They don't chat anymore. Adam won't tell me anything about the conversations they used to have. Made me want to scream back then. But that's Adam. If nothing else, he's loyal to a fault."

I shrug and continue watching the game while Abby processes the news. A girl passes the ball to Kate and she does an incredible fake, spinning around and kicking it right into the upper corner of the net.

Bloody brilliant.

She's the best striker I've ever seen. Hands down. I want to stand and cheer and scream her name, but can't risk the attention.

"It bothers me that she wouldn't tell Adam who the bastard is that did it," I say casually, my eyes still on the match. "She didn't happen to tell you, did she?"

Abby eyes me suspiciously. "No. She didn't."

"Hmph. It's for the best, I suppose. Because if I knew who he was…" I stop to control the rising fury. "I'd bloody well be in jail by now."

"We can't have that, now, can we?" Abby chuckles. "I wanted to find him and do terrible things to him as well."

I bark out a laugh. "You would too."

"I feel like the worst friend in the world," Abby says sadly. "I'm a psychology PhD candidate for god's sake! I can't get her to talk to me. About anything. I could have helped! I could have done something."

Abby's voice is rising, the sharp tone of hysteria bleeding through. I put a hand on her shoulder.

"Abby, calm down. How were you to know? It happened…" I pause, the familiar nausea welling up when I think about my role in the attack. "It happened right after Kate and I broke up.

Then... *that* happened. It's my fault, you know. For dumping her. She never would have been at a party drinking herself into a stupor if I hadn't been such a stupid idiot."

"What? That's ridiculous Dax. Hell, I might not be a licensed psychologist yet, but even I know that you can't blame yourself for what some asshole did to Kate."

I turn away from Abby, watching Kate run down the pitch. My heart squeezes painfully in my chest, knowing that this is as close as I'll ever get to her again. I can't answer anymore of Abby's questions, the hurt is still too intense.

"I have to go. Please don't tell her I was here."

Without looking back or waiting for a response, I stand up and leave the stadium, my heart lying broken on a football pitch in Southern California.

Kate

"ABBY! I'M LEAVING FOR WORK."

"Okay, Kate! See you later!" my flatmate Abby yells out from behind the bathroom door where she's getting ready for her internship at a counseling center. It's been a good job for her to have while she's getting her PhD here at UCLA.

Thank god she got in, because it means I still have my flatmate and best friend. At least for another few years.

Smiling, which is rare for me these days, I grab my bag, locking the door behind me. Summer in Los Angeles is brutal, so I shouldn't be so happy to be working outside, but I scored the perfect job after graduation. It's even within walking distance of my flat, which means I don't have to take the horrid, sweaty bus anymore.

Ten minutes later I'm entering an air-conditioned building that serves as home to ESAC, the European Soccer Association of

California, a top-notch academy that trains and develops future football stars. And I'm one of their trainers. While still at uni, I interned for their summer camps. When I received my degree in sports medicine last spring, they took me on full-time as a trainer.

I love working with the kids and continuing to have football, I still can't bring myself to call it soccer, in my life. In fact, I play for a local women's premier league team as well, simply because I can't imagine not competing in some form or another.

"Kate, you look lovely." Logan, one of the full-time academy coaches gives me a huge smile when I pass by his messy office.

"Logan." I should know better than to flirt with my sort-of boyfriend at work, yet I can't help but grin back. The way Logan blatantly adores me is almost addictive. He's good for my ego. "Missed me already, yeah?" We spent last night together having dinner out before he brought me home.

That's the other good thing about him. Logan is very patient when it comes to... sexual activities. I'm nowhere near ready for that.

"Whenever you're not with me I'm missing you," he replies with a wink.

Grinning, I head for the locker rooms to change. Logan is the first, the *only*, man I've dated since Dax and since that terrible incident with Wes.

It took me a while to accept that Dax was gone and never coming back. Some days, my heart still aches for him. I wake up and swear that I smell him on my sheets, feel his presence in my bed. It took just as long to begin to trust men or want to be intimate again. I'm thankful I had my friends there to help me through it. Well, one friend in person and one on the phone.

Most days, I'm able to move on with my life and be somewhat happy with Logan.

It only took watching five minutes of watching a Lila's television program to finally cure me of my fixation on all things Dax. At least, I tell myself I'm cured.

Work goes well, all of the girls are focused and driven. Logan has an adult league game of his own tonight. He's highly competitive, possibly the most competitive person I've ever known. Sometimes, I can't take it he's so bloody arrogant when it comes to footy. He actually had a tantrum once when I stripped him of the ball while we were messing around on the pitch.

But he worships me. I can deal with a little bit of a competitive streak.

Since Logan's not going to be around this evening, I quickly shower after work and walk the few blocks home to the little flat I still share with Abby.

"Kate!" Abby barrels into me the minute I come through the door. "Oh my god where have you been?" she screeches, hugging me tight.

"What the hell, Abby?" I check the time on my mobile. "I'm only a few minutes later than usual." I patiently wait for her to let go, but it's apparent that she isn't moving. "Can I put down my bag and get a drink?"

"Oh. Sure. Sorry." She drops her arms, hopping up and down on her toes as I get a Gatorade out of the fridge, chugging half of it down in seconds.

Abby is fidgeting excitedly while I drink, which in turn makes me incredibly nervous.

"What? Just say it. You're freaking me out." I clench the bottle of blue liquid in my hand. Waiting for whatever news Abby is about to drop on my head.

"There's a voicemail for you!" she squeals. "Go check it!"

"What is it?" I ask, irritated that she won't just tell me. I despise surprises.

"Go listen! Go, go, go!" She stays on my heels for the short walk to the table where we keep the house phone. Picking it up as if it were a bomb about to explode like in those old Mission Impossible shows on the telly, I dial the code for our mailbox.

A recording of a British woman with a Northern accent begins.

"This is Chelsea Lewis, coach for the 2012 Olympics women's football team to represent the U.K. I'd like to speak to you about trying out. London is the host city and we want to make a good show of it. Call me at..."

Dazed, I hang up the phone, staring blankly at the wall.

"They want me for the Olympic football team."

"I know!" Abby is jumping up and down, looking as if she might burst from excitement.

"England never has a women's football team in the Olympics," I mutter, more to myself than to Abby.

She stops bouncing immediately. "What? They don't? Isn't that like, your national sport?"

I explain to my oblivious American friend. "Women's footy isn't a big deal in the U.K. like it is here in the U.S. I don't know why, it just isn't. I was lucky to attend a school that had a program. It's the reason I had to come all the way here for university."

"Wow. I had no idea." Abby shakes her head.

"I don't really understand why they're having a team now," I admit.

"Then call the woman back." She points to the phone that's still in my hand.

"Right. Oh," I glance at the time and frown, doing the math in my head. "It's late there already. After midnight. I'll have to ring her tomorrow."

Abby wraps her arms around me in a big, comforting hug. "I'm so proud of you, Kate."

"I haven't made the team yet, Abby." Even though I'm being cautious with my excitement in case it doesn't pan out, I can't help the grin on my face or the way my spirits have been lifted.

"You will. I know it."

"I'm glad you think so," I joke.

Abby give me a serious look. "I *know* so."

I won't admit it to Abby, maybe not even to myself, but this is the most hope I've had for my future since Dax walked out of my life two years ago.

It never occurs to me that my first thought wasn't to ring Logan and share the good news, it was to ring Dax.

Maybe I'm not cured after all.

Dax

"THIS IS SO STUPID," I mutter to myself as I stop my Ducati in a large parking lot surrounded by a half-dozen green football pitches.

Kicking down the stand, I pull off my helmet and set it between my legs. There are players on every single field, ranging in age from primary school through young adult. The littlest children squeal in delight as they pass the ball back and forth. Wistfully, I remember wanting to play footy as a kid and my dad responding by having me hit a punching bag for an hour.

I don't know why I'm here. Maybe I just need to make absolutely sure Kate is okay. I've been replaying the conversation I had with Abby at Kate's football game over and over in my head for the last six months. Once I let the cat out of the bag about Kate's assault, I never got around to finding out if Kate was able to find some semblance of happiness.

For some reason I *need* to know.

Reaching down, I pull a hat out from the compartment under the seat and tug it down low. Hopefully, with my sunglasses on, no one will recognize me. It tends to be fifty-fifty when I go out alone without a beard or disguise of some sort. When I'm with Adam, it's one hundred percent guaranteed that someone will spot us. There are quite a few benefits in not being the lead singer.

I don't want to pass through the actual office building to get access to the pitches. There's too much chance in being recognized and then I'd have to explain my reason for being here. I walk directly over to the fence surrounding the property that spans the length of the fields. I'm passing the second pitch when I spot her not more than twenty meters away.

Heat spread across my skin, my heart pumping blood through my veins at a pace fast enough to feel my pulse throbbing in my neck. A lump forms in my throat. I try to swallow it down, but it refuses to move.

Unwelcome emotions flood my brain, emotions I've shut down every time they've tried to appear—longing, heartbreak, and most of all fear. Fear that Kate will turn me away, that she despises me for what I did.

She's speaking to a teenage girl, maybe fifteen years old. The girl is chatting animatedly, pointing down the pitch and making gestures as she speaks. Kate is smiling, her face radiant, nodding at the girl's words. Kate kneels down and flexes the girl's left ankle this way and that, doing some sort of clinical exam.

Watching her, the genuine joy on her face, reminds me of a time when *I* was the one who made her happy. I was the one who held her when her team lost a match, the one she smiled at when she aced her latest exam. Seeing her getting along without me is heart wrenching. I'm glad that Kate has found something that makes her happy, yet I'm upset that it seems she was able to move on.

What did you expect, Davies? For her to cry for two years?

No. All I can hope for is that inside, she's as lost without me as I am without her. That maybe some of the feelings she had for me are still there, even if it's only a tiny sliver.

The young player trots off towards the building and Kate begins to put her gear away.

Now or never, Davies.

I'm about to call out her name when a dark haired man dressed in football gear jogs up to Kate. I was wrong. Kate wasn't radiant when she was helping the girl with her ankle. She was merely doing her job.

When *this* bloke comes over, her entire face lights up in a way that makes radiant look dull. She's stunning. She's thrilled. She exudes happiness from every pore. The man lowers his mouth to hers, kissing her right there on the pitch.

Fuck. She's in love. And it's not with me.

16

Six months later

Kate

"KATE! KATE, WAKE UP!"

I gasp, shooting up out of bed, my heart racing in terror.

"You were screaming. Are you okay?"

My eyes adjust to the dim light of my bedroom, finding my poor flatmate crouched over me, looking scared to death.

"I'm sorry, Abby. It was just a nightmare." I fall back onto the bed, giving my trembling pulse a chance to slow down.

"Jesus, Kate." Abby sits down on the edge of the mattress. "Do you want to talk about it?"

I should. I really should. The nightmares have been getting worse. So bad, in fact, that I've stayed up late every night for a week. Maybe talking about them will help make them stop.

It's essential that they stop before I head overseas for the games leading up to the Olympics. That's all I need is to terrify a teammate with my screaming nightmares. We'd both lose enough sleep to be crap on the pitch the next day.

"Abby..." I pause, taking in a shaky breath. "I'd like to tell you about my dreams."

Abby's eyes go wide, the whites standing out in the dark room. Her hand digs under the sheets for mine, gripping it tight when she finds it. "Of course. We're best friends. Take your time. Tell me what the nightmare was about."

Embarrassingly, the damn tears start welling up in my eyes. "Crap." I use the corner of the duvet to wipe them off. How do I tell my best friend that I keep reliving the almost-rape from two and a half years ago? Only, in my dream, Dax and Lila are watching me, laughing.

I spend the next twenty minutes giving Abby a tearful version of the different nightmares. The fact that the incident happened in this very room. In this bed. Certainly makes them worse. Abby cries with me, climbing under the covers and stroking my head while I sob.

We lie there for a while, both of us emotionally wrung out. My stomach decides to growl quite loudly and inappropriately. Laughing, it breaks the somber mood and we decide to order takeaway.

"Nothing helps heal the heart like a giant, fatty meal," Abby chirps as she digs through a junk drawer for the menu to a local Chinese restaurant.

"Ha!" I say sarcastically. "I wish. I'd be all fixed by now if that were true."

Abby puts down the stack of menus, walking up to where I'm plunked down on the sofa. "Stop that, Kate. There's nothing wrong with you. You've been through some really fucked up shit, okay? You're allowed to *feel*. Even if it's not always good or happy, just feeling something means you're alive. No one expects you to be perfect and smiling all the time."

I stare at my fingernails, suddenly fascinated by them. "I know that."

She rips my hand away from my face. "Do you really know that? It's okay to take time to heal. It's okay to need to figure out who you are."

I start to get defensive. "I know that, Abby! Why are you getting mad at me?"

"I'm not mad, Kate. I just, I wish we talked sooner, more often. That's all. Maybe I could have helped before it got this bad."

"I'm sorry. Maybe I should have let it out and discussed everything. I just, I didn't want you worrying for me all the time." I start picking at the sofa cushion.

"Well I do that anyway. Do you feel better? After getting it off your chest?"

Do I?

"Yeah. I do."

"See. At least my education wasn't a total waste." Abby picks up her mobile and phones in our order.

While she does that, my own mobile buzzes from between the sofa cushions. I check it and immediately silence the call.

"Ignoring Logan again? When are you going to realize that Logan might care about you, but he's so jealous of your success that he can't see straight?" Abby flops down next to me, jostling me sideways. "He's been weird ever since you made the Olympic team."

"Hey! Buggar off! He's not like that." I say it confidently, but I know that Logan is exactly that... jealous. Since he found out I made the team, he's been taking his annoyance out on me. Not physically. He snaps a lot, is easily frustrated. Or maybe it's the lack of sex that's got him all wound up since I still won't go there with him.

Maybe the dreams aren't the only reason I haven't spent time with him lately. He's repeatedly attempted to move things forward physically, and had to deal with my rejection every time.

"Have you talked about what's going to happen with him when you leave the country next month?" She leans back with her arms folded across her chest.

"Well, no. Not exactly. But—"

"Like I said. You need to end things with him. At least have the decency to break up with him before you leave for Europe for a year."

I huff loudly, but don't feel the irritation to back up the sound. "He wants to come visit. At the Olympics, Abby."

Abby's mouth falls open. Her hands dart out and cover one of mine. "That's a terrible idea, Kate. He won't be able to deal with the attention you'll be getting. He'll make the proudest moment of your life miserable."

I know she's right. He will be an absolute shit if he goes with me.

"I'll break up with him before I leave," I tell her. I cut off her smile, adding on to my promise. "*After* my last day at work. No sense making everything awkward when I only have a few weeks left." I put my notice in since I'll be gone for so long.

She pats my hand. "Good idea. Just don't leave it until the last minute. He might be an ass sometimes but that's cruel."

A knock on the door lets us know our food is here. Abby get it and unpacks the bag onto the table.

"I won't wait until the last minute, mum. Can we eat now?" I ask, done with discussing Logan.

Abby doesn't respond. She simply picks up her chopsticks and stuffs her mouth full of tangerine chicken. I take that as a yes and dig into my own container of beef chow Mein.

DAX

"HELL THAT FELT GOOD," I exclaim as Adam, Gavin, Hawke and I head out of Ross' office.

"About time, yeah?" Adam punches my arm, grinning like a fool.

Gavin glances around with a nervous tic as we exit the lifts and cross the enormous lobby of our new record label.

"You alright, mate?" I ask, watching as his bloodshot eyes dart back and forth suspiciously.

"I'm fine," he snaps. Dismissing me completely.

Hawke grimaces at Gavin's back but keeps his thoughts to himself. Adam is going on and on about our new label and how great it will be to have more creative control.

Me? All I care about is the fact that I won't have to deal with Lila fucking Griffin and her mountain of bullshit anymore.

Gavin's Range Rover is waiting for us out front. Ross' secretary must have called to have it brought around. Outside, it's a real scorcher, even for L.A. in July. Hot enough to roast your bollocks if you stay in the sun too long.

Gavin hurries around the front of the SUV and jumps in, slouching down behind the wheel.

"What's up with him?" I nudge Hawke's arm and point towards Gavin with my chin.

"Oh, nothing. It's probably the heat, that's all." Hawke opens the passenger door and climbs in next to Gavin.

"Okaaay," I say to myself.

When I climb into the back seat, I turn expecting Adam to be following me, but I'm alone. I look outside and realize he's made a few new friends. A group of girls has him surrounded, smiling and taking selfies with their phones. Adam is grinning, playing along and signing whatever scraps of paper they come up with.

"Fucking asshole. Always gets the girls," Hawke mutters.

"Oh fuck off," I say lightly. "You get so much pussy you're buried in it."

That's no lie. Women really really like Hawke and his

tattooed, skater boy look. Hell, they like all of us, although Adam gets the most attention by far.

He makes it look so easy. You'd never know by his public behavior how miserable the bloke is. Adam's only sober this morning because we had a meeting with the executives for our new label and if he fucked it up for us, we'd have killed him. Inside that tortured mind of his, I'm certain he's counting the minutes until he can get his hands on his next drink.

Adam waves, expertly extracting himself from the groping hands. "Thanks ladies. Cheers!"

He climbs into the seat next to mine, grinning like an idiot.

"Can we go now, your highness? Or is your fan club still needing your service?" I ask, pointing at the now *very* large group of girls he's left squealing on the sidewalk to take pictures of the SUV.

Before Adam can answer, Gavin slams down on the gas, rocketing the massive vehicle out into traffic. A loud horn sounds as the squeal of breaks echoes up and down the street.

"Jesus, Gav, watch it!" Hawke yells from the front seat. "Fuck! That car almost hit us."

Hawke is freaking out over the near miss, hurling a slew of insults at his best friend. Gavin mumbles an apology under his breath, which only causes Hawke's face to darken with fury.

Adam and I exchange glances, but stay silent. Gavin's been off lately. Edgy, nervous, like a rabbit being stalked by a fox. He looks like something you'd find in the bottom of your bin, not the posh, well-dressed man I'm used to seeing.

Hell, between the four of us, you'd think at least one of us could be a normal, functioning member of society. But no, we're all equally fucked in the head, it seems.

Bloody brilliant.

~

GAVIN DROPS us off at Hawke's place, a nice house he bought up in the hills. We decided to grab a bite to eat and Gavin begged off, saying he had something to do. He tore out of the driveway so fast I'm wondering if he's stable enough to be behind the wheel.

Whatever is bothering Gavin, that near accident made Hawke shoot him a look so dark, you'd think Gavin went and dropped a clanger on his living room carpet.

"That was strange," Adam quips, before heading straight for Hawke's liquor cabinet.

I sigh, rubbing the back of my neck. Telling Adam not to drink does absolutely nothing. If anything, it makes him more determined, even if he does appreciate our concern. Banging my head against a wall isn't something I enjoy.

"Let it go," I tell Adam, though it's more for Hawke's sake. "If Gavin has something he wants to discuss with us, he will."

Hawke laughs, "Yeah, because we're all the type to sit down and have a sharing of feelings moment."

"Fuck off, Evans." I flip him the finger, American style, and smile.

Hawke and I set to making lunch, or in this case, pulling out food Hawke's housekeeper has stocked in his fridge. Adam plops down on the sofa with his drink, singing along with the XM channel he selected.

Miley Cyrus, wonderful.

I glance at Hawke and catch his eye. "We need to hurry," I whisper. I have to get him back to the hotel before he's too pissed to move."

Hawke nods. "I have plans later. I can't babysit his ass tonight, but he can crash here if he has to."

"It's your call, mate."

Hawke's dealt with drunk Adam before. Hell, we all have. He shrugs and I take that as a yes.

"Right then. I'll eat then call a cab so you don't have to drive me back to the hotel. It's only a few minutes away."

He agrees and we dig in, serenaded by international rock star Adam Reynolds as he belts his way through an impressive rendition of Wrecking Ball.

Fuck, if the public only knew.

AN HOUR AND A HALF LATER, I collapse onto one of the leather recliners in my hotel suite, new contract in hand.

No more Lila.

I close my eyes, trying to imagine how great it will be to work and go on tour and not have to deal with her. No more of that stupid bloody show of hers, either. Thank god for that. I've avoided her as much as possible, but she still catches me with those damn cameras now and then. When she does, I try to curse a lot so the footage will be useless.

I chuckle at the thought, my eyes still closed.

A sharp rap on my door breaks my little fantasy.

Hell, it better not be Adam. I'd be shocked if Hawke brought him home already. We both live in the Chateau Marmont. Each of us for similar reasons. Neither of us particularly cares for L.A. and neither of us wants to settle down in a house alone. That would be admitting that we'll never get our girls back.

Pathetic? Maybe. I can't be bothered to give a shit.

Stupidly, I yank open the door without checking who it is and find myself face to face with Lila Griffin, surprisingly without her camera entourage.

"What the fuck do you want, Lila," I growl, feeling the hostility heat the blood in my veins like a match to gasoline.

"Why yes. I'd love to come in," she says acerbically, shoving past me into the suite.

I slam the door a little, okay maybe a lot, too loudly. "Why are you here, Lila?" I cross my arms over my chest and give her my most intimidating stare.

She stands her ground. I'm impressed. She's either brave or stupid. "You think you've gotten rid of me?" she snaps out. "You haven't. Not by a long shot. I'll make you sorry that you left my dad... that you left me."

So she knows we've jumped ship from her dad's record label. "Like I give a fuck what you do." I stalk over to where she's standing, hands on her hips and a hideous, twisted grimace on her face.

Towering over her, I make myself perfectly clear. "Get out. Don't ever come back. If you do, I'll make your life a living hell. Daddy isn't going to be there to control me anymore so you'd better hope I never see you again."

Lila's eyebrows shoot up in surprise. She quickly contains her reaction, her mouth spreading into a flat evil grin. "You fucked up, Dax. You could have had it all. My dad's power and influence, my show to make you a household name, me. Now I'll make sure you know what it feels like to be fucked over."

Who the hell does she think she is? She's a bloody nutter.

"Leave. Now." I walk back over to the foyer and open the door. "Or I'll have you arrested for trespassing."

Lila does as I ask, swinging her hips as she teeters on those ridiculous heels of hers. I step back when she attempts to touch my chest as she walks by, her hand swiping nothing but air.

That smug smile of hers disappears. "See you soon, Daxey." Then she walks out the door.

And out of my life.

I haven't felt this good since... let's just say it's been a long time.

～

Kate

"LET'S GO OUT!"

"Abby, I'm knackered. I don't want to go out," I whine.

My flatmate comes into the lounge and frowns. "You're leaving in two days. I'm not going to see you in forever. You need to get up and do something with me. We're going out and you're not saying no."

"Ugh!"

"Quit moping. For someone who's about to embark on the adventure of a lifetime, you're not excited enough and we're fixing that tonight." Abby is serious, crossing her arms and staring down at me.

"But Abby, I'm about to go through brutal training. I'm trying to catch up on my sleep before I go." The whinging sound of my voice doesn't escape me.

She makes a dismissive noise. "Whatever. This is our last chance, sister. You've slept enough for the next four months. C'mon. Get showered and dressed. You look awful."

Abby grabs my hands and pulls me up off the sofa. "I'm going through a rough patch, Abby. You're not a nice friend. You should be spoiling me while you have the chance. Let me eat ice cream and watch the telly all day." I stick my lip out, pouting. Not that she knows the extent of my troubles. All she knows is that Logan and I broke up, she doesn't know how badly he reacted.

Is every bloke a complete and total bastard?

"You can't eat ice cream and watch T.V. all day, you're an Olympic athlete. You need to be in peak form. Now it's time to party. You broke up with a boyfriend who you say you didn't think you loved and had been acting like an ass so there's no point in moping. No more excuses. Go get ready."

She shoves me bodily into the bathroom and pulls the door shut behind me. Damn, she's stronger than she looks. And with her psychology degree, she's always analyzing my moods. It's like I can't have a bad day without her wanting to dive into why I'm sad and what happened to cause it.

Okay, so maybe I've had a lot of bad days over the last few years, but Christ, I've only just begun to stop obsessing over everything—Wes, Logan, my career, Dax. The last thing I need is Abby trying to crack into my head.

It's not like she hasn't been hiding something herself. Dodgy phone calls and unexplained absences. The only reason I don't ask is because I don't want her to turn the tables on me. And I'm afraid it might have something to do with Hawke, and that hits a little too close to home.

"I hate you!" I call out to the closed door as I strip and get into the shower.

"You love me!" she yells back.

Yeah, I do. Once I leave and don't have her there to keep me sane, I have no idea what I'll do.

~

"ADMIT IT, THIS IS FUN," Abby says loudly over the pulsing music of the club.

"It is," I agree. Abby decided we needed to dance, so she dragged me out to Phoenix, a popular club off Wilshire Boulevard.

"Another?" she asks, pointing at her empty glass. I look down and see that mine is empty as well.

I shrug. "Sure! But two is my limit." No way will I ever end up drunk again.

By the time we maneuver through the thick crowd to the bar and back over to the dance floor, we're both feeling the effects of the potent cocktails. Grinning, we spin around, swaying to the thumping bass. People our age surround us, all looking to get lost in the music.

I'm about to tell Abby that she's brilliant and this was a great idea when suddenly there's a commotion on the other side of the dance floor. Two bright spotlights stand out in the dim lighting of the massive room, creating a halo of light that appears to be following someone through the crowd.

"Cameras," Abby shouts in my ear. She takes one last look before continuing to dance. "It's Hollywood, I guess it's no surprise."

I nod, agreeing completely, yet not comfortable enough to lose myself again. My last encounter with cameras was that horrific day at UCLA during our final game of the season. Dax went crazy, punched a couple of security guards, and ended up arrested.

Then he broke up with me.

The bright lights come closer to where we're dancing. Well, Abby is dancing. I'm standing paralyzed—watching the cameras move towards us while an ominous feeling takes root in my stomach, gnawing and tearing at my insides. The group comes within view and the bottom drops out.

"Is that—?" Abby has stopped dancing again and is standing next to me as the horror plays out.

"Lila," I choke out. "Yes."

Lila Griffin and her reality show crew in the flesh. I haven't seen her since the day Dax helped me move out of our dorm room.

Now *she's* with Dax. At least, I think she is. He hasn't been on her show lately, not that I would watch that drivel. I've been told he's not been on recently. Okay fine, I might read the summaries on a gossip site. It's not a big deal. Everyone does it.

Not everyone has shagged the man in question, however.

"Don't let her get to you," Abby says, her arm sliding over my shoulders like a security blanket.

"I'm fine," I say so unconvincingly that I know Abby doesn't believe a single word.

"Let's go. I'm pretty tired." Abby reaches for my hand, but I can't move. I can't do anything. All I can do is think about Dax's hands being all over Lila's body. Despair hits me like a freight train, fast and hard. Seeing her here brings back every feeling I've tried to deny for the last four damn years.

Jealousy, hurt, betrayal, sorrow, anger... and worst of all, I feel completely and totally inadequate. Olympics or no, I'll never compare to Lila.

"Oh my god! Kate?"

No. No, no, no.

"Kate," Abby hisses, "let's get out of here." She tugs harder on my hand. I must be a sadist because I don't move an inch.

Suddenly, the small circle of lights grows to include Abby and me. I'm face to face with Lila Griffin, my slutty first-year flatmate from hell and current girlfriend to *my* soul mate.

"It is you!" Lila spreads her arms and pulls me into what has to be the most insincere hug I've ever experienced. She steps back, that familiar evil spark in her eyes. "It's been so long. How are you?"

The dark lens of a camera is less than three feet from my face. The reality of my situation smacks me over the head.

I'm being filmed for Lila's show. The show she has with her boyfriend Dax. He's going to see this.

"Ummmm, I'm great. Brilliant. It's good to see you." I glance over at Abby who seems to be itching to slap Lila right across her smug face if the scowl she's sporting means anything.

"That's so awesome! I can't believe you're here! I figured you'd have left L.A. by now. You know, to go back to that little town you grew up in."

Nice dig on my poor upbringing. "No. I'm still here—"

"Great!" She interrupts me before I can tell her what I really think of her or how I made the Olympic footy team. "Well, I gotta run. Daxey is waiting for me."

My mouth falls open as Lila leans in to air kiss both of my cheeks. Before I know it, she's gone, her bizarre little entourage trailing behind.

"I hate her so much," Abby says.

Me? I'm speechless. There is literally nothing I can say to make anything that just happened seem less humiliating than it is. Dax will see that. He'll think I'm a total failure. A pathetic waste of space.

They'll probably watch it together and have a laugh.

Abby manages to maneuver me outside and into a cab before the tears start pouring down my face.

17

D^{ax}

"WHEN DID THIS TAKE PLACE?" I bark into my mobile, my breath coming out in misty puffs.

"Dax, are you coming inside?" My mum is staring at me from the door of the conservatory with a concerned expression on her face. Her arms are wrapped around her middle to stave off the bitter cold.

"Hold on." I cover the mouthpiece of my mobile. "Mum, you go on in. I'm buying it for you and dad. It only matters if you two like the house, not me."

She nods, but the knot between her brows lets me know she's not happy. I rub my forehead, the stress so overwhelming I'm on the verge of losing my mind.

"Zane," I bark at my assistant. I hired the eager kid from the gym in L.A. "When was the bloody thing filmed?" The urge to chuck my mobile into the fancy koi pond is nearly overwhelming.

He's a great assistant, has been for a few years now. Unfortunately, he does take the brunt of my frustrations.

"Two months ago."

Clenching my jaw, I attempt to calm down. It's not Zane's fault that Lila is a psychotic bitch. It's not his fault she somehow found Kate at an L.A. nightclub and filmed it for her reality show. It's definitely not his fault that I found out about it airing while I'm over five thousand miles away in London, spending the holidays buying a house for my parents so they can get away from the dangers of Hackney. It took me two years to convince them to move, I had to jump on the chance to get them out of there as soon as they agreed to it.

A cold winter wind whips under my fleece, causing a shiver to wrack my body. The large back garden is laid out beautifully, with a stonework courtyard, bushes that are probably gorgeous in spring when they're blooming, and of course, a pretentious little koi pond complete with working waterfall.

"Get me a meeting with Rachel as soon as I'm back in town."

"You got it."

"Make sure one of the solicitors I have on retainer is there as well."

"Solicitor?"

"Lawyer, whatever you call it," I snap, taking out my irritation on my assistant.

"No problem. Did you want Mr. Evans present for the meeting?" Zach asks, continuing as if nothing happened. I like that about him. He doesn't take my mood personally.

"No. Not Ross. Get it set up and text me the time and date."

I hang up the call and tilt my head back to look at the grey English sky. Never in my life did I think I'd miss the chilly, rainy weather of London or any winter season for that matter, but after spending years in the constant L.A. sunshine, I find that I do.

I put together a plan in my head to take down Lila and her

crazy train. She's fucked with me for years, but fucking with Kate? She'll regret she ever met me.

Smiling, I go back inside the posh country home, joining my parents and their estate agent as they take the tour. I nod when the different amenities are pointed out, but I'm not listening. I'm figuring out exactly how I'm going to ruin Lila and her quest to be the next Kim Kardashian.

By the time I get done with her, Lila Griffin is going to wish she never heard of Dax Davies. Now, to let off some of this anger.

I pick up the phone, and dial Shaun.

"Oi! Little brother, how's it been?"

Shaun crosses the empty expanse of the huge warehouse that houses our family business.

"Fuck me! Are you bloody smiling?" My brother Shaun has smiled approximately four times since we were kids. It's a rare occurrence to say the least.

He doesn't even argue with me. He walks over, grabs my shoulders, and pulls me into a hug. Once he releases me, he smacks my arm gently. "Loosen up, Dax. You're wound tighter than a spring."

"Yeah, well, I'm under a lot of stress. So sue me."

Shaun holds up his hands. "Oi! Don't take it out on me unless you want to do it in there." He nods towards the cage that sits in the center of the room.

It's been a while since I've had a good brawl. It would make me feel better.

"Only if we wear padded gloves. I can't break my hands. We're recording when I get back to the States."

Shaun grins. "Still a pussy I see."

"Leave your brother alone, Shaun!"

I spin to see who has the guts to yell at Shaun and live to tell about it. A tiny girl with long, black hair bounces over to Shaun's side. He wraps her up in his arms and drops a sweet kiss on her head.

"What? Have I landed in another dimension? Are you having a laugh?"

Shaun? With a girl? One girl?

The two of them smile, my brother looking down at her like she hung the bloody moon. She's no better. Gazing up at Shaun as if he's some kind of prize.

As I stare at the girl, I realize she's familiar. "I know you."

Her face reddens and her eyes drop to the floor. Shaun steps forward, subtly pushing her behind his body.

"Leave it be," he warns, his tone indicating that it isn't up for discussion.

Ah. There it is. This is the Shaun I know.

"Alright then. I'm Dax." I wave at the girl who seems to have recovered her composure.

"Tasha, nice to see you," she says in a lovely voice.

I frown. I know that I've met her before. If I could only remember.

Shaun takes her hand, turning her away from me. "Tash, we're going in the cage. Can you grab Dax some gear and lay it out in the changing room, love?"

Tasha nods and hurries off.

I stare at my brother open-mouthed.

"What?" he asks. "It's not that odd."

"Uh, yeah it is, mate. You, *in love*. It's..." I struggle for the right words. "It's bloody mind blowing."

"Fuck off. Get dressed and get your arse in the cage, rock star. I'm gonna beat you silly."

I laugh. "Just like old times then."

Only it's not the same. Everything in Hackney is different. Mum, dad, Shaun, me. It's my home, only it's not. As I'm getting changed into my gear I realize what the problem is. It's Kate. She's not here. That's why it doesn't feel right. Without her, Hackney holds no fond memories for me. Nothing here will ever feel right again.

"C'mon ya nancy! Let's see what ya can do!" My dad's loud bellow shakes me from my moping.

Great. It really will be like old times. I'll get my ass beaten, dad will tell me how much I suck, and I can go back to being alone and miserable.

Sounds about right.

Kate

"GREAT WORK, CAMPBELL."

Chelsea Lewis, my new coach for the U.K. Olympic team, high fives me after I make seven out of ten of my practice free kicks.

"Brecken!" Coach yells out at our keeper, "you need to work on your left. Campbell figured your weakness in two kicks."

The redheaded keeper from Scotland waves in agreement. "Aye, Coach. I'll dae better next time."

I head inside of the training facility in Manchester, where our team is based.

"Ready for tomorrow?" I ask Colleen, a peppy blonde girl from Ireland.

"Oi'm excited we're startin' the matches," she chuckles, slamming her locker door shut.

I smile. Sometimes I think I need a translator for all of the different dialects we have on the team. We're all speaking English, but it doesn't always feel that way.

"New Zealand's a long way away. I hope there's a good in flight movie," I joke.

Colleen laughs out loud. "Dare better be. Oi git bored easily."

Grinning back, I join her, laughing until my cheeks hurt. Finally, I belong somewhere. Here, with these women, I'm welcomed with open arms. We all have the same love of the game, having dedicated most of our lives to excelling at it. Now we have the chance to show the world that we aren't a bunch of mannish munters.

The competition is fierce, but it feels unbelievable, like I'm alive and doing something incredible—for myself and for my country. Unfortunately, Logan disagreed. I think back to the conversation we had before I left.

"You should be free to see other people while I'm gone, Logan. It wouldn't be fair to expect you to wait for me."

Logan's steel-grey eyes pin me in place, the emotions in them indiscernible. "I thought you wanted me to go with you." Still, his eyes reveal nothing, not hurt, not anger, not anything.

"You can't just quit your job and follow me around the world. It's not right and it's not going to happen, Logan."

He frowns, those usually loving eyes turning hard. "What do you mean it's not going to happen? You don't want me to come with you? Is that it?"

Logan's tone is getting harsher and louder. A few people in the restaurant have glanced over at us. I should have done this in private, but I didn't want to be stuck having a four-hour weepy goodbye with tears and begging and whatever.

"Logan," I hiss under my breath, "calm down. For the first time in my life, I'm doing something for me. To make myself happy. I can't worry about your happiness as well. That sounds selfish, but it's true. I need to do this alone."

"Selfish?" He shouts. "It's not just selfish. You think you're better than me, is that it?"

"Shhhhh, please. You're making a scene." Now other patrons have

*turned their entire bodies in our direction to watch the show—and
lucky me, I'm the star.*

"*Making a scene? You know what, Kate... I've been waiting patiently
for you to get over yourself and this narcissistic streak you have. Go. Go
to the Olympics and worship yourself in the mirror everyday since you
love yourself so much.*" *He stands up, his cheeks red and his eyes glassy.
He tosses a few bills down on the table. "I'm out of here."*

*Choking back tears, I focus on breathing in and out steadily. He's
wrong. So wrong. I'm not doing this because I love myself. I'm doing it
because I need a reason not to hate myself.*

*I've got to prove to myself that I was good enough for Dax Davies
and still am. That I'm not a nobody from Hackney who hasn't done a
single useful thing with her life.*

MY MOBILE RINGS from somewhere in the hotel room, the sounds
of Katy Perry belting out a line about California Gurls pulling me
from a deep slumber.

After faltering for a moment, I find the offending device in my
luggage.

"'Lo?" My voice is thick with sleep.

"Have you seen the news?"

"Abby?"

"Kate," she huffs impatiently, "have you seen it yet?"

"Seen what?" I yawn, climbing back into bed and burrowing
under the duvet. January in Sweden isn't cold, it's downright
arctic.

"Oh my god, you haven't!"

"Abby, it's three in the morning," I complain. "I've got a game
tomorrow... sorry, today, and need to be rested."

"It can't wait, so get up and turn your computer on," she
demands.

Grumbling, I toss back the covers and shiver violently. "I hate you right now. It's below freezing out and you've got me walking around my room nearly starkers, hunting for my laptop."

"Put on a sweater and suck it up," she laughs. "You'll thank me when you see what I'm talking about."

"Fine." I open my laptop and boot up the computer. "What do I do?" I ask once my search engine is open.

"Go to *E! Online*."

"Abby..." I warn, not liking where this conversation is headed.

"Trust me. Would I want to psychologically scar you?"

Of course she wouldn't, she's getting her doctorate in psychology so she can be a counselor. "No, you wouldn't." I type in the web address. When the front page comes up, I gasp.

"Told you. Enjoy it, Kate. You deserve to savor every single word. Love you!" She hangs up before I can respond.

Another full body shudder has me convulsing from the cold. I scoop up the laptop and climb into bed with it.

I skim the article, my mouth gaping in disbelief. I have to read it two more times before it sinks in.

Dax Davies Speaks Out

Notoriously tight-lipped guitarist for the multi-platinum *Sphere or Irony*, released a statement today via his public relations manager. In it, he accuses socialite Lila Griffin, of using her father's position as producer for the band's first three albums as a reason to In it, he alleges that she manipulated events, photographs, and film clips from her television show in order to portray them as a couple, when that has never been the case.

The statement from Rachel Whatley at Accessible P.R. read as follows.

OVER THE COURSE of the last four years, Ms. Lila Griffin has subjected Mr. Davies to unwelcome advances, telling people that they were a couple and following him to various places including on tour, at recording sessions, and at public events.

In spite of being asked multiple times to cease her behavior, Ms. Griffin continued to harass Mr. Davies. Her father, Sebastian Griffin, the producer of Mr. Davies' last three albums, used his position of power to force my client to tolerate the actions of Ms. Griffin unless he wanted to face severe financial consequences including the termination of Sphere of Irony's contract with Underground Records.

Mr. Davies wants his fans and the public to know that despite what they see on Ms. Griffin's television show, they are not, nor ever were together romantically. It has taken until now for Mr. Davies to speak publically because with the completion of their latest album, the band has fulfilled their contract with Underground Records and are not resigning with the label.

Mr. Davies' legal team will be filing lawsuits in Los Angeles county superior court against Ms. Lila Griffin, Mr. Sebastian Griffin, and Underground Records for fraudulent misrepresentation, negligent misrepresentation, and coercion under threat of the loss of Mr. Davies' record contract. Their actions in falsely portraying a relationship between Mr. Davies and Ms. Griffin has caused Mr. Davies and his friends and family to suffer duress.

Mr. Davies hopes that this statement clears up any confusion or misunderstandings anyone may have as to the nature of his relationship with Ms. Griffin. He apologizes to anyone who may have been hurt by the rumors perpetuated by Ms. Griffin. Any further questions can be directed to my office at Rachel_whatley@accessiblepr.com. Thank you.

I SWALLOW past the lump that has formed high up in my throat. All of it was fake. Dax was never with Lila. In fact, he's suing her and her father for falsifying it all and forcing him to go along with it.

While my heart is soaring from this knowledge, it brings up more questions. One old question, actually.

If he wasn't with Lila, why did Dax break up with me?

I close the laptop and sink under the covers. Everything I thought was true turned out to be a lie. Dax didn't shag my horrid, disgusting flatmate. He didn't dump me because he was screwing her on the side and preferred her to me. My mind is racing with all of the thoughts and questions I have and will probably never get answered.

The only thing I know for sure is that I won't be getting any more sleep tonight.

DAX

"SHIT," I mutter to myself as I check the bedroom of my hotel suite for a fourth time.

Nope. My book still isn't there. I need my fucking composition book. Every single song I've written in the past six months is in there and it up and disappeared on me.

I have my mobile in my hand to ring up Adam when I remember that he's been in fucking rehab for the last month.

"Bastard!"

Right, think Davies. Where were you the last time you wrote? Obviously not at Adam's since he's been in some posh resort where celebrities go to dry out.

Got it!

My finger swipes over the tiny screen until I bring up the correct contact. I push send and wait on edge while the phone connects. Feeling a little wobbly, I drop onto the bed as it rings.

"Dax! You calling about Lila? Crazy bitch."

My grip on the phone tightens. "No, Hawke. I don't want to discuss that psychotic nutter."

Soon after the lawsuit was filed, Lila went officially mental. She was arrested after getting into an altercation in a popular L.A. club and refused to leave the premises. The police found several illegal and prescription drugs on her and in her car.

Of course, having a powerful dad, she was released within the hour. Last I heard, she was in mandatory rehab to stay out of jail. Being on loads of drugs would certainly explain a lot of her behavior, but I honestly think she was just obsessed with me. Plain and simple.

"Okay, okay. We don't have to talk about her." He chuckles What's up?"

"Hawke, you haven't seen my notebook have you? I might have left it at your place last week—"

"Hold on. Let me go down to the studio." Muffled sounds of the phone being carried crackle in my ear. Hawke's house has a soundproof room in the basement that we use when we're messing around trying to get our songs right. We've only gotten together the one time since Adam's been gone. It's pretty useless without your lead singer and main songwriter.

"Is it that black and grey book you always have with you? The one with the guitar on front?" he asks, knowing damn well that's the one. "Because it's here."

"Yeah. Thank god. I was going mental thinking I had lost it. A few of Adam's lyrics are in there. We wouldn't want anyone to get their hands on it."

My frantic pulse begins to slow. I wipe my sweaty palms off on my jeans. Hawke doesn't need to know that there's a song in there that I wrote about Kate. About us actually. Our journey. Needless to say, it's not a very uplifting song.

"Can't have that. Wouldn't want some other band winning a Grammy for our work," he says in an amused tone.

"No."

"So," Hawke says, "We're all going to the Olympics. Wild, isn't it?"

I sit up straight at this piece of news.

"What? What are you talking about?" I practically shout.

"Holy... relax man. We all got the same email, or at least Zane did. I thought he would have told you about it."

My hand grips the phone so tight that my knuckles begin to ache. "When did you get it?"

"Yesterday."

"Well fuck, Hawke. No I haven't heard about it yet. Hell, it's only been twelve hours. Zane doesn't usually start work until noon and it's only just eleven."

"Oh, okay. See? He was going to tell you." Hawke doesn't elaborate which in turn, begins to make me aggravated.

"Why don't you tell me what it said, Hawke?" I roll my eyes glad he can't see me. I swear, sometimes I wonder what goes on in that tattooed brain of his.

"Sure. So, because the Olympics are in London this year, and I guess because you and Adam are such big *stars*..." I laugh at the exaggerated way he says stars. "The committee invited us to perform for some big event. I can't remember exactly what or where we're playing. Sorry."

"Don't worry about it. I'll check the email. Did Ross already approve it?" I think about going back so soon after I was just in London buying my parents their house. It doesn't annoy me to go again. In fact, getting out of L.A. is probably a good thing. Away from Kate and the daily distraction of knowing she's only a few miles away and I can't do anything about it.

"I'm pretty sure. I mean, who wouldn't want to perform at the Olympics?" I can hear Hawke's doorbell ring through the phone. "Hey Dax. I gotta go. You want me to bring by the book? I'm headed out in a little while."

"Nah. Just pop it in your letterbox and I'll come round on the Ducati. I'm going to go out. I need a long ride to clear my head."

"Whatever you want. I'll stick it in there now." I hear a giggling female voice and muffled talking. "Catch ya later."

The call disconnects. I drop back on the bed, putting my arms behind my head. That's a big deal, singing at the Olympics in my hometown. The urge to ring Adam strikes me again before I remember he's tucked away.

Fuck that. He has visiting hours. I'll go there and see him. Ross told us to leave him be and let him get better but I need my best mate.

I grab the keys to the Ducati, shrug on my leather jacket, and pull the door shut behind me.

Kate

BEING BACK in London feels weird. It's as if I never really lived here and my entire childhood was only a fuzzy dream. Thankfully, I don't have to go back to Hackney. Too many memories, good and bad.

My mum and dad came to the flat I share with two other teammates so we can go out to dinner. Opening ceremonies are in a little over two weeks, so we won't see much of each other unless I catch them at one of my games. They wanted tickets to every single one.

"Kate, we have to get going. Traffic is terrible. There's been an accident on the A406 and it will take all night if we don't leave now." My dad is fiddling with his car keys while watching the traffic on the news.

"Dad, we just got back from dinner, are you sure you don't want to stay a while?" My mum and I exchange worried glances. She mouths *"your father is nervous about your thing tomorrow"* while dad's gaze is firmly fixed on the telly.

Ahhhh, that explains his odd behavior all night. I walk over and put a hand on my dad's shoulder. "Dad, I'll be fine. I know it's scary. Hell, I'll admit I'm scared out of my wits. I haven't a clue why they chose me, but they did and Coach said it's not only good exposure for the team but that it's a chance of a lifetime. Plus, it's just... it's something I need to do for myself, yeah?"

My dad turns and pulls me into a hug. I sink into it, missing the warm, comforting scent of him, the loving contact, missing my family. When he pulls back, there are tears shimmering in his green eyes. "I'm so proud of you, love. So very proud. This is more than I ever dreamed of when you were just a tyke in wee little footy boots running around the pitch."

He smiles, his face older than the last time I saw him, the creases a little deeper, the grey on his temples a little more pronounced, but my dad is still the same man I remember. Caring, handsome but a little rough around the edges, and the best man I've ever known.

"Thanks dad." My voice catches and even I have to wipe away a tear or two.

"Love, we really should go," my mum says, pulling me in for her own embrace. After a moment, she releases me, patting my cheeks gently as she smiles. "Good luck. We'll see you at your first game."

"I love you both. Thanks for helping me get here. I know it's been hard with me in the States—"

"Nonsense, love. We missed you, yes, but it was worth the sacrifice to see the woman you've become." Mum squeezes my hand. "Come Charles," she says to my dad. "Kate needs her beauty sleep for her big day."

A few more quick goodbyes and they're gone, leaving me in the quiet flat alone. Both of my flatmates are out for the evening. They aren't the ones with a terrifying photo shoot tomorrow. One that might change everything. It's scary, but I have to do it for me.

It takes forever to fall asleep, what with me worrying about bags under my eyes and the possibility of waking up with an enormous spot on my chin or some other ridiculous ailment. Yet at some point, I must drift off, because the next thing I know, it's morning and I'm climbing into the backseat of a posh car sent over by *Sports Illustrated* to pick me up at the flat.

"How was it?" Rose, one of our keepers asks as we stretch on the pitch the next day.

"Odd." I bend at the waist, wrapping my hands around my ankles as I press my nose into my knees. "Lots and lots of standing around. Honestly," I sit on the grass to stretch each hamstring individually, "I felt ridiculous. Posing and what not. At this point, I'm hoping they make me look less stupid than I felt."

Rose shushes me. "Don't be daft. You're bloody gorgeous. Of course you're not going to look stupid. If anything, you'll have hordes of blokes following you around drooling like dogs once that issue is released." She pulls back a leg, stretching her quad. "Come to think of it, when does it come out?"

I have to shade my eyes to look up at Rose. The bright sunlight behind her makes her blonde hair glow like a halo around her cherubic face. "Three days before the opening ceremony." The thought of it gnaws at my stomach, making me a little queasy. "For," I make air quotes, "*Maximum impact* they said at the shoot. There's even a big reveal party I have to go to."

Rose giggles, "What they meant by maximum impact was maximum money lining their pockets."

I laugh with her. "Exactly."

Coach calls us over for our pre-practice pep talk.

Before I get up, Rose leans in. "Hey. I want you to know, if anyone gives you any trouble over the magazine, we all have your back. The whole team."

It takes a lot to keep from choking up, but I manage to keep my voice steady. "Thanks, Rose. That means a lot to me."

She nods and we trot over to meet up with our teammates. Once Coach Lewis starts discussing strategies and formations, any worries I had are gone. I'm part of a team. My burden is everyone's burden, that's how it works. We're a family.

I catch my teammates' eyes while we huddle and I see it in each of their steady gazes—they're behind me one hundred percent.

For the first time in a long time, I feel as if I've accomplished something to be proud of. I'm no longer Kate Campbell, insecure nobody. I'm Kate Campbell, member of the Great Britain Olympic Football team and I deserve to be here.

Coach wraps up her speech, high fiving everyone as we run out onto the pitch. I look up at the bright summer sky, blue as the Caribbean Sea without a single cloud in sight, and smile.

Dax

"What kind of bloody party is this, anyway?" I grumble from the back seat of the hire car that is bringing us to our gig.

"Who cares?" Adam says. "We got free tickets to the Olympics for doing this. Does it matter what it is?"

Christ. I almost like pre-rehab Adam better. Now that he's sober, he's all enlightened or some shit. It's irritating. Especially when I'm in a crap mood. Which I am all the time now that I've found out Kate is competing for the women's football team. Plus, he won't admit it, but Adam had to have known that before we agreed to perform. Which has me even more aggravated—if that's even possible.

"I'm excited," Gavin says cheerily. For once, the haunted look he's been sporting for the past few months has faded. He looks healthier since we landed at Heathrow a few days ago. "I love *Sports Illustrated*. They do great features on surfing all the time."

"Shut up," Hawke snaps playfully. "You read it for all the pictures of half-naked men. We're not stupid."

Gavin laughs. "Well, there is that." He bumps Hawkes shoulder. "You read it for the swimsuit issue, so you're not any better than me."

I roll my eyes as they have a laugh. Whatever. The three of them are too much for me to take right now. They're all excited to be here and I'm the pissy bloke who wants to put his boot up someone's arse.

The car glides to a stop in the back of some posh new restaurant near King's Cross. Rachel had to stay back in Los Angeles, so she has one of her coworkers traveling with us. He hops out of the front and meets with the rep for *SI* at the back door.

"Okay guys. Let's go in." Cole, Rachel's replacement, opens our car door, herding us inside the building.

The *SI* rep introduces himself. "I'm Scott Kramer, one of the public relations liaisons for the Olympics. We're really glad you guys agreed to play tonight."

"What exactly is this party?" I ask. When Scott's face registers fear and he takes a step back, I realize I may have sounded a bit more intimidating than I intended.

"Ummmm," he stammers a second trying to squelch his reaction to my intimidating demeanor. "Well, we're unveiling our 2012 Olympic Issue tonight. The cover model is from London and is competing for the U.K. in the games, so we wanted a performance from a band that has roots in the area." He gestures towards Adam and myself.

"And," Cole interjects, "most of the IOC will in attendance, as will the London organizers of the games, and the mayor."

"IOC?" Adam asks.

"International Olympic Committee," Scott fills in for him.

"So what you're saying is that this is a party for all of the Olympic VIPs and what not?" I ask, trying to sound less threatening this time.

Scott smiles. "Exactly." He opens up the door to a very nice private dining room. "Your instruments are ready in the main room. You can wait here while we introduce you. It shouldn't be long. A server will be around to see if you need anything before you go on."

"I'm going with Scott to mingle with the 'VIPs'," Cole says, smiling. "Text me if you need anything, but like he said, your wait will be short. You play, there will be a few speeches, the reveal, food and drinks, then done."

We nod and agree and the two of them are gone.

"Bloody hell." I collapse into a nearby chair, rubbing my forehead. "I didn't know we were playing for the entire Olympic Committee in a tiny bloody restaurant with them all crammed up close. This is a huge deal."

Adam grins. "Yep. I can't wait. I'd love to pick the brains of the people who make the Olympics a reality. That's really impressive."

Jesus. Man up, Davies. You've played stadiums with tens of thousands of people. You can do this.

A man brings us all water and asks if we need anything. Adam orders a PG Tips with honey. The rest of us stick with the water.

"Ready?" Scott pokes his head in, his smile somewhat nervous. I note a light sheen of sweat on his forehead.

Hmph. Seems I'm not the only one who's nervous tonight. Of course, he'll probably be made redundant if this doesn't go well.

Adam puts down his tea and stands up. "Let's go."

We're lead down a short hall into a much larger dining area. The end nearest us is set up with a fairly large stage, our instruments in their usual spots.

Adam hops right up on stage and grabs the microphone. He immediately starts working the crowd, chatting on about the games, London, and anything he can think of while we take our places. Like I've said, when Adam is performing, he's bloody brilliant. The audience is eating it up.

He shrugs on his own guitar and waits for Hawke to start us off. It's our first time playing this song in public, one Adam wrote in rehab. He hasn't outright said, but it's clearly written for Ellie. In my opinion, it's the best thing he's ever written.

Hawke signals to start and the place fills with sound. The guitars, the drums, Adam's clear voice—it's perfect. At the end of the first song, I've relaxed enough to unkink the knots in my back. After the second song, I'm starting to have a good time. By the time we finish our set I can't stop grinning. This is the most fun I've had in a long time.

We're shuttled back to the small room to clean up and get a quick drink before Cole herds us back into the party.

"They're doing the unveiling now," he tells us right before ditching us to suck up to more VIPs.

The people who have surrounded us to chat turn their attention to the stage when Scott takes the mic.

"Thank you all for being here." Scott looks out over the crowd, exuding appeal. Not in the naturally captivating way Adam works an audience. Scott is less genuine, more rehearsed. He goes on and on thanking various people and organizations, causing me to check the time more than once.

Just as people become restless, a massive screen drops behind Scott on the stage. The lights dim and Scott begins his introduction.

"I'd like to unveil our 2012 Olympic Issue, featuring Women's Soccer, I mean Football player, Katherine Campbell of team Great Britain."

I stagger in shock and my hand clenches around my drink. I'm frozen in place as Kate, *my Kate*, appears on a twelve-foot screen wearing only a teeny tiny scrap of a bikini with the Union Jack printed on it.

When the real-life Kate walks out on the stage in a low-cut, too-short red dress, waving and smiling for the cheers of the audience, I nearly lose it.

I grab the back of Adam's neck, pressing my fingers down tight.

"Ow! Sod off!" He tries to shake me off but I hold on.

"Did you know about this?" I hiss under my breath.

"What? No! How would I know? They've kept the bloody cover a secret! No one knew who was on it, just that it was an Olympic athlete."

"Fuck!" I release his neck, only to fist my hands at my sides. My eyes turn back to Kate, who is finished with her speech already and is making her way down the stairs and into the crowd.

Scott holds out a hand to keep her from tumbling in her heels. The insane urge to rip his arm off and beat him with it roars through me. Kate has always been beautiful, gorgeous even. But she's always had a shyness about her, an insecurity that held her back from reaching her full potential.

Tonight, I see none of that. All I see is an absolutely stunning young woman, confident and successful and proud of her accomplishments. That confidence is dead sexy and every guy in here is thinking the same thing.

The thought of all these men mentally undressing her—fuck, they didn't even have to do it mentally with a twelve foot picture of her stripped down to nothing. It makes me want to wrap her up in my coat and drag her out of here so no one else can touch what's mine.

She's not yours, Davies. Hasn't been for years.

And doesn't that just make it worse.

"She must know we're here, mate," Adam says, tearing me away from my gawking. "She had to have watched us perform."

He's right. She knows we're here. Should I go over to her? I'm at a loss as to what to do next.

Adam shoves me forward. "Right, we're going to chat her up. I haven't seen her in ages."

"But—?"

My argument is short-lived when I see that Gavin and Hawke have already approached Kate and are exchanging hugs and kisses. My body goes rigid as their hands touch her bare skin.

Adam leans in to speak quietly in my ear. "Calm down, big guy. I can practically see the smoke coming out of your ears." He pats my back and continues pushing me along.

Kate is smiling at Gavin and Hawke, but it's strained. She's uncomfortable. This is supposed to be one of her proudest moments, a crowning achievement in her life, and I've gone and messed it up by existing.

Then those clear, green eyes meet mine and I no longer care —I don't care who's here or what the right thing is that I'm supposed to be doing, all I care about is her.

"Dax." My name comes out on a quick breath. That raspy voice of hers still does things to me. The memories send blood rushing south.

"Kate." The rest of the room fades away, like one of those cheesy Hollywood films. Until, that is, a swaggering bloke comes up, slides an arm around Kate's waist, and introduces himself.

"Hi, I'm Blake Marshall, Miss Campbell's date."

That's the last straw. I lose it. The anger, the frustration, a lifetime of denying any of my true feelings, it all comes pouring out in one lightning fast movement.

My hands find the lapels of Blake Marshall's jacket and I have him shoved against the nearest wall, snarling in his face, before anyone can react.

"Take your hands off of her, mate. Unless you want to lose them in an incredibly painful manner."

"Dax, stop it!" Kate is futilely trying to pull me off of her date, while Adam and Gavin successfully manage to separate me from the tall, dark-haired man.

"Calm down, Dax," Adam growls in my ear. "You're making a scene."

"I don't fucking care. He's touching my—" The harsh untruth of my outburst stops me cold. She's not mine. I seem to keep forgetting that bit.

My clenched fists relax, allowing Blake to stand on his own two feet. "Christ, Kate. Forget any more favors after that..." he snarls, shooting an appalled sneer my way, "disgusting display."

"Fine, Blake. It wasn't my idea for you to come here with me. Go." Kate shoos *Blake* away with a toss of her hair over her shoulder.

"Fucking hell. It was a setup and not a real date?" I ask.

Kate turns her furious gaze onto me. "Why hello, Dax. Nice to see you. How have you been?" she hisses so sarcastically I actually flinch. "Yes it was a bloody setup. Blake is on the Men's Football team and the committee thought it would look good for us to come together."

"Okay, so I could have handled myself better," I admit.

Kate's mouth drops open but no sound emerges. Her face begins to turn an interesting shade of crimson while the four of us look on.

Blessedly, Gavin breaks the silence. "Let's move to the back room. People are staring." He takes Kate's hand and nods to Adam who then grabs my shoulders. Adam spins me around, giving me a hard shove down the hall to once again end up in the smaller room.

The door slams shut. I glance back to see that Gavin and Adam have ditched us. We're alone.

Kate has her back to me, the gentle curve of her spine torqued into a straight line. I take a step closer, close enough to see that her hands are shaking at her sides. Kate's shoulders are shifting up and down with each rapid, shallow breath she takes.

The tension in the air is so thick, I can feel it vibrating, wrapping around my body and worming it's way into my empty heart.

It swells with emotion, overflowing after years of forcing it to remain hollow.

When Kate turns to face me, I move on instinct. Stepping forward I take her beautiful face in my hands and lower my mouth to hers.

Okay, so I wasn't thinking. The kiss could have gone horribly wrong, with Kate getting angry and slapping me across the face. She had every right to do just that.

She doesn't. Instead, she sinks into it, her body relaxing against mine as she opens up to me. Pure animal need overtakes my brain, the desire to make her mine so overwhelming I can hardly think straight. My hands go to her backside, pulling her hips against me as I devour her mouth.

Kate is like a live wire, opening those sweet lips so I can taste every bit of her with each sweep of my tongue. A soft moan escapes from her throat. It vibrates though me, igniting a primitive fire deep inside. I growl, leaving her mouth to lick and suck my way down her neck. When I reach the tender spot where her neck meets her shoulder and give it a sharp bite, Kate gasps and pulls away.

My eyes find the dark red mark I left behind and a rush of pride fills me. Now everyone will know she's mine.

"Dax," she pants, her breath heavy and erratic. She's gorgeous—her hair mussed from my hands, her lips swollen and red, her cheeks flushed with desire. But those green eyes, they look hesitant, sad. The sight sends a spike of fear into my chest.

"Kate, no. Please, don't make me stop. I—"

Do it Davies, man up and tell her. Shit, here goes.

"I love you, Kate. I haven't stopped loving you since we became friends in school. Just, don't leave."

"I-I'm not leaving," she whispers. "I have to go back to the party."

"Can we meet after? To talk?" Kate looks wary. I can't let her go without a promise to see me. "Hell, I'm not above begging, angel. Just say the word and I'm on my knees for you."

A smile breaks through. Kate averts her gaze as her cheeks stain crimson once more.

"Christ, you're even more gorgeous than you were at eighteen."

"You're different," she says softly.

God that sexy voice. She's trying to kill me with it.

"Different?" I ask, worried that this is a bad thing.

Kate smiles. "Yeah. Not only are you telling me how you feel, but I can finally *see* how you feel. No more Iceman," she says with a giggle.

I grimace. "Iceman? I don't think I like that."

Kate leans up and presses a small kiss on my mouth. "I don't like it either. This is much, much better." She pulls back and turns for the door. "I'll meet you here after the party, we can talk then."

She slips out of the room and disappears.

I can't help the ridiculous grin that stretches across my face. Then one of my dad's rules pops up in my head.

Rule 2—Never let your emotions show.

I continue smiling like an idiot. I'm done with that rule. Holding everything in has caused me nothing but pain and heartache and hurt Kate as well. If I have to turn into a romantic, sappy, love-song writing bitch to have Kate back in my life, then that's what I'll do.

I've finally figured it out.

Rule 1—Do whatever it takes when you love someone.

18

K ate

IT'S quiet in the back of the car as it makes it way to Dax's hotel. We have to talk. I need answers to so many questions I don't even know where to start. So instead, we sit there silently in the dark, ignoring the colossal number of issues that suffocate us like a heavy blanket on a hot day.

Dax escorts me through the lobby of the posh Warren hotel, guiding me with a hand on my lower back over to the lifts. Once inside, he slips his rough hand into mine, glancing over to make sure I'm okay with it.

I smile at his uncertainty. It's odd to see something other than brash confidence on his handsome face. Yet the fact that he can be vulnerable is endearing. It makes him more human.

"Here we are." Dax only releases my hand to fish out his keycard and open the door to his suite.

"Thank you."

"Drink?" he asks, making his way to a small bar area.

"White wine if you have it." I glance around the room. It's gorgeous. "You can see the river from here. There's the London Eye! Wow, and Kensington Palace."

Dax comes up next to me at the window, putting a glass of wine in my trembling hand. "I haven't looked." His large palm covers the hand holding the wine, steadying it. "I'd rather look at you."

My eyes jerk away from the view to meet his dark, soulful gaze. I've always been able to read his eyes... most of the time. But tonight the door that had been keeping me out has been blown wide open. I can not only read his eyes but his body and even that striking face of his. Everything is laid out for me to see.

He loves me. Of that, I no longer have any doubts.

There are still questions, of course.

"I've missed you so much," Dax says, sliding his hands up my shoulders to rest at the base of my throat. His fingers curl around behind my neck leaving his thumbs below my jaw, resting over my fluttering pulse.

I know he can feel the shudder that wracks my body, the hitch in my breath as I struggle to speak. He can definitely feel the way my blood is flying through my veins, pounding out a staccato rhythm under his hands. I ache for him to touch me, to bring us together physically and make me his again.

Questions can be answered later.

Reaching up, I thread one hand into that thick head of dark blonde hair, fisting it tight. A throaty growl rips from Dax's chest and that loving gaze turns primal. He relieves me of my glass and places it on the bar behind him without looking. Taking advantage of my empty hand, it joins the other one in Dax's hair, gripping it hard to yank his mouth down to mine.

We crash together, devouring each other in wet, messy kisses. Dax uses his bulk to muscle me back until I'm pinned against the cold glass of the floor to ceiling window.

"Fuck, I've missed this. Missed you... your scent, your voice, the feel of your skin." His hands are everywhere, touching, squeezing, caressing every part of me.

"Dax...I need you," I pant as he attacks my mouth again. His tongue forces it's way in, dominating the kiss in a way Dax does so well. "I want you to take me." I need him to erase what happened with Wes. For him to be the last man to have touched me.

He releases me, putting a hand on the window on either side of my head. Dax lowers his forehead to mine. Both of us are out of breath, struggling to control our desires. "Are you sure?" he asks with his eyes screwed shut.

He's so attentive to my needs. Even now, with his hair all disheveled, his dark shirt rucked up on one side, exposing a sliver of tan skin, and an unmistakable bulge straining in his jeans—he's worried about pushing me into something I may regret.

"Look at me."

He opens his eyes and those gorgeous dark irises lock onto mine. I put a hand on his chest, sliding it down until my fingers are hooked in his waistband. Dax's breath stutters and his hips instinctively jerk forward.

"I love you, Dax. Always have. I always will."

Those eyes widen, shimmering with disbelief. As quickly as it appears, the surprise is gone, replaced with naked lust.

"Dax!" I squeal.

In one swift motion, he has scooped me up, throwing me over his shoulder like a rag doll. I laugh, my hair hanging down and my face against his lower back.

Turnabout's fair play!

I lift the back of his shirt and lick a hot swath across the skin above the waist of his jeans. When I get to his side, I bite down on the muscle and suck—hard.

I'm rewarded with a grunt right before I'm tossed onto a

massive bed. Shocked, he tries to see where I marked him while I giggle.

"You little—"

I crook a finger, inviting Dax to join me. "Do you want to talk or do you want to come here?"

With shaky hands, I reach back and unzip my dress, wriggling out of it until I'm naked. Dax stares with blatant lust in his eyes and quite a bit of shock on his face when he sees I have nothing underneath.

I shrug and smirk wickedly. "The dress was too tight for proper undergarments."

"Jesus, Kate." His voice is husky and laced with hunger. Dax hurriedly sheds his clothes, quickly losing each piece while I take in every familiar—and unfamiliar—inch of him.

I'm in awe. "You have a tattoo." I scoot over, climbing to my knees so I can run my hands over his shoulders to his back. I wish I could feel the ink that marks his skin, but it's just as smooth as the rest of him. "What does it say?"

Dax turns around so I can see his glorious back, wide, cut and now, inscribed with a large tattoo.

I read it aloud as my fingers lightly trace the heavy, black Old English letters. "NO MORE RULES." Dax twists his head so he can see me over his shoulder. "What does it mean?"

He turns back towards the bed, taking my mouth in a passionate kiss. Assertive and unapologetic, Dax keeps kissing and moving forward until I'm corralled beneath him on the mattress.

He breaks the kiss with a gasp. "It means I'm living my life for *me*, not anyone else. I'm going to do what *I* want."

"And what is it that you want?" I ask breathlessly.

His sharp gaze pins me down.

"You."

Dax

NOW THAT I'M not holding back anything, the longing, the craving, the need for Kate burns my insides. My emotions are like an out of control car speeding towards a brick wall.

When I lower my body down on top of hers, skin touching skin, the car slams into the wall and explodes in hot, flickering flames. Kate's hips arch up into mine and I break our kiss with a huff.

"God, angel..." I groan long and deep from the tortuous friction of her slick flesh on my cock.

She tugs on my neck, bringing our mouths back together. I could literally devour her right now. Kate sucks on my lower lip, bringing it between her teeth.

"Ow!" I pull back, putting a hand up to where my mouth stings. "You bit me!" My finger comes away with a dot of blood. Even though it hurt, that was the sexiest thing I've ever had done to me

"My, my," I whisper, trailing a finger down her neck and between her breasts. "Someone has turned into quite the little deviant."

"I'm not a deviant," she rasps, "I just want to—"

"Want to do what, Kate?" I thrust my hips down hard, dragging a moan from her. "More of this?" *Thrust.* "Is that," *thrust*, "what," *thrust*, "you," *thrust*, "want?"

"Yes!" she shouts, wrapping her legs around my waist. "I want it and everything else! I want you!" Her heels dig into my backside and she uses her powerful legs to lock us together.

"Oh fuck. Kate, stop." She keeps grinding up on me and I'm a hairsbreadth away from coming. "Stop!"

Those toned legs fall to the bed, freeing me to sit back. "Christ. We were almost done before we began, angel." I stand up and locate my wallet, pulling out a condom.

"Come back," she groans wantonly.

"Fuck you're so bloody gorgeous, Kate." I stand there, appreciating her exquisite beauty as I roll on the protection.

"Stop talking and fuck me, Dax Davies."

The curse coming out of that sweet mouth stuns me. It sounds so perfectly filthy when she says it. Then she sticks her finger in her mouth and sucks on it, moaning as she closes her eyes and makes it a show.

A choked noise comes from my throat. It's all I can manage, what with Kate having turned from innocent schoolgirl to smoking hot seductress. Talking is unnecessary at this point. I climb up on the bed and lie next to her. Her eyes fly open.

"What—"

"Shhhhh," I pull her over to straddle me and thrust up into her tight heat before she can say another word.

"Oh god," she moans loudly. Kate sits up, bracing herself by spreading her hands across my chest. She rolls her hips slowly. "Oh, god."

I practically swallow my tongue, stuttering uncontrollably. "Y-you feel so g-goooood." Kate tilts her head back, those wicked hips never stopping in their mission to drive me insane.

We never tried this position before. Kate was always too insecure to be on top. My how things have changed.

I glide my hands up and down her smooth skin. "You look stunning riding me, angel."

Kate moves faster, moving her hands from my chest so she can bend back, putting her them on my thighs. I can feel the gyrations of her body all the way down in my toes. Too soon, the delicious tingle begins in the base of my spine, quickly building in intensity.

"Kate, Kate...shit."

I know I won't be able to hold it back, and from the noises Kate is making, she has to be as close as I am. With my hands on her hips, I thrust up and drag her back and forth while bucking into her to give her the friction she needs to come.

That's all it takes to send her over the edge, crying out my name as her entire body shakes with pleasure. The sight of Kate shattering so spectacularly while riding my cock is enough to pull me right along with her. Two more deep upward thrusts and I explode, shouting loudly and filling the condom with my release.

Kate collapses on top of me, her long hair scattering over my skin in soft wisps. I wrap her up in my arms, determined to never let her go. This moment is perfect. Truly perfect.

Kate stirs, sated eyes meeting mine. She gives me a small smile and a peck on the lips.

"We need to talk."

Moment ruined.

Kate

AFTER GETTING DRESSED and grabbing our forgotten drinks, Dax and I curl up on one of the sofas in the lounge of his suite. I can see the anxiety on his face, something that will take some getting used to. Stone cold is the only expression I recognize on him.

"So, err, what did you want to talk about?" Dax asks, rubbing the back of his neck in a classic display of stress.

My ears heat up. "Why, Dax?"

He looks up, his confusion plain as day.

"Why what?"

I swallow thickly. I can do this. I deserve answers.

"Why did you leave?"

I watch as this big, tough man, a man who never showed a hint of emotion until now, pales and his eyes shine with unshed tears.

He opens and closes his mouth several times before he can speak. "I...shit, Kate. I didn't want to ruin your life."

That is so far from the answer I expected to hear, I have no response prepared.

"I don't understand."

Dax shifts closer on the sofa, putting a hand on my knee. "The cameras, Lila, groupies, the stress..." He blows out a long breath. "After that disaster at your game, a game that was important to you, I realized that being with me would destroy everything you loved."

I reach out, skimming a finger down the sandpaper stubble of Dax's cheek. He leans into my touch, his eyes fluttering closed.

When his dark eyes open and focus on mine, the depth of the emotions behind them nearly steals my breath away. "Dax, the only thing I loved was you."

That's when the impossible happens. The Iceman sheds a tear.

Kate

I CHECK THE CLOCK AGAIN. The ninety-minute mark has come and gone. If we don't score soon, Brazil will win and our Olympic run will be over in the semi-finals.

One of our midfielders steals the ball and drives it down towards me. She feints, confusing her opponent, and chips it in the direction of our other striker. Using her body to stop the ball, the striker quickly turns to take it to the goal.

When she realizes that there's a defender between her and the goalkeeper, she arcs the ball my way. I'm known to be tough in the penalty zone, able to score in ways most strikers can't even fathom. Brazil knows this, so with the game on the line they're desperate to keep the ball from getting to me. And we all know that desperate people do stupid things.

I get under the ball, set up perfectly to send into the net with a perfectly timed header. As the ball comes down into play, a searing pain tears through my calf and I stumble to the ground.

The refs whistle sounds off, loud and long. I can only assume the referee holds up a red card, because while I'm gripping my leg where the player dug her sharp boot into me, holding back the scream that wants to burst from my lungs, half of the arena begins to boo and the other half cheers loudly.

Coach Lewis and our medic rush out on the pitch. Players circle around, watching as they help me hobble to the bench. While our medic tends to my leg, tears prick my eyes. My Olympic career is over.

Less than a minute later, the game ends and so does the United Kingdom's run in women's football. The team surrounds me, exchanging hugs and cheers for the hard work everyone put in. A few tears are shed as well. We went farther than most experts predicted. I couldn't be prouder to be a part of this team.

"Kate!"

I struggle to my feet—foot actually—as my left calf is swathed in white gauze, bright red blood already showing through. My name is called again, and this time I see him.

Dax strides purposefully down the sideline, his face a mask of concern. I'm not the only one who notices his distress, because the crowd of players and officials melts back to allow him through.

"Kate." He grabs me, lifting me off my feet and into his arms. "You alright, angel?"

Through the salty flood of tears, I smile. I no longer need to prove anything to myself. After our talk the other day, all of my self-doubt is gone. It only took seven years and two continents for us to be honest with each other.

Dax tenderly brushes my hair back from my face and gives

me one of the hottest, sexiest, toe-curling kisses I've ever had in my life.

The arena erupts in whistles and cheers, the fans going mental. Dax points up to the massive electronic screen where I spot us, ten meters tall, on display for everyone to see. We look... well, we look happy. I'm grinning from ear to ear cradled against Dax's chest, my bandaged leg dangling over one of his thick arms. Dax pulls his attention from the screen back to me, whispering in my ear, "I love you," before snogging me good and proper to the delight of everyone at Millennium Stadium.

"I think I'm ready to go home now," I tell him.

"Home?"

"With you."

Grinning like fools, Dax carries me off the pitch to begin our life together.

EPILOGUE

Dax

Two years later.

"DAX!"

I turn to see Adam rushing to catch me as I walk into the New York studio where we've been recording our latest album. It's a soundtrack for some movie I've never heard of, our first time doing one, which is odd seeing as we've been around a while.

"Dax, you won't believe what happened last night." Adam is panting from running through the building, presumably to locate me.

"What happened?"

His eyes dart around, looking for what, I have no idea. Adam grabs my arm and pulls me into the nearby men's room. He checks to make sure it's empty before calming down enough to speak.

"Is all this subterfuge really necessary?" I ask, rolling my eyes at his dramatics.

"Yes," he hisses. "I just got a call from London."

My mind goes a million different ways at once, mostly bad, mostly involving his fucked up family members. Did his dad die? His mum? His bastard of a brother?

"It was from a girl named Gemma. Gemma Spencer."

"So you ran after me to tell me that your number got leaked to a fan site again?" I ask irritably. "I have plans tonight, Adam. We need to start recording so I'm not stuck here late again."

He huffs impatiently. "No, not a fan site. Shut your gob and listen." I scowl at Adam, but wait for him to continue. "This girl, Gemma, she says she works with Ellie!"

Ellie? That isn't even remotely close to anything I was expecting him to say.

"What about Ellie?"

"She claims to be Ellie's best mate." Adam is positively beaming with excitement. I haven't seen him this alive since... well, since Ellie.

"Adam, she could be some nutter trying to trick you," I say, not wanting to destroy the first sliver of happiness he's experienced in ten years, but I don't want him to get his hopes up if it's just some cruel prank.

"No," he grabs my arm. "She knew things. Things only Ellie could have told her. She said Ellie's been trying to contact me, through email, through the record label, even through regular post. I've never heard a word about it." Adam's face becomes stormy, his eyes narrow in anger.

"They probably thought she was lying. Loads of people probably ring up the label and claim to be our friends."

"Right, well... this is the real deal. I'm going to London."

"What?" He could have knocked me over with a feather. "You're going to London based on the word of a random girl who rung you up?"

"No. I'm going because she's not lying. Ellie's mum is getting married. I'm crashing the party."

I laugh, bending over with the hilarity of it all until I realize he's not kidding. "You're serious?"

"Dead serious. I'm going and getting my girl, just like you did."

I'm speechless. Kate and I eloped right after the closing ceremonies of the Olympics. We didn't think there was any point in waiting after all those years apart. I wonder if Adam will come back married to Ellie.

"Oh, and I need to bring Zane with me. Can I borrow him?"

I sigh, my reminiscing coming to an abrupt halt. "Yeah, sure. What are best mates for?"

Indeed.

We have our best session in years, mostly due to Adam's upbeat attitude. He's so spot on we finish thirty minutes early for a change.

I hurry out, jumping on my brand new Ducati, zipping out of the car park. I speed through the streets, weaving around cars and take the Holland Tunnel to the Jersey Turnpike. Thank god for the bike, otherwise I'd still be sitting in stagnant traffic back in Manhattan.

An hour later, okay, so I broke the limit a few times, I pull into the lot at Jesse Owens Memorial Stadium on the campus of Rutgers University. I kick down the stand and lean the Ducati to rest. Heading toward the entrance with my helmet tucked under my arm, more than a few heads turn my way.

Most of them know me by now and pay me no mind, but there are always girls who get excited by my appearance.

"Dax Davies, wow!"

"We heard you came by, but I can't believe you're really here!"

I pose for a few selfies and excuse myself. "I have to go, ladies. Don't want to miss the start."

They giggle and huddle together whispering like girls tend to do. I wave at Andre, one of the regular security guards at the stadium.

"I got your bike covered man," he says as we shake hands.

The first time I brought the Ducati, students climbed all over my unattended bike, snapping pictures and messing around with it. It fell over and had quite a bit of damage. After that, I made sure to park close to the entrance and have someone watch it for me. The guards here know me and never mind keeping an eye out.

"Thanks mate."

I find my usual seat and relax. It's a perfect evening for a game, unseasonably warm for late September in New Jersey. Kate spots me and smiles. The stadium is still filling up, so she takes a minute and walks over to my section. My seat is in the front row, just off the pitch. There are perks to being married to the head coach.

"Hi angel." I lean over and give her a kiss, just a small one since she's at work. Nowhere near the sloppy, wet, tongue kiss I want to lie on her.

"Dax. You made it in time tonight." She winks. Kate knows that I've been frustrated with all of the late recording sessions that have made me miss more than one of her games.

"Yeah, well, Adam was in a good mood today. We got done early if you can believe that." I'll tell her about Ellie later. No need to distract her before a game.

We ignore the whispers and pings of mobile phones as people nearby sneak pictures of us. We're used to it by now. Everyone who sits around me is friends and family of the staff and players. They're used to me and treat me like a regular bloke. It's nice to be normal.

The video of Kate and I at the Olympics went viral minutes after it happened. By the next day, most of the world had seen it, or was talking about it. It took forever for the attention to die out.

No more hiding behind the front man anymore. I'm thoroughly recognizable all on my own.

I lean over the half wall. "Is your helmet still in your car?"

Kate eyes me curiously. "Yes."

"Ride home with me." We have a beautiful house about a half-hour north, midway between here and the city.

A spark of interest flashes across her face. "Why?"

I lean in as close as I can get. "So I can feel that fit body pressed up against me while the Ducati growls between your thighs, angel. Why else?"

"Dirty, dirty, Dax." Kate pulls back and smirks. I can tell she likes the idea.

"I'll bring you back tomorrow to fetch your car. What do you say, Mrs. Davies? Ride with me?"

Kate shifts to whisper in my ear, her hot breath causing me to shiver under my leather jacket. That raspy, sexy voice of hers sends testosterone racing through my veins. "I'll do anything for you, Mr. Davies. Anything."

Kate winks, then turns and trots over to her team. I watch that tight ass and sit back in my seat, loving the hell out of my life.

Fuck the rules, my way is much, much better.

The Rules

1. Family first

2. Never let your emotions show

3. No fucking, shagging, wanking, sucking, or getting off for seven days leading up to a fight. You win, you get your reward.

4. Women who act like slags can be treated like slags, but never disrespect a proper lady.

5. Defend what's yours.

THANKS FOR READING *STRIKE.* I hope you enjoyed it!

CURIOUS TO KNOW **what happens with Hawke and Abby?**
Continue reading for a sample of Wreck.

Hawke

Laughter surrounds me from all sides. I high-five my way through the crowd of jocks and rich princesses filling the hallway. I want to shrink down, hunch into myself, but my parents expect me to be like them—popular, fun, the guy everyone likes.

So I do it, and I do it well. Too well.

"Hawke! Call me."

"Bro! Text me later about the party!"

I wave and nod my head as classmates call out greetings. It takes everything in me not to turn around and shove the entitled assholes into the wall and tell them how shallow I think they are. I think about it all the time but never do a thing. It's just easier to maintain the status quo, be the popular guy I'm supposed to be, even though it's killing me.

Waving and smiling at everyone, I walk out into the bright Los Angeles sun. My car is all the way across the sprawling parking lot, a fifty-yard minefield of idle gossip and "bro" pats on the back standing between me and my escape from what I imagine a teenage Dante would have used as the seventh circle of hell if the *Inferno* had been written in the twenty-first century.

Luck is on my side, because I make it through row after row of high-end luxury cars to my vehicle without a single person stopping me. The black Audi R8 was a present from my parents. Present for what? I have no fucking clue. For existing, maybe? For being cool and popular among the children of Hollywood's elite? They mean well and they love me, but they have no idea I'd rather go to the public school with normal kids than these spoiled brats.

"We want you to be with the best, Hawke. Greater Malibu Prep is the best high school in southern California."

I wonder if my big shot Hollywood agent dad and my gorgeous ex-supermodel mom would think the school was so great if they knew half of the student population was high at any given time, including the "cool" kids they want me to be friends with. My parents probably wouldn't care if they knew about the drugs. I mean, my mom and dad were the epitome of cool when they were my age. Hell, I know for a fact they both did their fair share of drugs back in the day.

Begrudgingly, I expend the necessary time and energy to be important in a group of kids that would kill to be me. In my mind, it's a complete waste of time sucking up to the vapid, entitled, trust-fund babies just to achieve a social status I don't want, in order to spend time around people I can't stand. But I'd do anything to make my parents happy, and seeing me go to endless parties with well-known socialites on my arm makes them happy.

I sigh and start the car, its engine growling beautifully under the shiny black hood. Another day done. Only a little over a hundred more until I graduate and get out of here.

Crap. I hope I can last that long.

THE BEAT of the drums vibrates through my body, every part of me moving with the rhythm. All of the stress in my life transferring from my hands to the sticks, to the sounds created by my frantic yet controlled movements. Sweat beads up on my forehead and trickles down between my shoulder blades as I use every muscle, every limb, every part of me to create the complicated beat that fills the sound studio built into the basement of my parents' huge mansion.

My eyes close, the tempo taking over my mind and body—not thinking, simply *feeling.* Here, in this sanctuary, there is only me and the sound I create. I'm in charge, and with that power I can create something magical. If my classmates knew how much time I spent in the studio drumming, they'd turn their surgically perfected noses up in the air.

"Henry Walker!"

I fumble the drumsticks and they go flying in different directions. "Mom! You scared the crap out of me!" I fist my shirt to keep my heart from flying out of my chest.

"Sorry, honey." Mom doesn't look sorry at all. She looks... *amused*. "It's not my fault. You didn't answer the first five times I called your name." She shoots me a smirk. This isn't the first time Mom's caught me unaware in the studio. I'm sure it won't be the last.

"Whatever. You didn't have to go all middle name on me." I pout, sticking out my bottom lip in a way I know my mom can't resist. My mom is awesome. Both of my parents are, even if they're completely oblivious to my disdain for keeping up my social status at school.

She smiles, her eyes shining with love. "Come upstairs, Hawke. Sebastian Griffin and his daughter are here." Mom pats my shoulder sweetly. Ugh! Lila Griffin is a first-class bitch. My mom is clueless to the amount of contempt I have for Lila, who is the biggest spoiled brat I've ever met.

I roll my eyes. "You don't need me, Mom. Lila and I will catch up later."

Lila Griffin has no idea I hate her guts. At least once a month, she tries to get me to go out with her. Every time I say no, it probably kills her to not get her way. Lilia, popular and pretty, has a dad who is a big time movie producer. She isn't used to not getting what she wants.

Lila's dad is here because my dad represents a lot of the actors and directors Mr. Griffin uses for his movies. Unfortunately, they work together a lot. But Lila? There are only two reasons for Lila to be at my house—one is that she wants to tell people she hung out with my mom, famous supermodel Vickie Hart. The other is to get her claws into me.

"Don't be stubborn, Hawke. Come upstairs. *Now*." My mom gives me her serious "mom" stare, which doesn't keep her from looking drop-dead gorgeous, and heads out of the studio.

Never able to say no to my mom, or anyone in my family, I grab my drumsticks and shove them in my back pocket. Great. I can't think of anything I'd rather *not* do right now than hang out with Lila. A girl who thinks most people are lower than the scum on the bottom of her designer heels.

This is going to be fun. As fun as a root canal without Novocain. I trudge up the stairs, resigned to my fate of listening to the musings of someone who has less between her ears than the pocket-sized dogs carted around by half the snobs in LA.

Why is she in *my* house? This isn't school, where I have no choice but to deal with her and her nonstop innuendos and invites to get in her designer pants. I should be able to come home without having to fend off any more of her advances. My safety zone. She's in my safety zone.

Deep breath. I lift my chin and steel myself for the inevitable, patented Lila Griffin eye flutter-lip pout combo. There it is. Lila's moony eyes meet mine and she gives me a small smile. Crap. I almost can't hide my contempt.

"Hawke," my mom says, interrupting my bewilderment. "Sebastian was just saying that Lila is going to a party at the beach. You should go with her, honey."

Jesus, Mom! Embarrassment fills my face and ears with prickly heat and a healthy dose of "Hell no!" dangles from the tip of my tongue. I already knew about the party, and had planned to skip out for once, trading hours of menial chatter about rich kid problems for a night at home in my studio.

"Mom—" I complain, trying to think of a way out of this. Naturally, wanting to get her perfectly painted claws into me in any way possible, Lila doesn't let me beg off.

"Hawke, come with me. It's going to be fun. Cookout on the beach, volleyball, bonfire when it gets dark." Her shrewd eyes narrow, a sly smirk cutting across her face.

She knows she's got me right where she wants me. My family is my kryptonite and I hate disappointing them. The hopeful look on Mom's face has me resigned to my fate.

Ugh. Maybe they'll cut me a break. "I would love to go, but—"

My dad doesn't let me finish my excuse. He stares at me from behind his signature black-rimmed glasses. "Son, go. It sounds like a great time. I remember the beach parties I went to when I was your age." He chuckles and Lila's dad joins in.

"I know I had a lot fun in high school," Sebastian says, wiggling his eyebrows. *Asshole.*

"Go and have a good time. Sebastian and I have a lot of work to do and you'll be bored hanging around here with a bunch of old farts, then we're probably headed over to the Tannens' for dinner." Dad waves me away, all but shoving me out the door.

"I don't think—"

Loud music erupts from upstairs, the heavy bass vibrating all the way to my bones.

"That kid, I swear." My dad laughs, the fine lines around his blue eyes crinkling. My younger sister has recently taken to testing the limits of her top of the line sound system. Her taste in music is decent, more rock and less bubblegum pop, so I never complain.

"Honestly," Mom says, smiling. "Excuse me, Sebastian. I need to have another talk with my daughter about volume control."

As my mom turns toward the stairs, I jump at the chance for a minute away from the pressure of my parents practically shoving me into Lila Griffin's arms. "I'll tell her to turn the stereo down," I offer, bounding for the staircase. "I have to change clothes anyway."

Halfway up, I glance back at Lila. The calculating look on her face disappears the second she catches me looking. Her features morph into her usual sultry expression. *What is she planning?*

I shake off the disgust and head to my sister's room, slamming the door shut behind me. I immediately grab the remote and turn down the music.

"Hey!" My sister, Hannah, flings her long dark hair over her shoulder and scowls from the center of her bed. She's sitting cross-legged with her phone in her lap, surrounded by pillows. "What the heck, Hawke?"

"Shhhhh." I cross the room and sit next to her on the bed. "Lila Griffin is downstairs."

Her big, golden-brown eyes widen and she scoots closer. "What?"

Hannah is the ultimate Malibu rich girl. She loves clothes, music, and gossip. Fortunately, she's managed to keep a smart head and isn't a raging bitch like most girls I know. Hannah is loving and kind and a genuinely sweet person, which is impressive for a thirteen-year-old.

Hannah is well aware of Lila's obsession with me and when I tell her about the party, she wrinkles her little nose in disgust. "Ewwww. When is she gonna give up on you?"

"I don't know. But Mom and Dad are making me go with her." Hannah loves me and couldn't care less how popular I am. She knows I only go through the motions, supporting me even if it does confound her that I don't want to associate with the socially acceptable assholes at school.

"Don't go, then," she says easily, shrugging.

"I don't know, Han. Dad loves Lila. He really wants me to go." My shoulders sag in exhaustion from keeping up pretenses all the time.

Hannah puts a hand on my knee and looks me in the eye. "First of all, you would be pretty cool even if you weren't the most popular guy in school, dummy. And second, Dad will get over it. If you don't want to go, you shouldn't."

I smile at my sister. "You're pretty awesome for an annoying little sister." I have the best family and wouldn't trade them for the world. If anyone ever pulled any shit with my sister, I'd kill them. The day she starts seriously dating is a day I'm dreading as much as my dad. Possibly more since I'm more inherently protective than he is.

She laughs. "You're pretty awesome for an older brother."

Hannah wraps her skinny arms around my shoulders, giving me a tight hug. No way she can't feel how tense I am. "You're going to go to the party, aren't you?"

I sigh. "Yeah. I can't disappoint Mom and Dad, Han. I just can't."

My sister pulls back and bites her lip. I can tell she's thinking hard since I do the same thing. "Well, take this then." Hannah leaps off the bed and snatches something off her nightstand. She grabs my hand and presses a cold, smooth object into my palm. "I found this a few weeks ago. I've been carrying it around, but you can borrow it."

Uncurling my fingers, I find a perfect, heart-shaped rock. "Cool." I pull my brows down in confusion. "What's it for?"

She shrugs, giving me a brilliant grin. "For luck, silly."

I have a feeling I'm gonna need it.

Abby

"Nick? You home?"

I toss my backpack onto the old kitchen table and toe off my shoes.

"Nick?"

A quick search of our modest house turns up nothing. I pull out my phone and shoot a text to my mom.

Me – I'm home. Nick not here

I DON'T BOTHER WAITING for a response. Mom is at work and can't check her phone often, but she'll want me to let her know my older brother is MIA. He was supposed to come straight home after finishing his class at the local community college.

Worry pulls at my gut, twisting my stomach into a tight ball. I grab a Coke out of the fridge, hoping the sugar will calm the acid churning inside. How is a fifteen-year-old girl supposed to be responsible for her nineteen-year-old brother?

I worry about him even though Mom keeps reassuring me that Nick isn't my responsibility. I'm only supposed to give her updates when she's not here. Yet I can't help but feel that I should do something to help. Every time Nick doesn't show up when he's supposed to, or blows off school, or goes into one of his moods, I feel like I'm letting everyone down.

Mid-mope, my phone alerts me to an incoming text. Relief surges as I snatch the device off the counter, hoping it's my mom. I'd even take Dad at this point, regardless of the fact that he's out of town on business.

EM – Mall? Pleeeaasse? It's been 4ever.

I SAG when the text is from my best friend, Emily. Not that I don't want to hear from her. I'd just feel better if Mom answered me. Like I was actually doing something about Nick. Having my mom know Nick is late would help ease my anxiety.

Whatever. Mom told me he's not my problem. She keeps telling me Nick has issues he's working out and there's nothing I can do.

My mood does a one-eighty like only a teenager's can. I quickly type out a response.

*M*E – *Yes. Pick me up?*

*E*M – *Be at yours in five*

GOOD. I need to get out of here. My little brothers have lacrosse today and Mom picks them up on her way home from work. Hanging around the house, waiting for my bipolar brother to get his act together and stop being so selfish, has gotten old. Anger surges inside me, directed at Nick for making me feel helpless. A heartbeat later, guilt takes over for thinking badly about my brother. He didn't ask for mental illness, didn't ask to be tormented by his own mind.

A horn blaring from my driveway shakes me out of my funk. I grab my wallet from my bag and my phone from the countertop. Biting my lip, I take one last look around the kitchen, wondering if I should just wait here for Nick to get home, or at least until my mom texts me back.

The thought of sitting here alone yet another long afternoon —worrying about my brother, waiting on my brother—makes me nauseous. I shake my head and slam the door shut, locking it behind me.

Nick will just have to take care of himself today. For once, I'm putting myself first and acting like the fifteen-year-old girl that I am. I've missed out on so much already, I'm going to take advantage of a rare day of doing what I want.

I trot out to Emily's banged up Honda Civic and climb in. She squeals and cranks up the radio, singing along to a popular song as she pulls out of my driveway. As the car turns the corner, I glance back at my house, wondering if I'm doing the right thing.

"Ooooohhhh, I love this one!" Emily elbows me, laughing. "Sing with me, Abby!"

The house disappears from view and I force the nagging thoughts out of my mind, determined to have fun. We sing at the top of our lungs, windows down, all the way to the mall. By the time Emily parks the car, I'm honestly enjoying myself for the first time in a long time.

Feeling normal shouldn't be a big deal, but it is. It really is.

Hawke

"Just take one, Hawke. We're all doing it." Lila purrs, rubbing against my side as she holds out her palm, a small packet of white powder balanced in the center.

"C'mon, man! It's no big deal. It's just ecstasy." Truman Briggs, world's biggest douchebag and the son of the head of a major film studio, is egging me on. He snatches the packet off Lila's hand, opens it up, and dumps the contents under his tongue. After a few seconds, he grins and opens his mouth, showing everyone the powder is gone.

"I've done X before, asshole." I glare at Briggs who is shirtless, wearing only a low-slung pair of board shorts. It kills me not to roll my eyes. The dude lives to show off his six-pack.

Lila produces a second packet, holding it out for me to take. I glance around, a half-dozen faces I recognize from school waiting impatiently for me to take the drug.

Fuck! Why the hell not? I'm supposed to be cool, don't really give a shit about these people, and despise hanging out with them. If taking a hit of ecstasy will give me a break from feeling surrounded by douchebaggery all the time, I'm in. Besides, my parents probably wouldn't even care. It's only X, not heroin.

I take the packet, putting on my cocky face. Six sets of eyes watch as I peel open the end and dump the powder under my tongue without hesitation. They laugh when I screw up my face at the bitter, yet somehow sour, taste.

"Yeah," Briggs says, elbowing me in the ribs hard enough that it'll probably leave a bruise. I stifle the urge to plow my fist into his nose. "Tastes worse every fucking time. But damn..." He closes his eyes and tilts his head up to the sun, a look of total bliss on his face. "It's so worth it, man."

Lila opens her own packet, taking it the same way. The others all grab one, copying her movements. They laugh and shove each other playfully while I stuff my hand into my pocket, finding Hannah's stone so I won't have to share any more "bro-hugs" with these idiots. Lila grabs me, dragging me across the sand to the edge of the volleyball court.

Music is playing and my classmates are laughing and joking around with each other. What would it feel like to be with people I genuinely like? I mean, there are a few people here who are cool, but most are like Lila. As fake as ninety percent of the perfect bodies in Hollywood.

After an hour of chatting inanely and concentrating on not running away screaming, I get a second wind. Suddenly, sitting on the sidelines talking, watching everyone have a great time seems stupid. Joining is a much better idea. Briggs is dancing with Harper, a stunning redhead whose dad is a big time actor. They're grinding together sensually, eyes locked, bodies slick with sweat.

I lick my lips, realizing how dry my mouth is. The sun is still a good ways from the horizon and it's fucking hot out.

"Here." Lila appears, pressing a bottle of water in my hand. "Drink."

I chug back half the bottle. Lila stares at me, taking the water back without breaking eye contact. She wraps her full lips around the opening and takes a drink, her tongue swiping over her mouth when she's done.

Jesus. My jeans are suddenly really tight. The outline of my dick would be obvious to anyone who looks. Despite the fact that my dick should never get hard in front of Lila, I can't seem to be bothered to care. In fact, when I look at Lila, I realize she's pretty fucking gorgeous.

Why do I hate her again?

Needing... something, I take the bottle out of Lila's hand and finish the rest, still meeting her heated gaze. I toss the empty container to the sand and grip her tiny waist. With a quick tug, I pull her up against my crotch and she gasps.

Without a word, Lila wraps her arms around my neck and we begin to dance—grinding, rubbing—the sensuality of her touch near overwhelming. It's both the strangest and most thrilling experience of my life.

"Your eyes are so beautiful," Lila murmurs, her fingernails scratching up and down my neck before trailing into my hair. "Brown and blue. One of each."

"*You're* beautiful," I respond, my voice husky from my still parched throat. Fuck it's hot out. "I never noticed before." My hand finds her face, shining with a light sheen of sweat, and I trail my thumb across her lower lip. Lila opens her mouth and bites down, sucking my thumb into her hot, wet mouth. The intense heat ignites a fiery blaze that trails down my spine and straight to my cock.

"I've noticed you," Lila whispers, twirling her tongue around my thumb.

My head is spinning with a barrage of incredible sensations. I feel invincible, as if I could do or have anything, and what I want right now is Lila. The intensity of my attraction is so high, my body is running on pure instinct. I lower my mouth to Lila's, her flesh so hot it nearly singes me. Lila groans hungrily, sucking my tongue between her lips. I grip her round ass and tug her even closer, craving the connection, the intimacy, the touch of another human being.

Lila pulls back, her eyes dark, pupils blown wide. She trails a finger down my chest, stopping at the waistband of my jeans. "Let's go to my car."

She takes my hand and I let her lead. Right now, I'd do anything she asked. Absolutely anything.

It feels fucking great.

Abby

"Thanks, Em!" I slam the car door shut and wave as my friend drives away from my house. Happy and smiling, I put the key in the lock and walk inside. Exhausted, I drop my one purchase on the floor and drop onto the sofa, tucking my feet up under me.

I'll only close my eyes for a minute, then I'll do my homework.

"Abby!"

The sharp tone of my mom's voice startles me out of a deep sleep. "Mom?"

"Abby! Where's Nick?" I rub my eyes, listening to the footfalls of my mom's shoes on the stairs. "Nick?" The loud bickering and stomping of my two little brothers entering the house and dumping all of their lacrosse gear drowns out her voice.

My head spins when I sit up too fast. I check my phone—five o'clock! "Mom? I fell asleep. What's going on?"

Her feet pound down the stairs until she's standing over me, all five foot two inches of her. "He never came home?" My mom's blue eyes are wide and worried, blonde hair falling out of its usual ponytail, the loose pieces curling around her face.

"I-I don't know. I came home, he wasn't here. Then Em came and picked me up..." My heart stutters. What if something happened to my brother because I wasn't here? What if he came home and went back out since no one was here to talk him out of it?

"Don't," my mom warns. "I know what you're thinking, Abby. Nothing Nick does is your fault. It's bad enough you have to be responsible for watching Jace and Evan after school. Nick isn't your problem, honey."

She's given this speech before, and she'll probably give it a hundred more times. Hearing it doesn't make my response different or the guilt any easier to bear. My older brother is an unpredictable mess at best; at worst, he's a danger to himself and others. His moods have been stable lately, but you never know when he'll turn on a dime and you'll be left with a depressed wreck or a reckless risk-taker.

"Come on." Mom grabs her keys and purse. "We'll drive by the school and see if his car is still there."

"Aw, Mom! We were gonna play Xbox!" Jace whines.

"Yeah, Mom. I'm hungry too," Evan chimes in.

Despite their protests, we all follow my mother outside. I struggle to hold back the tears that burn behind my eyes and swallow against the thick lump in my throat. Nick might not be perfect, he might cause our family a lot of stress, but I love him. He wasn't always like this, and even now I catch glimpses of the real Nick between the periods when his mind takes away any traces of his true self.

"He told me he was taking his meds," Mom murmurs, more to herself than to me. She inhales a shaky breath. "He'll be okay, Abby." She gives me a sad smile and turns back to focus on driving.

Two hours later and we haven't found any trace of Nick. Mom stopped at the college, the local hospital, and a few of his favorite hangouts. No one has seen him. When we return home, our moods are dark. The boys are sated with the bags of fast food they're clutching. My mom, like me, is too guilt ridden and worried to eat.

Mom calls Dad, then goes to her room to call the police. She knows they won't do anything about Nick until he's been missing forty-eight hours, but she still reports his absence. This isn't the first time he's vanished without saying anything, nor is it the first time we've had to involve the authorities.

Reluctantly, Mom tells me we need to get some sleep in case Nick shows up or calls us to come get him. She's right, of course, but sleep doesn't come. Instead, I lie in my bed, staring at the shadows on the ceiling as I alternate between hating Nick for putting us through so much emotional stress, and loving him so much that the thought of something bad happening to him has my anxiety levels through the roof.

When the phone rings at four in the morning, I'm still lying awake, utterly exhausted. The sound has my heart racing in fear. *Please let it be Nick calling for a ride.* My bedroom door cracks open and my mom's tired voice cracks.

"They found him. Let's go."

I use every bit of strength and concentration I can manage to force back the panic threatening to overflow so I can pull on a pair of pants and stuff my feet into my shoes. All I want to do is fall to the ground and sob, but somehow, I stay upright and do as my mother says, helping her get the boys out of bed and dressed.

This is only the beginning.

Hawke

My body is crumpled up in an odd position. One arm is twisted underneath me, one sprawled up over my head, and my legs are curled up into my abdomen. I try to sit up and immediately regret moving. A white-hot, stabbing pain pierces my skull, radiating out the back. It's as if the entire chorus of Riverdance is stomping on my head at once. Moaning, I dig the heels of my hands into my temples, pressing hard in a pathetic attempt to alleviate the pain.

"Fuck."

Once the world stops spinning, I take a look around. It's pitch black out and the only sound is the crashing of waves on the shore. It takes a minute for my eyes to adjust and I finally figure out where I am. I'm lying on the sand next to the remains of the bonfire. The party is over. No one else is anywhere nearby.

Lila left me on the beach? Alone? Fuck, I knew she was a bitch. Anger like I've ever known wells up inside. I'm so furious if anyone were here, I'd punch the shit out of them.

I pull out my phone and check the time. Almost midnight. Not super late then. The party started way early, or more accurately, we started partying too early. My finger hesitates over the button, but really, do I have a choice? It's not like I have a bunch of friends I can call to come get me. Everyone I know was here with me, and left me behind. Hell, I don't even have Lila's phone number to call and rip her a new one.

Still pissed, I push the button and tap the fingers of my free hand on my knee, drumming out a random rhythm to calm down.

"Hawke?"

"Mom? I think... I think I need your help."

"Honey? What's wrong?"

I swallow back the anger and my parched throat is on fire, as if someone took a blowtorch to it or shoved a glowing hot poker down my esophagus. "I need a ride."

"What happened to Lila, sweetie?"

Scowling, I stop tapping and dig my fingers into my leg. I have to bite the inside of my cheek to keep from taking out my rage on my mom. "Lila took off. I don't have a way home."

There's a pause, and for a moment, I wonder if my mom is deciding whether or not to leave me here. Or maybe she's questioning how I ended up stranded at a party.

"Where are you? We'll be right there."

"We?"

"We just left dinner with Sebastian, honey. We ate, then went to visit Reid Tannen and Eva Allen. The men lost track of time talking about their new project. Hannah wanted to see Sydney, so she's with us too. Where are you?"

I drop my head into my hands and groan. Great. The entire family gets to witness not only my humiliation at being ditched by my friends, but my craptastic drug hangover that has me seething mad.

"Zuma Beach."

"We're on our way, sweetie. Meet us in the parking lot."

"Fine."

I hang up and rub a hand down my face. Shit. What the hell was I thinking coming here with Lila? I must have been fucking insane to do whatever the hell I did last night. My head jerks up and the phone slides out of my hand, landing softly on the beach.

Lila. Holy shit. Images of the two of us grinding together, kissing, clothes coming off... stumbling into the backseat of her car. My headache explodes into unbelievable agony. *Oh my god.* I had sex with Lila Fucking Griffin.

I must be the stupidest asshole on earth. I pick up the phone and jam it into my pocket. It cracks against the smooth stone Hannah gave to me.

Some good luck charm. It turned me into a total fuckup.

My self-flagellation is interrupted when a pair of headlights shine across the beach, casting the sand in a yellow-gray glow. Before I can bring up another awful memory from earlier today, I brush off my clothes and hop into the backseat of my dad's car.

"You look like crap," Hannah whispers, her eyes half closed.

I ignore her and lean against the window, pissed off and ashamed. Mom looks over her shoulder and gives me a worried smile, but otherwise, the car is silent. My parents are so awesome. Somehow they understand I don't want to discuss anything tonight. I'm sure tomorrow my mom won't be as understanding and will want at least a few details of how I became stranded on a deserted beach in the dark.

I laugh to myself. Maybe some good will come of this. Maybe they'll realize what a bitch Lila Griffin is and—

I'M WET. It must be raining. Another drop hits my cheek, rolling up my face toward my hair.

Up? Can it rain up?

My head hurts so fucking bad it's difficult to think. Intense throbbing clouds my mind, pounding so hard it's as if my heart is beating inside my skull. Slowly, painfully, I reach up and wipe the dampness from my skin right as another large drop splats next to the first.

"Shit."

I rub the moisture away and crack open my eyes. Blackness. I'm surrounded by total blackness, the only exception a gloomy blue glow a few feet away. *What the fuck?* I'm so confused, I can't tell where I am or what direction is up or down.

Another drop of warm water hits my skin and I immediately swipe at it, bringing my fingers a few inches from my eyes to get a better look. Even with very little light, it's obvious the liquid isn't clear and much too dark and thick to be water. In fact, my hands are stained an eerie purplish-black color in the faint blue light.

When I try to move my head to see where the water—or whatever it is—is coming from, a feral scream rips from my chest and throat. Pain like nothing I've ever felt turns my body inside out. I'm on fire, every part of me burning white hot and searing at once.

My neck is somehow twisted at an odd angle, my skin is sizzling with the agonizing sting of a thousand tiny paper cuts, and my arm won't respond to my brain's instructions, instead lying limp while my shoulder shrieks in agony.

The heartbeat in my skull speeds up, hammering out a rapid, drumming beat. Using my other hand, I attempt to push my useless body off the ground, wincing when the bites of hundreds of bits of glass dig into my palm. Minutes... hours later—I'm not sure it matters how long it takes, even if I could figure it out—I finally manage to maneuver my body into a sitting position.

My chest is filled with liquid fire, heaving from the effort expended. Every square inch of my body is raw. There's not a single part of me that doesn't hurt. When I feel another dark droplet hit me, this time landing on the top of my head, I look up to find the source.

And promptly lose the contents of my stomach before passing out from the pain.

Thanks!

So, so many people to thank for helping make the stories that plague my mind a reality—my betas (you gals know who you are by now), my street team-The Dirty Fangirls, all of the hard-working bloggers out there who bust their butts for their love of books, my family, my awesome friends, and everyone who reads one of my books and finds it worthwhile.

xoxo HCL

STALK ME

Heather C. Leigh is the author of the Amazon best selling Famous series. She likes to write about the 'dark' side of fame. The part that the public doesn't get to see, how difficult it is to live in a fishbowl and how that affects relationships.

Heather was born and raised in New England and after living outside Atlanta, GA for 15 years, currently lives near Houston, TX with her husband, 2 kids, French Bulldog, and a Hedgehog named Nina.

She loves the Red Sox, the Patriots, and anything chocolate (but not white chocolate, everyone knows it's not real chocolate so it doesn't count) and has left explicit instructions in her will to have her ashes snuck into Fenway Park and sneakily sprinkled all over while her family enjoys beer, hot dogs, and a wicked good time.

Stalk Me

heathercleighauthor.com
heathercleigh@heathercleighauthor.com

19

ALSO BY HEATHER C LEIGH

D*ark Romances*
         Junkie- Broken Doll 1
         Jagger- Broken Doll 2
Killer- also available via KU program

R*OCKSTAR* R*OMANCE* (S*PHERE* of *Irony*)
   Incite — Adam
   Strike — Dax
   Resist — Gavin (M/M)
   Wreck — Hawke

T*HE* F*AMOUS* S*ERIES*
   Relatively Famous
   Absolutely Famous
   Extremely Famous
   Already Famous (Drew's POV)
   Suddenly Famous (a novella)
   Reluctantly Famous (a novella)

RICOCHET— Military Romantic Suspense
  Locked & Loaded
  Friendly Fire
  Extraction Point

AS LEIGH CARMAN- **M/M Romance**
  Players of LA -by Dreamspinner Press
  Match Point- Volleyball (Summer)
  Fair Catch- Football (Fall)
  Power Play- Hockey (Winter)
  Full Count- Baseball (Spring) coming soon

CLICK below to get updates on new releases by Leigh Carman

~

www.ingramcontent.com/pod-product-compliance
Lightning Source LLC
Chambersburg PA
CBHW021328250626
47155CB00002B/640